GRACELESSLAND

To Sherri,
I hope you enjoy it
as much as I enjoy your
bread!

Gracelessland

A NOVEL

ADAM LINDSAY HONSINGER

ENFIELD
&WIZENTY

Great Plains Publications gratefully acknowledges the financial support provided for its publishing program by the Government of Canada through the Canada Book Fund; the Canada Council for the Arts; the Province of Manitoba through the Book Publishing Tax Credit and the Book Publisher Marketing Assistance Program; and the Manitoba Arts Council.

Design & Typography by Relish New Brand Experience
Printed in Canada by Friesens

LIBRARY AND ARCHIVES CANADA CATALOGUING IN PUBLICATION

Honsinger, Adam Lindsay, 1963-, author
        Gracelessland / Adam Lindsay Honsinger.

Issued in print and electronic formats.
ISBN 978-1-927855-14-0 (pbk.).--ISBN 978-1-927855-15-7 (epub).--ISBN 978-1-927855-16-4 (mobi)

        I. Title.

PS8615.O505G73 2015   C813'.6   C2014-907243-0
                                           C2014-907244-9

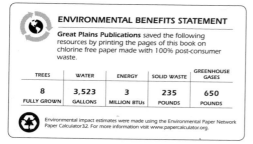

ENVIRONMENTAL BENEFITS STATEMENT

Great Plains Publications saved the following resources by printing the pages of this book on chlorine free paper made with 100% post-consumer waste.

TREES	WATER	ENERGY	SOLID WASTE	GREENHOUSE GASES
8 FULLY GROWN	3,523 GALLONS	3 MILLION BTUs	235 POUNDS	650 POUNDS

Environmental impact estimates were made using the Environmental Paper Network Paper Calculator 3.2. For more information visit www.papercalculator.org.

FSC
www.fsc.org
MIX
Paper from responsible sources
FSC™ C016245

This book is dedicated to my parents, John (1929–1997) and Barbara (1931–2011) Honsinger

Dramatis Personae

KEPLER PRESSLER	Narrator
DR. ATWOOD	Psychiatrist
BRUCE	Orderly
OPHELIA	Patient
HAM	First chimpanzee to survive a launch, orbit and return from space
ELVIS	Icon
WALTER PRESSLER	Kepler's father
ALICE PRESSLER	Kepler's mother
AUNT JUDY	Alice's sister
MR. PHILLIPS	Neighbour
CARL	Dispatcher at Bluebird Cab Company
MR. LEMON	English, Math and History teacher
MISS JONES	Guidance Counsellor
MR. WATERS	Principal
BENJAMIN	Classmate
MILLY	Kepler's girlfriend
CETUS	Constellation
INFINITE MONKEY	A Theorem

1978

CHAPTER ONE

As the enclosure door swings open I feel a sobering blast of adrenaline, a euphoric mixture of excitement and fear, followed by the pungent smell of excrement. This is it. Pan Troglodytes Verus—the Western chimpanzee. The article that I have cut out of the newspaper says their names are Oscar, Wilma and Pluto. I take a deep breath, place the bolt cutters back in my gym bag, and then scan the enclosure with the flashlight. It looks more like a kindergarten classroom than a forest in the wilds of Africa. The three chimps are huddled in the far corner under a platform made of logs and rope, staring into the beam of my flashlight like a family of annoyed, captive primates trying to determine why they have been woken up at 2:37 in the morning.

The plan:

One. Lure the chimps out of their cage, through the pavilion, over the fence and out to the forested area of the valley surrounding the zoo.

Two. Orient them to their new surroundings—teach them to hunt, forage, and implement strategies of avoiding captivity, etc.

Three. Leave them to live the rest of their lives free and happy among the trees.

The first banana I toss lands with an unappetizing thud on the concrete floor in the middle of the enclosure about ten feet away from me.

No reaction.

I throw the second one a little harder; it splits open when it hits the floor and then skids to a halt in front of the little one, who glances at the overripe and gooey offering, curls back his lips and begins to snort and cough.

The third banana I toss lands a few feet closer to where I'm standing at the doorway.

Still nothing.

I peel a fourth banana and take a bite. "Mmmm," I say, and wave it in front of me. Their eyes follow the motion of my arm. The one I assume is the mother picks up a burlap sack and pulls it over her head.

It is obvious that, despite my peaceful intentions, Oscar, Wilma and Pluto are in no mood to participate in their own liberation. I hadn't really considered this. I just assumed that every caged thing spends its time sitting around waiting for either rescue or an opportunity to escape.

But whether they understand it or not, I have to save them, need to save them, even if I have to take each one by the scruff of the neck and drag them kicking and screaming to their freedom.

I take a deep breath, drop the half-eaten banana onto the floor, bend down, pick up my gym bag and step into the cage.

For a split second it feels as if the air has been sucked out of the room.

The beam of my flashlight illuminates the brightly coloured, plastic furnishings. A soccer ball, a single rubber boot, and three orange pylons cast long shadows across the floor.

I look up at the roof and try to imagine the blue light of a star-filled sky flickering through a canopy of leaves.

I feel my heart beat once loudly in my chest.

Time stops.

And then all hell breaks loose.

There is something almost choreographed in the sudden-ness of their response—like a huge flock of birds simultane-ously alighting from a telephone wire. The three chimps tumble and thump, leap and howl. They move so fast and furiously that it is difficult to take it all in. And even though I should be terrified during all this spitting, chest pounding and feces throwing, I sit on the floor, take the typewriter I have stolen from the principal's office out of my gym bag and resort to plan B: if all else fails, compose suicide note.

> To whom it may concern,
>
> Read any newspaper, flick on a television, or go to a zoo and you can feel it—happiness is built on illusions, a false sense of hope brought to you by Walt Disney, Maxwell House, and the Metro Zoological Society. And when you strip away the advertising, the laugh track and the price of admission, there's nothing left but a dull, aching bore-dom, reminding us that at the end of the day, William Shakespeare, Elvis Presley, and our forays into outer space aside, we haven't really come very far from the trees we descended from.

And then, just as my finger hits the period at the end of the paragraph, I spot what I think is a Goodyear tire sailing through the air. In the fraction of a second between being struck by that tire and the solid thump and rattle of my head hitting the Plexiglas wall behind me, I think about the famous French philosopher Emile Borel's hypothesis, and I paraphrase, a monkey hitting keys at random on a typewriter will eventually type out the complete works of Shakespeare. In the thick, weighty darkness that follows, I surmise that this same monkey, given a microphone, a pair of mirrored sunglasses and a white jumpsuit, would eventually become an Elvis impersonator—and, if this same monkey had been raised by an alcoholic, taxi-driving, amateur astronomer and a disillusioned manicurist, I suspect that it would eventually cut its wrists as well.

My next three observations: I am not dead, I have a terrible headache, and I am heavily sedated. Everything around me is moving fast, and yet, I'm moving slowly like a farm tractor leaving bits of straw and cornhusks on the shoulder of a busy highway. And then, when my shoulder bangs stiffly against something hard, I wince as a jarring pain shoots up my neck and settles in the foggy muddle of my mind.

"Sorry," a voice says behind me.

I open my eyes and realize that I'm in a wheelchair. I painfully twist my body until I see Bruce (he's wearing a nametag). His stern face is a mile above me. I wonder if he's a giant. Why isn't he playing basketball, replacing light bulbs or rescuing kittens from the branches of neighbourhood trees? I turn back to make sure he's not going to plow me into anything else. A crew of nurses, orderlies and janitors waltz chaotically around us as we continue down the hall. The peach-coloured walls are decorated with framed floral prints and there are signs everywhere— This is the First Day of the Rest of Your Life, or Laughter is the Best Medicine—that sort of thing. Bruce taps me on the shoulder and points at things, naming them as we move along: toilets, telephone, cafeteria, but I'm having difficulty connecting the words I'm hearing with anything I'm seeing. Eventually, the hall opens up on the left to a large room where five or six sad-looking people are sitting in fold-up chairs staring intently at a television, a chorus of munchkins imploring Dorothy to follow the yellow brick road.

I turn to Bruce. "Television room," I say—each syllable scrapes against the back of my throat as if I haven't spoken in a million years.

Bruce nods and points at a big red sign taped to the wall above the TV set.

TELEVISION PROGRAMS ARE
TO BE SELECTED DEMOCRATICALLY.
ABSOLUTELY NO TALK SHOWS, OR ANY PROGRAMS WITH
VIOLENCE OR SEX ALLOWED.

As we swerve suddenly around a guy vacantly staring at the ceiling, I spot a woman about the age of my mother who, when our eyes meet, starts gesturing with her hand between her legs as if she's stroking a very large penis. It's a little disturbing but I give her the thumbs up sign. Bruce flicks me in the back of the head, leans in and says, "Mind your own business."

Farther down the hall, just past the nurses station, Bruce stops, engages the brake on the wheelchair and then holds a door open for me. "Welcome home," he says.

The room is small. It looks more like a monk's chamber than a hospital room—no pictures, no signs, just a barred window, a bed and a chair.

I heave myself up, and though my elbows and knees won't cooperate, I manage to shuffle across the room and collapse on the bed. I bruise a rib when I land with a thud on the hard mattress. The muffled sound of Dorothy talking to the Tin Man down the hall gives way to a song and dance routine, and then I'm asleep.

When I wake up there is a red glow from the emergency exit sign in the hallway illuminating the little window in the door. The room is all dark shadows, a still foggy silence. A dull ache thuds in my temples. My legs are numb, and there's a crusty paste at the corners of my mouth. As I stare up at the ceiling images of a barren suburban landscape—car dealerships, recreational centres, strip malls—are juxtaposed with glimpses of the three caged chimps.

I watch Bruce duck his head slightly as he enters my room in the morning. There is about an inch between his neatly coiffed hair and the top of the door. He doesn't actually need to duck but I suspect that he does this out of habit, having banged his head on one too many chandeliers or ceiling fans. I drag my legs over the side of the bed. Still stiff.

"Where's my wheels?" I ask.

"No more free rides," he says.

I heave myself up and follow him out the door. It feels as if I'm walking on the bottom of the ocean with weights around my ankles—pulled in two directions. Bruce stops me in a large open foyer, points at the clock and then nods towards a long, straight and orderly queue. I will myself forward, but it seems to take a second or two before my legs respond.

The line moves slowly. We are scarecrows, lions and tin men, misfits lacking the essentials—brains, hearts, courage—a clear and cogent sense of reality. Several minutes pass before I realize that Oz is a window through which a nurse disperses daily rations of pills and cigarettes. The thought of smoking makes me want to throw up. My heart aches. Is that a good sign? I stay in line contemplating the potential currency of a cigarette stash should I ever need a favour in this place.

Like the others ahead of me, I swallow my meds, tuck my cigarette behind my ear and head for the smoking yard where Bruce, or someone dressed like Bruce, stands holding the door open for us while swinging the keys on the end of his finger. All the orderlies are ex-basketball players it seems.

I take a seat on a wooden picnic table in the shade of a single tree that has claimed the only patch of earth in the centre of the concrete yard. I consider the cars and people going by and estimate that the fence is about twelve feet high. I notice a taxi idling across the road. I calculate the damage the barbs at the top of the fence would inflict on my hands and other parts of my body should I attempt a hasty climb, but then a twinge of pain arcs across my temples and I realize I've been thinking too much. They probably have a sign somewhere warning against this. I settle back into my sedated lull.

We aren't allowed to have lighters or matches so one of the orderlies has to light the cigarette for each patient. Hands cupped to block a nonexistent wind, they look like they're sharing secrets, the first deep inhale filling their lungs, a satisfying reprieve from their madness. I sit alone under the tree breathing air instead of smoke.

As the day slips by, I discover that Bruce's duties include waking me up, escorting me to appointments and activities. I can sense him behind me as I drag my feet down the hall. It's like being followed too closely by a steamroller. And yet, I find that I'm comforted by his economy of words. Mostly, he firmly places his large hands on my shoulders and steers me in the direction he wants me to go, or he shakes his keys to get my attention and then mimes his orders—a finger raised to his lips to indicate that I am talking too loudly or saying something that the facility deems inappropriate, a tap on the wrist to indicate that time is up, a rapid circular motion over the belly to indicate mealtime. I decide to think of him as the game warden. I adjust my stride and adopt a posture of resignation as we move from one appointment to another. By the end of the day I'm exhausted. I lie down on the hard bed and wait for someone with bolt cutters and a bunch of bananas to rescue me.

Dr. Theodore Atwood, BSC, MA, PhD, PSC, a.k.a. head shrink, is an impressive man. If you narrow your eyes, he resembles Dr. Zaius from *Planet of the Apes*. He makes the expanse of the oak desk in front of him look like the tray of a high chair. Everything about him is large with the exception of a pair of rectangular glasses perched on his nose, the thin wire arms splayed outward on either side of his temples barely reach his ears. The top of his head seems small compared to the enlarged architecture of his face. The collar of his shirt and the knot of his tie disappear into the fold of his neck. Every time he inhales, his chest swells and he looks like he's on the verge of belching. The buttons on his shirt strain and his face flushes in a slow wheezy cycle.

He intentionally, I think, tries my patience. Not that I'm in a rush or anything, it's just that he spends what feels like a year trying to get the lid off his coffee. The smell of industrially manufactured floral cleaners mingling with an air of authority, aftershave and the clinging odour of stale cigars makes me feel like I'm sitting in the principal's office all over again. I find myself staring out the window at the donut shop across the road. It's a fast food world, why can't this be a fast treatment facility? By the time this guy gets around to acknowledging that I even exist, I could have ordered a double-double, a blueberry muffin and enough rope to make a noose.

Atwood fingers a package of Sweet and Low, hesitates and then drops it back into a brown paper bag. While he continues to dally about, I take the time to scan his bookshelf: *Psychodynamic Interpretation of Dreams, Experiographic Conceptualization of Dreams, Archetypes, Lucid Dreaming,*

Dreams and Reoccurrence of Feelings, Webster's Concise Dictionary.

A soft grunt directs my attention back to Atwood. He is trying to tear the little tab off the plastic lid of his coffee cup, but his fingers are too large to manage such a delicate operation. Several more minutes pass before he finally stirs what must now be a cup of room temperature coffee with his finger and takes an onomatopoeic slurp. I have scanned the rest of his bookshelf and counted the tiles in the ceiling by the time he clears his throat and indicates with a wave of his hand that he wants me to approach. I get up and sort of stagger over to his desk.

"Sign these, please," he says.

I take the forms and settle back into the couch with an exaggerated sigh. A quick glance at the forms confirms that I can barely read. What the hell are those pills they're giving me?

"So tell me," his voice is now less authoritative, almost kind, "how are you feeling today?"

I don't answer. I'm not sure yet if I want to make this hard or easy for him.

He glances at his watch, leans back in his chair and takes another sip of coffee. "We don't have all day," he says.

Moronic or ironic, I wonder.

"I feel fine," I say, but it's a lie. I feel like a safe fell on my head.

"Do you know why you are here?" he asks.

Vague images of music stores, pinball arcades and parks where old men sit on benches feeding pigeons race through my mind. Second-hand bookstores, theatres that play old movies, Chinatown, fresh fruit and vegetable stands, and then those damn monkeys again—I don't know what he knows, but I can see that the file on his desk is disturbingly thick. "Well, if you ask me, I'm here because we moved to the suburbs," I say.

"The suburbs?"

I find myself shaking my head—"It was so much better when we lived in those crappy apartments downtown, when my parents' dream was just a dream, something out of reach. I mean, they acted as if becoming homeowners in the suburbs was the greatest achievement in the world. I'd take the broken elevators, the noisy neighbours, the cockroaches, the silverfish and the earwigs over the boredom of the suburbs any day."

"Hmmm," he says. And then after a long pause, "You sound angry."

I close my eyes, hoping that my other senses will be more acute. I want to lie down. My heart is breaking all over again. I've seen enough doctors to know that he wants to hear my story. He needs copy in order to make his diagnosis. But I have a history of being uncooperative in this regard. It's not intentional. There are parts of my past that blur the lines of so-called reality. And I am prone to bouts of amnesia, which I am dismayed to realize I am suffering from at this moment. I scratch under my arm and try to focus, which is when I realize that I'm drooling. I look down. There are little wet dots of saliva on the papers I'm still holding in my lap. I use the blue sleeve of my hospital gown.

"If you're going to fill out those forms you'll need this," the doctor says.

When I look up he is holding what looks like a very expensive pen.

I ascertain that he expects me to get up again, walk the six feet between us and take the pen. I stay where I am and eye the forms suspiciously. "What's in it for me?" I bargain. I remember hearing somewhere that all contracts are negotiable.

"What do you want?" he asks.

I pretend like I'm giving the question some thought, as if I have never considered what my soul is worth, and then I tell him. "A typewriter. The monkeys destroyed mine."

He scribbles something quickly in my file and holds the pen up again. "Sign the forms, and I'll see what I can do," he says.

As I walk back to his desk I notice that my left wrist is bandaged. I have a moment of clarity—I remember the pills, the shaving of my eyebrows, breaking into the zoo, but just about everything before that is balled up in a fistful of newsprint. "There were three chimps," I say taking the pen—but it all feels vague and distant, as if it was something that happened to someone else, something I read in the newspapers or saw on television.

The doctor takes another sip and then empties the paper bag on his desk. "Go on," he says tearing open another packet of Sweet and Low.

"—Setting free a family of monkeys isn't as easy as you'd think," I say, falling back on the couch, "but I suppose you'd rather hear about Plan B."

Atwood empties the sweetener into his cup, takes another sip and dabs his mouth with a hanky that I notice has a cursive "A" embroidered in one corner.

"What's Plan B?" he asks.

"Plan B..." I exhale loudly and point at the bandage on my wrist. "This is Plan B. I tried to kill myself, remember?" The words feel as if they are attached to something lodged in the back of my throat. When I inhale I choke on each vowel and consonant as they return to the pit of my stomach.

Atwood eyes me as if he's trying to assess whether he might have to call Bruce in to administer the Heimlich maneuver or something.

I cough a few hundred times but that just makes my eyes begin to water and my breathing accelerate. I lean forward holding my chest. I know what's coming. These symptoms always precipitate a seismic tremor, a tectonic shift. The epicenter this time appears to be located across the street. I feel the floor rumble, the glass in the window vibrates and darkens with soot and smoke. I can smell burning crullers, coffee beans, Styrofoam and polyester. Atwood doesn't even flinch. I try to catch my breath. One Mississippi, two Mississippi, three … breathe.

As the smoke settles it feels as if there is nothing below me but fathomless space, and for a second, I'm suspended there like Wile E. Coyote in that moment he realizes he has stepped off the cliff. As I fall, I'm blinded by the headlights of a reversing car. I feel the sting of gravel, an Elvis song receding into the distance. And then I hit the ground.

I need to press down on the edges of this, hold the spine of it flat so that I can figure it all out. I need to start at the beginning, alphabetically—aardvark, accident, alcohol … I follow the thread back a year to my 16th birthday—August of 1977.

"Sorry," I say, "I have this condition—Catatonic something or other."

"Catatonic Dementia Praecox," Atwood says, looking down at my file. "But CDP is the symptom," he adds. "What I'm after is the cause."

He then casts his gaze upon me as if we're sitting in a court of law, assessing my worth and the appropriate pharmaceutical sentence. "I'd like to help you with all this," he says, "but first you have to sign those forms."

I push myself up off the couch, carry the forms back to his desk, and as I scribble my name at the bottom of each page, I notice that I have wet myself. I stumble backwards and collapse dramatically on the couch again.

"Thanks," he says.

"Hmmm," I say.

"Too early for an accurate assessment, but I think we're dealing with a hyperactive imagination possibly stimulated by cyclothymia as a direct result of unresolved post-traumatic stress. I'm recommending weekly therapy, rest and a trial dosage of anti-depressant pharmacology."

It takes a moment before I realize that he's talking about me, not to me, and that he is addressing a little tape recorder on his desk. He makes a few notes and then picks up the phone and mumbles something into the receiver. A moment later the door opens and Bruce steps into the room. He stands by the door with his arms at his sides like a bodyguard. I notice that the sleeves of his shirt are too short.

Dr. Atwood scribbles away for what seems like ten years before he looks up again. "Bruce here will remind you where the washrooms are located. As far as the typewriter goes," Atwood adds, "I'll see what I can do."

CHAPTER TWO

Dinner is served prison-style by a guy who has clearly been in the cafeteria business too long. He slops mashed potatoes onto my plastic plate, reaches back, scoops up some green beans and then drops a thin slice of meatloaf on the floor. He picks it up with the spatula, dabs his apron at it and then slides it onto my plate. I discreetly blow on it a few times when I get to the table. The beans are a little undercooked, but the food is good. I don't remember the last time I had a square meal. I devour everything in a matter of minutes. And then, as I'm finishing a cup of chocolate pudding, the crazy lady who made the rude gesture to me in the television room yesterday, last month, or whenever it was, limps into the cafeteria. She bends in weird places as she walks, as if she's made of straw. I have my head down, staring at my empty plate when she sort of crashes into the chair on the other side of the table. "You don't belong here, do you?" she says.

I shrug, because even though I don't want to be here, I'm not sure yet if I should be or not.

"No," she says, "I can tell. I saw you before. You were being chauffeured by Bruce."

Her name is Ophelia. She has a nametag on her shirt. I glance down and notice for the first time that I have one too.

She says, "You escaped from the story, didn't you?"

I casually scan the room for an empty seat at another table.

She leans in close. "Have you ever read Hamlet?"

"To be or not to be," I say with a vaguely British accent. The escaping from the story thing begins to make sense.

"I'm a number four like you," she continues. "Us number fours have to stick together."

Pistachio, I think to myself.

"Pistachio what?" Ophelia says.

Holy shit, how did she do that, I wonder.

"Do what?' she asks.

And then I realize that I must be thinking out loud.

"A number four," Ophelia informs me, "is an access restriction code. Number four, being the highest, carries the condition of constant supervision. Number four patients are a high risk of suicide, a danger to other patients and staff."

"A pistachio," I inform her, "is a type of nut."

She is not insulted. Instead, she offers to trade her meds with me. It turns out Ophelia is an expert on sedatives, tranquilizers and hypnotics. I guess she's been here a while.

"Careful with the red ones," she says. "Take them too many times in a row and you got a terrible case of Akathesia—never mind a caffeine buzz, those little buggers will send you to the moon. And the little blue ones," she scrunches up her face and tightens both hands into fists, "will give you the worst case of constipation."

"And I was worried about the meatloaf."

"You're funny," she says as she grabs the little salt and pepper packages and quickly stuffs them up the sleeve of her cardigan.

After dinner, Ophelia follows me to an occupational therapy class where we play games, do charades, and my personal favourite—work on puzzles. She pulls a stick of lipstick out of her pocket and applies it with the expertise of a four-year-old without a mirror. "You can't be sure who might be in the audience," she says, while puckering her lips and drawing a red line that veers from her bottom lip to her chin.

I need some elbowroom. I glance around and spot a table with one chair in the corner. "Gotta go," I say.

But before I can get up, she grabs the cigarette behind my ear and places a small handful of pills in my hand.

Time moves excruciatingly slow. I know I should be bored as hell, but I suspect that the drugs keep me subdued and complacent. There are paper chain-link decorations taped to the walls and fake flowers placed in plastic vases. Everything looks pretty much like a cross between an old folks' home and fucking kindergarten class. I watch the activities around me as if from the portal of a submarine, as if there is a pane of thick glass between me and everything else. I am trying to hold it all together and stay calm, but there's a momentary lapse of time between my thoughts and actions, a delay of about three seconds during which I can't be sure of anything. I spend an hour one afternoon watching a couple waltz back and forth down the middle of the hall. At first I'm impressed with how fluidly the dancers move together, but then I notice that the man, who is about six inches shorter than the woman, is standing on the top of his partner's feet. I begin to realize that if I don't get a typewriter soon I will simply go nuts.

"Memory," Dr. Atwood says, "is the ability to store, retain and recall information."

I nod.

He taps his fancy pen several times on my file and then spins it expertly between his fingers.

I suspect that the coffee on his desk is not his first of the day.

"—But memory is not truth." As he says this, he raises his hand, his chubby index finger pointing to the ceiling.

I look up.

"—It is a construct of our perceptions and experience," he continues. "And in order to get you on your feet again, we've got to stabilize you, and work on your cognitive imbalances."

I am thinking of my mother, how she started placing the milk container in the cupboard, sugar in the fridge, leaving cryptic notes all over the house. "A construct like a jigsaw puzzle?" I venture.

"Yes, well that's a fairly accurate analogy," Atwood says. "Memory can indeed be broken down into bits and pieces of sensory information, images, sounds, smells, feelings. The people, places and events that we recall define our sense of self within the world. These things are all filtered through our psyche where the memory is modified and edited and adjusted so that the pieces fit together into a cohesive narrative."

"And this cohesive narrative," I add, "should resemble the image on the box."

"The box?"

"The box the puzzle comes in."

Atwood scratches at his chin. "You're funny," he says.

He then pushes his chair back and struggles to get himself out from behind his desk. The amount of energy this simple maneuver requires is kind of amusing and pathetic at the same time. If I ran for the exit this man would never catch me.

"This cohesive narrative is the story of our lives," he says as he drags his comfy-looking office chair behind him across the uncooperative dusty rose shag. He wheezes with each step until he finally parks the chair next to the couch and takes a seat. "What I have in mind for today is called regressive hypnotherapy. All you need to do is relax."

Since I've been selectively trading my meds with Ophelia, I've developed a taste for the little yellow ones that leave my brain wrapped in cellophane. I've been having trouble sleeping though, and so I look forward to an opportunity to recline on a couch far more comfortable than the hard furniture outside this office. "Relax," I say it like a mantra. "Relax, relax, relax…"

"—Memory," Atwood interrupts, "serves us in every decision we make. It provides context, and without context we cannot learn, we are doomed to a cycle of repetition and chance."

He takes a deep breath and then he's up again, limping across the room to the wall-unit bookcase where he opens a cabinet door and presses the play button on a tape deck. The sound of gentle waves lapping on a beach fills the room. The waves are eventually accompanied by a badly played piano. I expect Anne Murray to start singing at any moment.

"Think of it as a journey," he says, as he groans back into his chair. "Just like when you open a photo album and revisit the moment when the pictures were taken." His voice is neutral now. He pronounces each syllable clearly as if he's reading a recipe from a cookbook.

I listen to the soothing waves and try to surrender, letting my mind wander like channels changing on a television—Firestone Tires, Calgon Laundry Detergent, Polident—and in between each commercial there are two or three channels with no reception. As I focus on the static, I have the strange sense that I'm in two places at once.

"It's your dad's birthday," I hear my mother say. "Get your shoes on. We're going shopping." I'm already wearing my sneakers so I just sit there. It's like I'm having a dream within a dream, as if the glass around me is now two panes thick.

"Earth to Kepler."

I try to focus. Past, present, future. The channel changes again.

My mother is holding the door open at the mall. "Jesus Christ, Kepler," she yells, "I don't have all day."

As we stroll past the bank I stop to watch a lady trying to lift a kid off one of those coin-operated horses while it's still galloping. The kid seems terrified, he's crying, but he won't let go of the reins. "I've got you," the lady says. "For the love of god, just let go, Colin."

I feel my hands tighten into fists. No, I want to say, never let go. Hold on. Hold on as if your goddamn life depends on it.

I turn just in time to see my mother disappear into a store. I can hear the cellophane crinkle, the channel changes again, and I'm standing in the Hobby Barn.

"Puzzles are the perfect gift," the salesman says. He has a large black mustache complimented by a pair of thick eyebrows that make his deep-set eyes difficult to read. "They stimulate the mind," he adds, pointing at his temple, "and the imagination." He points his other finger at his other temple. "We just got a new one in of Batman. Your mother tells me you like Batman."

When did my mother tell him that I liked Batman, I wonder.

"It's for my dad," I say. "He's an astronaut."

"Dad owns a telescope," my mom adds.

The salesman reaches over and ruffles my hair. I decide that I hate it when people ruffle my hair. I look at the racks of puzzles and ask him if he has anything with a picture of Carl Sagan on it.

The salesman smiles and reaches for the top of my head again. "How about something to do with space," he says.

"Carl Sagan has everything to do with space," I say.

"This Carl Sagan fellow a friend of your dad?" he asks smugly, looking over at my mother. He then turns to lead us further down the aisle. His finger runs down the line of boxes as he shuffles along. "Here we are, the expert puzzles, five thousand pieces and up. Let's see, The Last Supper, The Great Barrier Reef, Wild Mustangs, The Solar System, The Mona Lisa—"

I give a sharp tug on the sleeve of his shirt. "Go back," I say. The words go back echo in my head.

I have to tread water for a while until I can get my bearings. It feels like I've been stuck for a while between floors in a broken elevator. I guess I'm one of those people who is easy to hypnotize.

"Kepler, you okay?"

I recognize Atwood's voice, but I keep my eyes closed for a moment until I can feel my body again. But as I settle in, I feel a weight on my chest and I realize I have dragged something back from the memory. I don't know why, but I start to cry, and when the tears come, it's like a heaving, snot-filled storm.

Dr. Atwood passes me a box of Kleenex. "What's going on, Kepler?"

"My dad started working on the puzzle as soon as he got home," I tell him. "We had to eat dinner that night with our plates perched on the edge of the kitchen table because there were puzzle pieces all over the place. 'Move your glass of water, there, Alice,' my dad said. When my mom picked up her glass, my father laid down a piece with some red on it. 'There's no water on Mars,' he said. My dad worked on the puzzle all evening. By the time he went to bed he had about eight square inches of the puzzle complete. My mom didn't complain until the next evening at dinner, but by then he was working on Saturn's gaseous rings. 'It took god seven days to create the universe,' he said. 'I'll have it done in six.'"

A little bell chimes.

"Good," Doctor Atwood says. He gets up and turns off the tape. "We've got you connected. That's a very good start."

I don't want to get up, but Atwood is holding the door open.

I peel myself up off the couch, and as I shuffle over to the door, it feels as if he just yanked the stitches out of an unhealed wound.

"Just the tip of the iceberg, Kepler," he says with a satisfied smile.

Ophelia is waiting for me outside the door. Bruce goes over to the water fountain to give us some space. Ophelia has done a horrid job applying her makeup again. And I'm a little disturbed that I'm actually happy to see her. It's like she's my dear old aunt and all the rest of our family has passed away and we're stuck here on this weird television show together. But then I look at her and think I must be losing my mind to have her as a friend, and I want to go screaming down the hall pulling my goddamn hair out.

"Doctor wants three thousand words a week," Bruce says as he places the typewriter at the foot of my bed. I wait until he closes the door before I even bother to sit up.

The Remington is a thing of beauty with all its workings exposed, a much nicer machine than the one the monkeys destroyed. Atwood must have dug this antique out of somebody's attic. I poke at a few keys, press the carriage release lever, pull it closer. It weighs about as much as the complete works of Shakespeare. I know because my mother had all thirty-seven plays stacked neatly on the back of the toilet.

Bruce opens the door again, "Sorry. You'll need this," he says, and drops a package on my bed. I tear the wrapper open and scroll in a piece of fresh white twenty-pound typewriter paper, press the space bar and then hit a random key. It's a D— for drunk, doghouse, dream... I look down and aim my pointer finger at the E key and then the A. The T and H keys almost glow. Every tragedy ends this way, but this is how mine begins.

My fingers tingle, and when I start hunting and pecking, each letter hits the ribbon with a satisfying snap. The words "cohesive narrative" echo in my head and before long I hear the clatter of a million primates in garbage dumps, thrift shops, insane asylums (wherever we can get our banana-stained hands on a typewriter) pounding away in one miraculous chorus.

CHAPTER THREE

(I)

I remember how matter-of-fact it sounded when my mother told me my aunt had died. "They found her on the toilet," she said. "They figure she got up in the night to go—you know—and she had a heart attack."

My mother tossed three frozen pork chops onto a baking sheet, and then handed me a bag of frozen corn. "Open this," she said.

I tore a hole in the top corner and handed the bag back to her.

"Which aunt died?" I asked.

"Aunt Judy. Jeeze, Kepler, I only have one sister."

I watched her maneuver the bag of corn awkwardly over a pot of water.

"Have I ever met her?"

"Of course you've met her," she said placing the pot of corn in the oven, "she's your aunt."

"Mom, you got it reversed," I said, "the pork chops go in there."

She took a quick step back as if she had dropped something on the floor. "Not again," she whispered.

After placing the pot on the stove she stood there for a moment, her eyes fixed on the sheet of pork chops. "Anyway," she finally said, "if we're going to a funeral, I'll have to get my nails done."

I had faced all manner of nightmares as a child, moderated parental arguments, been shoved around by a number of schoolyard bullies and not one tear. But as I watched my mom hesitate and then place the pork chops in the oven, it seemed like a cloud had drifted in front of the sun, or the bulb in the light above the stove had been replaced with a lower wattage. That lesser quality of light felt unsettling, like a filter newly shrouding the world. And that subtle atmospheric shift drove me to my bedroom where I fell down on my bed, and for no explicable reason that I could name, I began to bawl my eyes out.

I had to wear a maroon and grey pinstriped jacket that my father got second-hand at the Ex-toggery. The jacket smelled horrible.

"Christ," my dad said. "You look like Howard Hughes."

My mom made a funny face. "Mothballs," she said. And after digging around under the sink for a minute, she stood up with a groan and sprayed me with a can of Lysol.

My dad wore his blue suit, the only suit he had, which, aside from the Elvis 1968 comeback special commemorative necktie he was struggling with, was pretty much what he wore every day. My mom squeezed into a red dress that was, as my father pointed out, at least two sizes too small. But it matched her freshly painted nails, her lipstick, and her shoes. When I think about it now, it probably looked like we were going to the Oscars not a funeral.

The service was punctuated by my mother's curses as she made adjustments to the hem of her dress every time the minister asked us to stand. While my father discreetly snuck a couple of sips from a flask that he had secreted in the inside pocket of his jacket, I sat quietly confused about the whole production. I didn't quite get it. But then after about an hour of singing, and praying, and sermonizing about God's inscrutable will, the affirmation of life, and immortality of the soul, it hit me. When the minister mentioned the bit about how we must look to the future with faith and hope in the presence of grief and despair, I just cracked. Despair—the word awakened something in me, something I had been feeling since earlier that day in the kitchen, the uneasy feeling that I could not articulate now had a name—the state of being without hope; a feeling that nothing good can happen.

As the word settled into my gut like a black hole, the gravity of the ceremony sunk in with it. I couldn't shake it. I grew up watching Charles Bronson and Clint Eastwood dispatch justice in slow-motion on television practically every Saturday night—but this was the other kind of death, the kind that happens to ordinary people, the kind that sneaks up on you in the middle of the night when you get up to use the damn toilet. I was suddenly struck by the permanence of it, one minute you're there having a crap and the next minute you're gone—you don't even get a chance to wipe your ass.

Despair. Holy fuck.

On the way home, my dad was in a mood. "What a farce," he said. "Everyone going on about how fabulous she was."

"That's the way it works, Walter," my mother said. "It's called respect. We'll all pretend you were a real prince when you go, too."

My dad gripped his hands on the wheel tightly. "When do we get possession?"

"Possession of what?" I asked.

"Never mind, it's a surprise," my mother said.

"We're moving," my dad said.

"Walter."

"Again?" I said.

"No, not again, into a house—our very own Graceland."

We didn't actually get possession of my dead aunt's house for another two months, but my parents started packing the day after the funeral, which meant we spent a lot of time reopening boxes looking for things that got packed too early, like the can opener and the take-away menus. But nothing could upset my mother during that time. She marked off each day on the calendar with a ballpoint pen, and then ripped the whole page off when each month was over.

"Three more weeks, Kepler."

My mom ran a strip of tape over a box with the word "fragile" markered on its side.

"Two more weeks, Walter."

I caught my parents hugging in the kitchen.

"One more week, Alice."

Blast off.

I didn't know where we were going, but as I sat there on the empty birdcage placed between the two seats of the rental van, that hole in my gut seemed to expand.

"It's a new start," my mom said. "No more landlords. No more bugs. And no more damn streetcars outside the bedroom window."

"It's also darker in the suburbs," my father added, "less light pollution, so my telescope will work a hell of a lot better."

It was like my parents had caught the same happiness disease.

"You'll have a yard to mow, Kepler," my dad said. "Your mother can grow some flowers. We can get a barbecue and a croquet set."

My mother sort of smiled. And with that, my dad thumped his fist on the horn a couple of times.

Lawn mowers, croquet. The suburbs. I didn't like the sound of it one bit.

A half hour later we pulled off the highway and headed south on Markham Road.

"Smell that?" my father said, rolling down the window. "Fresh air."

"Smells like cow shit," I said.

My father jabbed me with his elbow, but he was still smiling. "I bet there are some great golf courses out here."

"Since when do you play golf, Walter?" my mother asked.

"I taught Arnold Palmer everything he knows," my dad said, winking at me in the rearview mirror. "—Hey, look, there's a school," he yelled. He said it like it was the first time he had ever seen one, and that if we didn't look quick enough it might vanish back into the land of magical surprises. A few minutes later we were driving through the tree-lined boulevards, streets and crescents of our new neighbourhood. My mother pointed out that each house had its own antenna. "The reception must be great out here without all the tall buildings."

But all I felt was the trouble in my gut. Out there beyond the dirty windshield I counted seven gas stations, nine car dealers, six donut shops, and three dead squirrels. By the time my dad pulled up to the curb and jammed the gear into park, I was ready to trade my new life in for an asthma attack, epilepsy, or a brain hemorrhage. Anything would have been better than how depressed I was feeling.

"Okay, here we are," my dad said pulling the keys out of the ignition. "145 Easy Living Street."

My dad was out of the van first. I waited for my mom to maneuver herself out the passenger side, and as my parents strolled up the walkway, I stood on the boulevard under a decrepit looking tree taking it all in. Our driveway was the only one on the street that wasn't paved, and the lawn was covered in a mixture of dandelions, dog shit and cigarette butts. I don't know what my parents were excited about, but the obvious fact that this house was not only the loser of the block, but a million light years from anything remotely interesting didn't seem to faze them at all.

"I see a snowman on that lawn next winter, Kepler," my dad said. "We can string up some Christmas lights once I get the eaves repaired."

While my dad fumbled with the key ring, my mom looked down at the pile of soggy newspapers on the cracked porch, back at the cigarette butts all over the patchy lawn and then over at the neighbour's blooming rosebush bordered by a row of blue petunias and marigolds. "C'mon, Walter," my mother said with the first hint of real irritation I'd heard in weeks.

"The damn lock is rusty," my dad said, as he tried another key.

It felt like we were breaking into someone's home.

There were still cigarettes in the ashtray, a light was on above the stove and the kitchen had the faint odour of macaroni and cheese. While my mother slammed the cupboards and unpacked the cleaning supplies, my dad headed for the basement. I went straight to the bathroom where my aunt had died. I don't know what I was expecting, but the only thing I found was an empty pack of cigarettes, a half roll of toilet paper, and a few dead flies on the windowsill.

My dad spent the weekend in the basement, and by Sunday afternoon there were about a dozen garbage bags at the curb. That evening he sat on the stoop of the front porch smoking. "It needs a bit of work," he said, "but this place has a lot of potential."

You didn't have to do much more than look both ways up our street to see the problem with it—out house was a neglected mess, but what was even worse was that the houses in the whole borough were a variation on three different designs. The brick and shingle colour varied along with the placement of shrubbery and potted petunias, but the houses were otherwise the same. My dad even managed to pull into the wrong driveway the next evening when he came home from work. He actually had one shoe off when he spotted a woman down the hall in the kitchen with nothing on but a cooking apron.

"Who the hell cooks in the nude?" my dad said when he was telling the story. "We just stood there staring at each other. I was thinking, what the hell is this naked woman doing in my kitchen? And then she dropped her spatula and screamed so loud I could hear the crystal rattle in the dining room hutch. Helluva way to meet your neighbours."

My mom called it Freudian. "How could you possibly mistake their house for ours, Walter? They have an interlocking brick path framed by a row of snapdragons leading to the front door. And nudists or not, their lawn is mowed."

In my dad's defense, it was dark out, and he just finished a double shift—that and he was more than likely drunk.

I admit that the sense of despair that had made its home in the centre of my stomach coloured my perspective, but there was something claustrophobic about that house. I wouldn't go so far to say it was haunted, but I was convinced that my Aunt Judy's death was responsible for the overcast atmospheric conditions of the place. Even my parents' enthusiasm and the familiar sight of unpacked boxes was not enough to evict the despondency and sadness that seemed to be present in every room. In fact, the junk of our former life as apartment renters just accentuated the fact that, though we were now in a house, at the core of it, nothing had really changed. The couch still looked like hell, the plates in the kitchen still had chips in them, and I, to my father's chagrin, was still sleeping with my sock monkey.

We ate Sunday dinners in front of the television, and for a while my mother's only complaint was that my father was developing what she called "bourgeois attitudes." After having a few beers he liked to look out the window and assess the neighbourhood. He had an opinion about everything—hedges, cars, the breed of the neighbourhood dogs. "Why would anyone associate themselves with a poodle?" he said. "It's embarrassing."

I liked animals and had been feebly petitioning for a dog since my seventh birthday, not a poodle of course, something my dad would approve of like a German Shepard. Truth is I would have settled for a hamster, but my father made it clear one morning that having a pet in the house wouldn't be such a good idea. I was helping him wash the car when he got down on his knees and started making gentle little purring sounds. It took a moment to realize that he was trying to coax a tabby out from under the car. A moment later the cat was arching its back and rubbing up against my father's shins expecting a scratch behind the ears. It was then that my father reached for the bottle of Windex. "Next time I'll use the hose," he said, as the terrified animal bolted across the driveway. He then placed the Windex bottle back on the hood of the car and gestured over his shoulder. "That's the little bugger that's been shitting all over the lawn. But we're homeowners now. We don't have to take crap from anybody."

My dad made several trips to the hardware store in those first weeks—tools, washers, fuses, but most of his repairs involved duct tape, a hammer, and a lot of cursing.

"Looks like I'll need a wrench," my dad called out from under the sink.

"Crescent, pipe or open-end?" I asked.

My mom was standing at the ready with the mop and a bucket just in case.

My dad groaned. "Ah, better bring them all. And grab me a beer while you're at it. This may take a while."

As my parents valiantly tussled with the expenses and labours of their newly acquired dream of being homeowners, I immersed myself in the newspapers that, despite my mother's call to cancel my aunt's subscription, still came every day. I couldn't seem to resist the headlines. *Civil war in Lebanon, the death of A.Y. Jackson, apartheid in South Africa, genocide in Cambodia.* It was the dawning of my realization that the darkness that I was feeling was not limited to the house I was living in. And just when I was thinking that it couldn't get much worse, I saw a back to school ad that reminded me that there were six more days till the end of summer holidays. It was just a matter of time before I was in yet another new school, sitting in yet another Guidance Counsellor's office trying to articulate why I was chronically late, didn't do my homework, and had no friends.

Miss Jones was wearing a tight black skirt, which accentuated the roundness of her hips and kept her knees locked together when she walked. "I'm here to assess your future goals and to facilitate your transition into a new academic environment," she said. Her lips seemed impossibly red, and her eyes were so dark you could barely distinguish the irises from the pupils. I hated her from the moment I saw her, and yet within a minute, she had me confessing my despair for the world. "240,000 people died in an earthquake in China." My voice came out a couple octaves higher as I unfolded the newspaper and flattened it out on her desk.

"Yes, I heard about that," Miss Jones said.

"Death is everywhere," I said.

I couldn't stop looking at her lips.

"It might be better if you focus on the things that you can control, Kepler."

"Like what?"

"Like your attitude. You have to cheer up a little."

"What's the point in being happy if a giant crack in the earth can suddenly open up and swallow us?"

"Earthquakes aren't really cracks in the earth," she said. "They're more like vibrations, shifts in the earth's tectonic plates. And we don't really have to worry about earthquakes in this part of the world."

She was wrong. I could feel the earth shifting at that moment..."How can that many people die at once? How will they bury them?"

"Slow down and breathe, Kepler."

She got up from her desk, came around behind me and placed her hands on my shoulders. "They'll probably hold a memorial for all of them together," she said.

All I could think of was a stack of coffins as large as an apartment building, that and the tube of lipstick that I spotted next to her little thingy of paperclips. I closed my eyes and breathed in the bawdy scent of her perfume.

"You're a smart kid, Kepler. I know you'll be all right."

When I exhaled, my breath came out embarrassingly loud. She went back around to her desk, and when her back was to me, I reached forward and grabbed the lipstick. I don't know why I did it. I'd never really stolen anything before.

"Is there anything else bothering you, Kepler?"

I wanted to tell her that ever since we moved into my dead aunt's house I had the sense that something horrible was going to happen. "No," I said. "Aside from the earthquake, every-thing is fine."

A week later, I pocketed some cheap eyeliner from the drug store. Not long after that, I stole a pair of my mother's earrings. I couldn't help myself. I hid the stuff under a pile of towels in the cupboard in the bathroom. There was something terribly exciting about it. Those secret stolen things gave me a sense of both power and anxiety, which took my mind off how depressed I was.

And then one night I found myself in the bathroom piercing my ear with an ice cube and a sewing needle. I was altering myself, flirting with the impending doom that my parents couldn't seem to see. I took the lipstick out and ran it across my lips, drew a dark line across my eyelids with a short black pencil. I looked different, feminine, sort of. Did I look anything like my dead aunt? I took several deep breaths and sat down on the toilet. But nothing happened. The lights didn't dim, a chilling breeze didn't blow across the back of my neck, there was no shrouded figure beckoning me towards a graveyard. As a matter of fact, I felt very calm and relaxed.

And then the bathroom door swung open.

My mother's eyes moved quickly from the cosmetics on the counter to my face, and then back to the cosmetics. The sudden pounding in my chest made me think that the horsemen had in fact arrived. When she screamed, I felt the drywall strain, the porcelain sink vibrate, and when my mother slammed the door, a section of the wallpaper peeled back in the corner above the toilet.

The next evening when my dad got home from work, my mom was waiting for him in the kitchen. While they talked I thought about jumping out the window, but instead, I just sat on my bed hugging Ham. I heard my dad open a beer. They talked some more and then my dad opened another one. I could hear the old house groan, something expanded and contracted in the ceiling, my dad's footsteps were loud across the floor. When he pushed my bedroom door open he took three steps forward and stopped. "Give him to me," he said. He had a look in his eyes that gleamed with both violence and humour.

I was crying again.

"Jeezus Christ, Kepler."

"No," I said.

If I could go back, I would hand him over willingly. I would wipe my hands and toss him in the trash myself, but at that moment, that sock monkey seemed like the most important thing in the world. I'd had the damn thing since I was five. He was the closest thing I had to a friend. He knew all my secrets.

Despite my efforts, my father left the room with a beer in one hand and Ham's left arm in the other.

There's a heavy thump at my door. I pull the page out of the typewriter and crumple it in my fist. It's a gut reaction, a reflex. I hear my name and then what sounds like a cry for help. I get up and look out the window in the door and see Ophelia being dragged down the hall by two orderlies. When I push the door open I'm on autopilot. I'm not really thinking or sure of what I'm doing, but part of me believes I am coming to the rescue. One of the orderlies turns and sees me stumbling down the hall towards them. He stops and lets go of Ophelia with one hand and points at me. "Go back to your room, Kepler," he yells. The tone of his voice is enough to slow me down. And as the two orderlies drag Ophelia around the corner, I realize how out of breath I am. I stop and look down at my feet. I'm all bone and tendon and veins. I am suddenly aware that in a Darwinian sense, I'm simply not very well equipped to rescue anyone. Hell, I couldn't even rescue a sock monkey.

I go back to my room, pull the door closed behind me and sit in front of the typewriter—this is all I can do. I pick up the crumpled page and flatten it out on the floor. I need to refocus. I need to concentrate. I put another sheet in the typewriter. This is my ticket out of here—I need a story. Everyone has a story—without one you're nothing.

CHAPTER FOUR

(I)

Eventually, the honeymoon came to an end. It's no secret that my parents fought in the past, ask any of our old neighbours, but the growing silence between them seemed much worse. No one mentioned the incident in the bathroom, or the skirmish with the sock monkey again. The quiet tension that had been lurking in the shadows began to expand and manifest itself in ways that were more conspicuous. I could smell its presence at the kitchen table every morning when my mother burnt her toast, I could it hear in my father's incompetent repairs under the sink where the pipe incessantly dripped into a bucket. It was in the tone of the anchorman as he reported on the news each evening, and by the time we went to bed each night, it was there in the darkness, in the quiet that surrounded us.

By Thanksgiving, the tension was palpable, but I was determined to enjoy the reprieve that holidays usually inspired. While my mother placed the turkey that had been thawing in the sink all night into a roasting pan, my dad sat down at the table silently smoking a cigarette. It was my job to keep things running smoothly, which I managed to do—plugging in appliances, cleaning bowls. I peeled potatoes, ran to the store to pick up butter, cigarettes and bread. By the afternoon, the smell of roasting turkey and a beam of sunlight cutting through the swirling dust put a spell on us all. As I stirred the gravy, my father got up, went into the living room and put an Elvis record on. Outside the window, the trees were bare and the days were getting shorter, but at that moment I could almost believe that maybe things would be okay after all.

My mother shook her head when I placed the Elvis salt and pepper shakers in the middle of the table. "Not tonight," she said, "get the clear glass ones off the back of the stove."

I had to go through the stack of unpacked boxes against the wall in the living room to find the good plates and the tablecloth with the embroidered edges. Even though the table was square and the frilly white covering was round, it covered enough of the table to make the setting feel festive and elegant. We used my dead aunt's silverware, and even though it was a little tarnished you could appreciate the weight and beauty of it.

When my mother pulled the turkey out of the oven she let out a little sigh as if she was tired but satisfied. "Perfect," she said.

And it was perfect, the three of us sitting down and tucking our napkins into the front of our shirts—the music, the candlelight. But as I reached for the bowl of potatoes that my mother had passed to me, the Elvis record ended and my father cleared his throat. "Am I the only one with an ounce of respect in this family?" he asked.

It was the first words he had spoken all day.

"Oh, Christ," my mother said.

"I'd like to take this opportunity," my father continued, "to give thanks, as is customary on Thanksgiving, and pass down our oral history to my progeny."

"You're drunk," my mother said.

I put down the bowl of potatoes.

"Ignore her, Kepler," my dad said. "She doesn't appreciate the importance of ceremony."

I held my breath waiting to see what my mother would do, but she just closed her eyes really tight for a moment and lowered her head so that the fat of her neck rolled out under her chin.

"There's the stories," my dad continued, "the stuff I can tell you, but there's also the qualities and nuances, the stuff you get through the bloodline."

I was torn, because even though I knew my mother was clearly not in the mood for one of my father's "blathering sessions," I loved my dad's stories.

"It's my obligation to share our history with my son," he said, turning to my mother, "and it's his obligation to listen. As far as I'm concerned, you can plug your ears."

My mother put her elbows on the table and pressed her hands up flat against her temples as if she was trying to keep something contained in her skull. I closed my eyes and wished we were back in our shitty little apartment in the city, where being homeowners was nothing more than a brief conversation that made my parents eyes go sort of distant and dreamy.

My father stood up and unscrewed the cap of the wine and filled each of our glasses. "Well, come on, stand up. I'm making a toast," he said. This declaration was followed by a brief coughing fit, which resulted in a wine stain on the white tablecloth. My father waited until my mother and I pushed our chairs out and stood up. "Ahem—Now, the important part of the Pressler family history begins in the year 1786 when Johann Pressler, a Protestant winemaker, sailed with his wife and two sons from Niederhöchstadt, Germany to America, fleeing the Catholic dominion." My father used his hands, gesturing dramatically to simulate the Atlantic crossing.

More wine was spilt.

I could feel the cutlery vibrate when my mother sat down again and reached for the potatoes.

"Johann, et al," my father said, ignoring my mother, "arrived in New York, as all ships did at that time, and set about looking for work. Now, for untold reasons, one son headed south—"

"Probably because the weather is better," my mother interrupted.

"—while the other went north, leaving Johann and his wife who, as the story goes, settled and died uneventfully in the Albany region."

My father paused to add effect, I think, to what he thought was a solemn moment.

"Günter, the son that came north, eventually got a job at a post office," he continued. "And in his spare time fixed his neighbours' broken clocks and watches, which he returned on his rounds when he delivered their mail."

My mother looked at her watch.

"One generation later, Peter Pressler took his father's tinkering to a new level when he opened a watch shop in Berlin, which later became Kitchener, Ontario." My father gestured with a sweep of his arm behind him as if Kitchener was on the other side of the wall. "Peter had two sons, Hermann, who apprenticed with his father in the family business, and Francis, who bought a couple of acres and started a winery in the Niagara area."

"What about the son who went south?" I asked.

"I'm saving the best till last. Now where was I?" He shook his head. "Jeezus, Kepler, now I've lost the damn thread."

"The traditions of his ancestors," I offered.

"Yeah, yeah, yeah. At least someone's paying attention." He glared at my mother who was slicing a piece of white meat off the turkey. "Anyway, the winery failed, some say because of the extensive tasting on the part of the wine master." Here my father laughed and took a generous sip from his glass. "Now Francis—" (Francis, Hermann, Peter, Günter, Johann, I was already confused) "—fathered nine children—seven girls and two boys, the last of which died at birth with his mother. Francis never recovered from this loss—" (whether the loss referred to his wife and child or the winery was never specified in the telling) "—and is rumoured to have abandoned his kids and returned to Germany, which by this time was in the throes of a revolutionary reconstruction of spirit led by a young upstart named Adolf Hitler."

My mother shook her head and gulped her whole glass of wine, her bottom teeth clinking against the edge of the glass. My father turned to her. "Oh, looks like someone's thirsty tonight." He reached for the bottle of wine and placed it where my mother couldn't easily reach it.

"Now Francis's youngest brother, Hermann, the watch fixer who never married, took the abandoned children into his home and never missed an opportunity to remind them that their father was a drunk and a dreamer."

"Sounds familiar," my mother said as she stuffed a fork full of carrots in her mouth.

Here my father refilled his own glass. "Raised by seven older sisters, the one boy, Walter, yours truly, ran away when he was twelve. He got a job at a bowling alley on Kingston Road, where he held the scoring title for three years straight. That is also where he met a beautiful woman." My father nodded in my mother's direction. "Believe it or not, Kepler, your mother once had an hourglass figure."

"Your father's as homely as he was the day I met him," my mother said.

Now they were both drunk. I knew where this was going. As my parents argued I picked up my glass. I knew the story; we all knew the stupid story. "To make a long story short," I said. "During the Civil War, the Pressler that went south, changed his last name to Presley." I took a sip of wine, and for a moment I was my father standing tall commanding the attention of the room. "...and on January 8, 19 something or other, Vernon, descendent of the very same Johann who landed in America all those years ago, fathered Elvis Aaron Pressler, I mean, Presley in a two-room house in Tupelo, Mississippi. The rest, as they say, is history."

My mother stood up, reached across the table, grabbed the bottle of wine and refilled her glass.

"35," my father said. "Elvis was born in 1935 ... so, if you do the math," he said, "the king and I are—" He paused as if he was waiting for a drum roll. "Cousins of some sort. And that makes us rock and roll royalty. Same damn tree, just a different limb."

Without any further direction, I sat down and tucked my chair in to eat.

"Ya see?" my father said. "He got the date wrong. That's why these stories need to be retold."

I'm not sure where the genetics of all that hip shaking and singing began, but none of it seemed to have come north with our side of the family. My father couldn't harmonize with a canary. But then that wasn't a prerequisite for his profession anyway. As my dad confirmed, "No fame and fortune for this Pressler. No sir, the engineers, researchers and aviators that the Canadian Space Society employs have to maintain an uncelebrated undercover operandi."

I can still hear my mother grinding her teeth.

"Unlike our cousins to the south," my dad said, as he pushed a carrot around on his empty plate, "we can't celebrate our successes publicly. All on account of the Russians." He turned his eyes up to the ceiling and then brought a finger up to his lips as if the house might be bugged.

"Stop it," my mother said without looking up from her plate.

My dad got up from the table, "Have some more potatoes, why don't you?" he said, and headed for the front door.

Where are you going?" my mother asked.

"Work. Where else?"

"There's pie for dessert," she said.

"It's probably cold like the rest of the damn meal."

As Atwood taps the bottom edge of my story on his desk like a giant deck of cards, I suddenly realize that this so-called therapy could all be used to put me away forever. I'm sure that what I have written points to the damn iceberg. And you don't have to be a shrink to know what you need to know about icebergs.

Atwood holds up the stack of pages and places a paperclip in the top corner.

"Where are you going with this, Kepler?"

I shrug my shoulders. "I don't know, I mean, I don't know anything for sure. We had a new home, but our old russet couch still had two fold-up TV trays on either side of it holding two mismatched lamps. Our black and white television still sat on the empty box it came in. The living room walls were still bare—there were no family portraits, pallet-knife landscapes, or wildlife prints, just hairline cracks filled in with Polyfilla. My parents couldn't seem to see that all we had done was move all our problems to a different place."

There's a moment of silence between us. I think I have disappointed him. Atwood just sits there looking at me as if we're playing a game of high stakes poker. And then he says, "Elvis died last year, didn't he?"

My eyes start to water. "August 16th, 1977," I say.

"Why are you crying, Kepler?"

I reach for the tissue. The idea of Elvis's death radiates like sonar into the icy blue depths outlining everything I have tried so hard to forget.

"Elvis and the house are external features of your troubles, Kepler. You've got to go deeper."

But every story begins with a bit of exposition. You need context in order to properly appreciate the conflict. My dad, troubled soul that he was, taught me that.

It snowed a lot that winter. I remember because I had to shovel the driveway with a spade. I even complained once, but my dad said keeping the damn driveway clear was a privilege and an obligation of being a homeowner.

"I just think it would be a lot easier," I said, "if I had one of those big snow shovels like the ones on the porches of the neighbour's houses."

"Never mind the neighbour's shovels, I'll get you a snowplow for Christmas."

Of course I never did get a snowplow, let alone a decent shovel, but whenever we had a big storm in the night, my dad would wake me up around five in the morning and I'd shovel the drive while he scraped the ice off the windshield of the car. My father's exact job description at the Canadian Space Agency was never conclusively disclosed, but it seemed to involve research, experiment and the occasional secret missions to various interstellar locations. It was something that I shouldn't talk about because the current political climate with the Russians was so unstable. It was a bonding force between us, something only rarely mentioned, but often hinted at with a wink or some other coded reference. When he left for work on those cold winter mornings, he'd tap out CSA in Morse code on the horn as he pulled onto the street, which in the strange and beautiful glow of winter light made him seem heroic to me. How many other kids in that horrible suburb had a father heading off on a perilous mission, possibly never to be seen again?

In January my dad discovered the Triple Blue Bowling Emporium, which became a regular pit stop on his way home from work. He couldn't seem to resist popping in for a quick game and a drink or two. My mom tolerated his drunkenness, but she hated it when he was late for dinner. His tardiness seemed to cut at something deeper and more pointed between them. When my dad failed to come home for dinner for the third time in February, my mother finally snapped. She got up from the table, tossed my father's plate into the sink and started storming around the house, flicking the channels on the television, opening and closing cupboard doors. While she made her way down the hall manically drawing the curtains in every bedroom I went to the stereo and put on an Elvis record. As soon as she heard the first chord of "Crying in the Chapel," she slowed down, and by the time Elvis was half-way through the first verse, his soft and sad voice had lulled her into the living room where she started swaying gently in front of the window.

"Maybe he got sent on an emergency mission," I said quietly as I sat down on the couch. But she just looked at me as if I'd interrupted her favourite television show. "Shhh, Kepler."

Elvis had that power on all of us. He could tame the beast, soften what was troubling us, and at least for the length of a song, make us forget about the curtain rod that had come away on one side, and the toolbox on the top of the television where my dad had left it after spending a few agitated minutes looking for a set of drywall plugs.

When my dad eventually walked in the door that evening, my mother got up from the couch and instead of giving him hell, she turned off the lights as if he wasn't there, and left him standing in the dark.

"I hate it when she gets depressed," he said as he picked at a plate of cold baked beans. "And I hate it when she doesn't put my records back in the album sleeves."

"Why don't you just call if you're going to be late?" I asked.

He got up and went over to the fridge. "It's the nature of my job, Kepler." He grabbed a jar of mayonnaise and a loaf of bread and sat back down at the table. "Do you have any idea how big the Canadian Space Agency is?" He dipped the fork that had baked bean sauce on it into the mayonnaise jar. "If something breaks down I'm the one who has to fix it." He slapped the two pieces of bread together and took a bite. "And it's not like there's a phone booth next to every turbo rocket accelerator."

I got up and headed for the living room.

"Hey, where are ya going?"

When I turned around he was on his feet.

"I'm going to put the records away," I said.

"Leave it," he said. "Grab my telescope. It's in the front closet."

When I came back into the kitchen, he had made another sandwich and was stuffing it into his jacket pocket. I followed him out the back door into the yard, and watched him as he started climbing the antenna. I could hear the beer bottles he was carrying in his jacket pockets clinking together. Halfway up, he turned and looked down at me. "They're gonna be launching the Enterprise Space Shuttle test flights soon."

After the telescope was set up, he blew into his cupped hands and cracked open a beer. "I bet we're the only ones up on their roof in the whole neighbourhood," he said. And then he took the mushed up sandwich out of his pocket and offered it to me. "Want a bite?" he said.

I shook my head.

"You can't be picky about what you eat when you're six thousand miles above the earth. You have to eat whatever the Space Academy puts on the menu."

We sat there for a while looking up at the stars, and for a moment, I forgot that it was freezing out and that we had moved to the stupid suburbs. And then, as if he just remembered why we were sitting on the roof in the middle of the night, he named a few constellations. "Orion, Pegasus, Ursa Major."

"Where's Capricorn?" I asked.

"The constellation of Capricorn," my father said, "is there to the left of Sagittarius."

I followed his arm to the tip of his finger and then I aimed the telescope.

"See it there—a goat with a fish's tail."

"I think David Bowie is a Capricorn," I said.

"David Bowie?"

"He was half a man and half dog on the cover of one of his albums."

My dad shook his head dismissively, tossed an empty beer bottle down onto the lawn and opened another. "The story goes," he said, "when the goat-god Pan was attacked by the monster Typhon, he dove into the Nile to escape—the parts of his body above the water remained a goat, but the parts under the water transformed into a fish."

All that stuff about the gods of the nighttime sky fascinated and frightened me. The anthropomorphic characters of the universe were like an alternate reality—it was easy to get caught up in the weave of the stories, the math of the universe falling like space junk around beautiful goddesses, bull-headed warriors and jealous kings. My dad called it, "a tapestry of tragedy and passion." But he was always quick to point out that the drama the Greek astronomers placed on the solar system had practical applications as well. "In my opinion," he said, "it makes things easier to remember. For example, in the case of my personal favourite constellation NGC 4631, the Greeks gave us Canes Venatici, the realm of Cetus the whale." When he talked about the stars it seemed to me that he was sharing the story instead of telling it. And up there on the roof that night I could imagine the man my mother fell in love with.

"What the hell is going on?"

We could just make out the bulk of my mother in the dark down on the lawn below us.

"Time for bed," my dad said. "The beast has stirred."

Two days later, my dad missed dinner again. I sat on the couch that evening with my mother watching television, eating Cheez Whiz spread on sticks of celery. After a particularly bad episode of *The Love Boat*, my mother made a pot of tea and took a seat in a chair that she positioned so that she could watch television, and with a glance, keep her eye on the driveway. By the time I went to bed she was in a frenzy again, the empty teapot on the floor beside her where she had spent the last hour vigorously cleaning the silverware with a toothbrush.

I wasn't sure what time it was when I was woken up by the sound of the vacuum. I climbed out of bed and shuffled out into the hall. I was feeling my way through the dark when I tripped over a cord, which must have dislodged it from the socket, because the loud howl of the vacuum slowly expired into silence. When I got to the dining room I turned on the light. My mother was bent over, flicking the switch on the vacuum cleaner.

"Mom," I said. "What time is it?"

She looked over at me. "Damn thing's broken," she said. "It was working a second ago."

I looked out the front window and of course my dad's car still wasn't in the drive. When I missed him, I simply scanned the night sky. There was always something up there that my imagination could convert into docking lights or a booster flare from his spaceship. But my mom didn't like it when I mentioned space stuff.

"Maybe he's working a double shift," I said uselessly.

And that's when the random Shakespearean quotes started. "There is nothing either good or bad," she said, "but thinking makes it so."

My mother's passion for Shakespeare wasn't a secret, she  kept a boxed-set of his plays on the back of the toilet wherever we moved, and she'd never let you forget about her great moment playing Lady Macbeth in a high school production, how her performance had made her a celebrity. Where my father had a million stories, my mom had the one, and she hung on to it.

I turned off the light, and left my mother in the dark.

The vacuum was still in the middle of the living room floor the next morning. The hose and the top of the canister had been dismantled and there was a screwdriver lying in a pile of dust and dirt.

I found what looked like a slice of apple pie in the fridge and sat down across from my mother, who was asleep with her head resting on the kitchen table. I pushed my plate towards her when she woke up.

"Is your father home yet?" she asked.

"I don't know," I said. "I just got up."

"Put the kettle on."

I got up from the table, and as I was filling the kettle I noticed a yellow note with the word "BROKEN" taped over the back left burner.

"Maybe he's in the basement," my mother said with a vaguely British accent.

"I don't know," I said again, turning on one of the smaller front burners, "I just got up, remember."

"Check the basement."

My dad often retreated to the basement when things got tense with my mother, but it was too early in the day for that. I walked over to the door and stood at the top of the stairs. All the lights were out.

"Dad?"

I waited as if there might be a reply, and then I turned back to my mom. "He's not home."

"Check the roof."

I walked to the front hall, put my shoes and coat on and stepped out the door, and even though it was about an hour early, I headed to school.

I had a crap day at school. They made us practise vaulting in the gym, we were studying World War II in History, Chad Whitman was demonstrating his karate skills and my locker was right next to his. My mother was on the couch eating cereal out of a box when I opened the front door. I knew my father still hadn't come home because his car wasn't there, and there weren't any fresh tire tracks in the snow. At my mother's insistence, I called the bowling alley. "He's not there," I said, hanging up the phone. It hurt when I talked, which made me wonder if one of my ribs might be broken.

"Screw your father," my mom said, slamming the cereal box down on the coffee table. "We'll just celebrate our damn anniversary without him."

I wanted to hug her, but she didn't look like she was in the mood for that. "How many years has it been?" I asked.

"How old are you?"

"Fifteen," I answered.

"Well, then, it's been fifteen years."

She handed me two bags of returnable pop bottles and sent me up to the fish and chips store for dinner.

We ate in the living room, straight from the greasy box with our fingers. When we were done, my mother told me to put some music on. Anything. Anything but Elvis.

My father had been gone for three weeks when he showed up at my school. He was driving a blue taxi with a long scratch across the passenger's side door. It wasn't the first time I'd seem him driving a cab; it was his go-to job every time there were funding cuts at the Agency. He honked and waved me over, and even though it had started to rain, he came around and opened the door for me like a chauffeur.

"All aboard," he said, as if he hadn't been gone at all.

Part of me wanted to hug him, tell him I love him, and part of me wanted to, I don't know, call the police, have him interrogated, make him pay for making my mother so crazy.

"Come on, Kepler, get in. It's goddamn raining."

I jumped in the cab, but he forgot to close the door for me so I pulled it shut myself and waited for him climb in the driver side. There was a little plastic Elvis mounted on the dashboard. Its hips swivelled when my dad slammed his door closed.

"Who's my first mate?" he said.

I didn't say anything.

"Don't worry about the cab, Kepler. Everyone at the Space Academy has a second job," he said. "Hell, Elvis used to be a truck driver. Did I ever tell you that?"

"About a million times."

He pulled out a comb and dragged it back through his thinning hair, which was longer than normal so it curved back in a wave, and because he hadn't shaved, his sideburns made him look like Elvis might look if he had never been discovered and drove a truck all his life.

"You kind of look like him," I said. "You could be one of those impersonators."

My dad glanced in the rearview mirror, curled his lip and launched into a rendition of "Heartbreak Hotel." "*Well, since my baby left me*—Well, stands to reason," he said. "I mean we're related to the man."

He sat there for a long minute, just staring at the windshield wipers.

"Where were you?" I asked, breaking the silence.

"I had to work," he said, putting the car in gear. "Special mission. Can't really talk about it. Anyway, things weren't going so well so I came up with a plan B. Every good captain has a plan B."

He was in what my mother called one of his manic phases.

When he accelerated the plastic Elvis on the dashboard swivelled his hips again.

"Elvis here is our good luck charm," he said, "our navigator, he'll make sure we make it to port in the storm." And then, despite the rain, he rolled the window down and rested his arm on the door, his elbow catching the current of wet air. "Gotta enjoy the mild weather while it's here," he said. "That's the key, Kepler. You don't complain, you just take what life dishes you, and you enjoy the good bits. Eat your broccoli and your French fries."

I couldn't remember the last time we had broccoli, but I knew what he meant.

He drove slowly into another long silence. When he turned to me, his hand was trembling on the wheel. "How's your mom?"

I wasn't sure how to answer that question. Something was happening to her. I couldn't exactly say what it was. "Fine," I said.

"Is she mad."

"Something like that."

We drove in silence again, passing a used car lot, several low-rise apartment buildings and a movie theatre, and then, when we came to a red light he flipped down the sun visor and a folded square of newsprint fell onto his lap.

"Read it," he said as he handed it to me.

I unfolded the paper. Enterprise Space Shuttle makes its maiden flight atop a Boeing 747 Shuttle Carrier Aircraft.

"What is it?" I asked.

"That's the future," my dad said. "You know, being homeowners is all great, Kepler, but it won't be long before we're living in domed cities on Mars."

Another long silence followed.

"What do you think, Kepler. Isn't it fantastic?"

"What's on Mars?"

"Well, nothing yet, but—"

When we came up to the house my dad slowed, but we drove on by. I saw him look over so I knew he didn't miss it.

"I think mom's losing weight." I said. We both were, probably because there wasn't any food in the house.

As we came around the block to our house again, he pulled up to the curb and put the cab in park. "That'll be eight dollars," he said.

I unbuckled my seatbelt and reached for the door.

"Hey, hey, not so fast." He reached into the glove box and tossed two chocolate bars on the seat between us. "One's for you," he said.

I grabbed the Aero bar.

"Not that one," he said. "I hate Coffee Crisp."

I picked up the Coffee Crisp and opened the car door.

"Jesus, Kepler, I haven't seen ya in three weeks. What's the rush?"

I settled back and pulled the door closed.

"Truth is, things have been a bit quiet at the, ah, Space Academy—" He took a bite of the candy bar and chewed it slowly. "The long and short of it is, I've run into a difficult chapter—that's all this is. Life is a story Kepler, and some chapters are nefarious—"

"What's that?" I interrupted.

"Egregious, atrocious, diabolical. Hard times, Kepler. But anyway, like I said, you've gotta roll with the punches because sometimes amazing things can happen, even when things aren't going so well."

My mother said there were at least ten versions of every story my father told, and she had heard them all. She said none were actually true. But whether the story was true or not didn't really matter to me because when he was telling it, it seemed, at least for the moment, like it was, and I was just happy to go along for the ride.

"So what amazing thing happened?" I asked.

"This," he said holding up a cassette tape. "It was there on the backseat. I don't know who left it—" He took another bite of the Aero bar and then wiped at the side window which was beginning to fog up. "Anyway, the point of all this is...well, guess what it is?"

"I have no idea what the point is."

"Not the point, Kepler, the cassette."

I shrugged.

"Come on, Kepler, this is the point. Take a guess."

"David Bowie."

"David who? Why would I ask you to guess if it was David Bowie?"

"I don't know," I answered.

"It's an Elvis tape," he said. "A damn Elvis Presley tape, and it's a pretty rare one, too. Son of a gun, can you believe it?"

My dad tossed what was left of his candy bar onto the dashboard.

"The problem is there are rules. Every damn company has rules, Kepler, and guess what rule number one is at the Bluebird Cab Company?"

I shrugged my shoulders again.

"Rule number one is, all things left in the cab are the property of the Bluebird Cab Company until claimed by the owner. I figure, okay, if I keep the tape and the some guy calls about it and I haven't turned it in, I'm fired there on the spot. So, despite the fact that it's a tape that happens to be one of Elvis's rare and hardest to find recordings, I pull into the depot and drop the tape off in the lost and found—which is a big cardboard box that must have had a washer or a dryer in it at some point. Anyway, the second I drop the tape in the box, Carl the dispatch guy turns in his chair. What was that, 3742? He annoyingly refers to me by my cab number, even in person.

"'A brick of gold,' I said. 'Sounded more like an eight track.' I told him it was a cassette. He glanced a me and squinted his eyes a moment. 'Really? What of?' 'Elvis in Person at the International Hotel,' I said. He went back to his magazine. 'Elvis sucks,' he said."

My dad glanced up and adjusted the rearview mirror. "Now, you have to realize that it took a degree of willpower to turn that cassette in, and then it took all the willpower I had left not to punch Carl in the jaw. Anyway, I jump back in my cab and I pick up a couple of drunks, a prostitute, and some old fella in a really nice suit, and then as I'm pulling over for a coffee I notice a pair of sunglasses on the seat. These exact ones." My dad reached forward and opened the glovebox.

"They fit perfectly," he said as he put them on. "These are the exact pair Elvis wore on his 1972 World Tour. So then, at the end of my shift I drop them in the box. 'What now?' Carl asked. 'Sunglasses.' I said. 'Really?' 'Really,' I said. Carl pushed off from the edge of his desk and rolled across the floor on his chair. 'Hmm, Liberace in town?' 'Don't know. Maybe Elton John,' I said. 'Elton John sucks,' he said.

"Next shift I'm out picking up fares and halfway through the night, same thing. I drop an old drunk couple off in front of Fran's Diner and I find a little plastic hip-swivelling Elvis on the back seat. That one there." My dad pointed at the dash. "Elvis in a blue blazer and black drainpipe trousers … 1968 comeback tour. Didn't make sense. They didn't look like Elvis fans. As a matter of fact, Elvis made a career out of offending older folks with his controversial hip shaking. When I stuck him on the dash my eyes started watering and I started feeling really sentimental. Your mother and I got married in Vegas. It was an Elvis wedding. Did I ever tell you about that?"

I'd seen the photos, heard the story a billion times, our house was full of the souvenirs. We both sat there staring at the Elvis on the dashboard for what seemed like a year. I was really relieved when my dad started talking again.

"The point of the story is, I knew that the tape, the sunglass-es and this little guy here were no coincidence. I was intrigued. Intrigue, before you interrupt, means the development of a complex or involved situation. Every good story should have it. Anyway, when I got back to the depot I pretended to acciden-tally drop my keys in the box, which meant I had to empty out half the stuff on the floor of the office. Carl swivelled himself around to see what I was up to. As I started to put the things back in the box, he reached up to the portable cassette player on the shelf next to a dead poinsettia. He ejected the tape, held it up, and pushed my sunglasses onto his forehead. 'Looking for this?' he said. He tossed the tape to me. 'Just remember, before you get any ideas. I get first dibs; you can have whatever I don't want.' As I placed the tape neatly in my shirt pocket, I nodded at the sunglasses. He took them off and said, 'You're not seri-ous?' 'I'm a big fan,' I said. 'These are gonna cost you.' I gave him five bucks and the three remaining cigarettes in my pack.

"I waited until I was alone in the cab before trying the sunglasses on. I don't know how to explain it but the glasses seemed to change the way I saw things, charging my synap-tic whatevers. I couldn't look at anything without really look-ing at it. The steering wheel, the tops of my shoes, everything suddenly had a personality. Streetlights looked like patio lanterns, reflections in glass and puddles seemed to have sparks or electricity in them, fire hydrants looked like noble chess pieces. And when I stuck the tape in the deck I fell in love all over again. I mean, it was like hearing Elvis for the first time. That album is a work of genius, effortlessly moving between sentimental love songs, rock and roll, gospel and blues. I felt like a teenager riding my first motorcycle, bowling my first turkey, my first kiss, Christ, it was the soundtrack of my life."

When my dad took off the sunglasses and tucked them into the sun visor I knew the story was over.

"But that doesn't explain where you've been for the last three weeks," I said.

"Yeah well, there's more," he said, reaching into the back seat. "It's a long story, Kepler." He had a mess of white flowers in his hand. "I'll tell you the rest some other time. Come on, let's see if your mother is home."

"She's home," I said, "you can see the blue flicker of the television through the curtains."

CHAPTER FIVE

(I)

"So your father was a storyteller." Dr. Atwood says.

"No, well yes, kind of, no." I thought I was clear about this. "A more accurate description would be to say, he made shit up."

"You sound a little angry, Kepler." Atwood leans forward, his tie with golf clubs all over it falls across his desk. For a moment he looks like he's going to throw up or something, but then he looks up at me and says, "I'd like to hear more about your mother."

I'm sitting down. And yet, for a second, I'm off balance. I steady myself and wait for the vertigo to subside. "I read this morning that McDonald's just opened a restaurant in Japan," I say. I don't know why this bothers me so much.

Atwood settles back into his comfy chair. "I recommend we stay focused on the work we are doing," he says. "There will be plenty of time down the road to worry about the rest of the world."

I had always thought of my mother as a bit-part actress in the drama of my father's life. Her life began or ended, it seemed, when she gave up her name in marriage—when she decided to fall for the self-absorbed attention-needing neon sign that was my father. Other than her thwarted acting career, I didn't really know much about her.

"The thing about my mother," I said, "is that she once auditioned for a part in a pilot on television. It was about two roommates who share a dorm in college. I heard that story once when I was in the hall closet. My mother was standing at the door having a conversation with a Jehovah's Witness. She turned every personal question they asked into a long-winded opportunity to talk about her failed dreams, as if she were a missionary herself trying to convert these trespassers into certified members of her sorry and hopeless life. The part in the pilot she auditioned for was the role of a mature student—a housewife who returns to college, but because she's so out of touch with the younger students, she finds herself the butt of all manner of freshman hijinks. The thing my mother loved about the part is that the character had a thing or two to teach the younger students in each episode. Anyway, the lead chosen to play the rich girl had an impressive cv—she'd done a tampon commercial, and a brief spot on a soap. Turns out, she didn't like what she called my mother's 'chemistry.' Long story short, that pretty much ended my mother's big break. 'Shot down,' my mother said, 'by a spoiled little prima donna with fake eyebrows. Story of my goddamn life.'"

"What were you doing in the closet?"

"Pardon?"

Dr. Atwood starts writing vigorously in his notes. "You said you were in the closet."

"I thought you wanted to hear about my mother?"

"Now I want to hear about the closet."

"It's nothing, I sleepwalk sometimes..."

"Since when?"

"—Since we moved to my dead aunt's house, I guess."

"What happened?"

"One morning, when my dad was still gone, I woke up with my face pressed into the tread of a boot. It took me a few seconds to realize that I wasn't in bed, and a few more to determine that I was in the front hall closet. I had no idea how I got there, but once the initial disorientation subsided, I began to feel embarrassed, like I had wet my pants or something. The awkwardness was exasperated by the fact that my mother was looking for me. I could hear the anxiousness in her voice escalating as she continued to call my name. And then the embarrassment subsided too, and as I listened to the doors being opened and closed, as my mom made her way through the house, I began to feel a sense of satisfaction, as if part of me was finally getting the attention I had been craving. I stayed in the closet until I heard her unlock the front door and step outside. After that, whenever I wanted some attention, I'd hide in the closet.

"Good," Atwood says.

"Good? How is that good?"

"Your mother plays a bigger part in this than you seem willing to admit."

At lunch, Ophelia sits down next to me.

"I gotta show you something," she says quietly. She glances over at Bruce and then pulls a spoon out of her sleeve. "There's a crack in the wall in one of the stalls in the men's washroom," she whispers. "We can take turns digging."

It's weird. She looks and sounds so much like someone you'd picture knitting or playing canasta as opposed to plotting desperate escape plans.

"How do you know about a crack in the men's washroom?"

"I was in there last night. Someone jammed up the toilet in the women's and I was having an intestinal emergency, so they let me use the men's."

I want to tell her that I may be on to something with this writing therapy, but I feel that this would be some kind of a disappointment to her. I push the spoon back. "Sounds risky," I say.

She nods and pushes the spoon back to my side of the table. "Anything worth the effort is risky," she says. "Don't let me down." She winks, gets up and disappears down the hall.

I don't know how I've become an accomplice in her madness. I get the impression that she thinks I'm really crazy like her. I pick up the spoon and tuck it into the waistband of my pants.

My mother cried when my dad walked in the door. She sort of huffed and snorted and then the tears came. She made a big deal about getting up off the couch and then she took the flowers that he was holding and strolled down the hall to the kitchen. I could hear her banging around in a cupboard and then the tap came on. My dad stayed where he was in the front hall with his hands in his pockets waiting to see what would happen next. A moment later my mom came back down the hall carrying a plastic milk jug with the flowers in it. She carefully negotiated a chunk of plaster on the floor just outside the bathroom door that had recently left a jagged hole the size of a dinner plate directly above in the ceiling. Her face was so intense and puffy that it was difficult to tell if she was going to start crying again or maybe wallop my father over the head with the jug of flowers. My dad seemed to sense this himself and relaxed a little when she strolled past him and placed the flowers on the coffee table. A moment later she was on the couch again. My dad kicked off his shoes, looked up at the hole in the ceiling in the hall, down at the mess on the floor, then at the dusty footprints that led to where my mother was sitting. "Jesus," he said. "What the hell is going on here?"

My mother sniffled and wiped her nose with her sleeve. "The place is falling apart."

My dad did a quick survey of the living room, eyeing the new cracks running through the walls as he went over and sat on the arm of the chesterfield. "You look like hell, Alice." His voice was quiet, almost tender.

"Shhh."

It was strange to see her with the upper hand like this.

My dad fidgeted with his tie until a commercial came on. And then for the next minute they both sat there acting like they were interested in buying some new steel-belted radials. When the commercial ended my dad sort of slipped off the arm of the couch onto the cushion.

"I'm sorry," he said.

"This is the last time, Walter." My mother eyes were still on the television. "You do that again and I'm changing the locks."

For the next couple of months my dad did his best to both stay sober and stay out of my mother's way, which wasn't too hard because he was working shifts now. He continued to spend a lot of time banging around in the basement, and in the evenings, when he was home, he'd sit out on the front porch with a coffee and say hello to anyone who strolled by, make some comment about the weather and offer his five-day forecast. Though it was obvious my father was behaving like a man on matrimonial probation, he was still prone to flights of passion and couldn't seem to bring himself to temper his point of view when canvasing the neighbours' opinions on issues concerning home improvement. He got to know a lot of neighbours this way, including Mr. Phillips next door, an older gentleman who didn't appreciate my dad's opinions or the state of our property. I was taking the garbage out one evening when I got pulled into one of their arguments.

"Kepler," my dad said, as I stepped by them on my way to the curb. "What would you rather have, a swimming pool or an air conditioner?"

I dropped the bag and shrugged my shoulders. "A swimming pool, I guess."

"There, ya see. Any kid would rather have a pool," my dad said.

"My kids have all grown up and moved out," Mr. Phillips said. "The wife and I are very happy with our central air."

"But a pool has an esthetic quality. You can jump in and cool down, get some exercise."

"Speaking of esthetics," Mr. Phillips said, pointing at our lawn, "you should invest in some grass seed, fertilizer and a proper lawn mower."

"That's the other thing," my father offered up quickly, "a pool means less lawn to mow."

When my dad came in about an hour later, he grabbed the Yellow Pages and stormed into the living room.

"We're going to get a pool," he said.

I was relieved that my dad's entrance coincided with a commercial. My mother looked up from the *TV Guide*.

"An in-ground pool," he said. "We'll have it built on the front lawn. And even when we get a damn heat wave we won't invite that damn prick, Edward Phillips, over."

"What are you talking about, Walter?" my mother asked.

He flipped another page in the Yellow Pages. "A pool. A built-in pool in the front lawn."

"Here we go," my mother said. And then she waved her hand at him as if he was a cloud of cigarette smoke. "You're blocking the television."

He looked over his shoulder. "It's a commercial," he said. And then he looked over at me for encouragement. "Come on, Kepler, you just told me you wanted a pool."

"I can't swim," I said.

"Don't tell me you're siding with ol' Phillips there."

My mom tucked the *TV Guide* between her hip and the arm of the couch. "While you're up, change it to channel nine," she said.

"A damn pool," my father said again, holding the phone book out with both hands.

"Okay, Walter, if you want a pool, go and grab a shovel and start digging. Just get the hell out of the way."

My dad shook his head and flipped the channel. "All right, all right," he said. "Never thought I'd see the day that a damn television show was more important than a nice swim in a pool."

When the theme song for *Three's Company* came on, he took a step back and flopped down on the couch between my mom and me. "I'll teach ya to swim myself," my dad said, dropping the Yellow Pages in my lap.

And for the next two hours we sat there together on the couch watching reruns. And even though my parents argued a couple of times over what to watch next, we were together, and no one was fighting, and at least in my mind, that was a million times better than a pool or air conditioning.

And then, as if the gods had decided that two or three weeks without a major catastrophe was enough, one rainy day in May my dad walked into the living room with a gallon of sky blue latex paint, a stack of newsprint and a stepladder.

"This place needs a facelift," he said.

"You've gotta be kidding, Walter. What do you think this is, a nursery?"

"It was on sale," he said.

But I knew he found the paint in the shed in the back-yard—I'd broken the rusted lock on the door myself.

"This is *my* sister's house," my mother said, "and it's not going to be baby blue. And anyway, *The Rockford Files* is on tonight and you know how paint fumes give me a headache."

It was surprising to see my father give up so easy, but instead of volleying back with some kind of elaborate sales pitch, his shoulders dropped and the excitement vanished from his face, and I could tell that all the energy it took for him to get along and do as he was told had run out. He left the paint can, newspaper and roller and the ladder on the floor and marched off to the basement, the glass shelves in the buffet that held his bowling trophies rattling as he stomped down the stairs.

His work in the basement at that point amounted to a lot of sawing and hammering, and the purchase of a small second-hand beer fridge, which I was enlisted to help him carry down the stairs. It fit nicely under the frame of what I could see was a roughly made bar. There were several sheets of drywall leaning against a frame of studs that, according to my father, would eventually be a laundry room. He had also put up a dartboard, which I happen to know he found in the shed as well. That same evening he turned on the skill saw, and despite my mother's cursing, he didn't turn it off until she stood at the top of the stairs and hit the light switch.

That night, I was awoken by a noise coming from the spare room.

"Well, since my baby left me. I found a new place to dwell…"

My father jumped when I pushed the door open.

"Jeezus, Kepler."

I put my finger up to my lips, "Shhh, you're gonna wake up Mom," I said. I could hear her snoring in the living room.

"Have you ever noticed how good the acoustics are in an empty room?"

I shrugged my shoulders. He was holding a paintbrush, which after smearing a bunch of random strokes of blue paint on the wall, he was using as a microphone.

It was obvious that he was drinking again.

"Once I'm done with the basement, we can turn this room into a recording studio."

He had already made a mess on the floor and had somehow managed to get a smudge of blue on his forehead.

"Blue is Elvis's favourite colour. Next to white, he loves blue," he said.

"Keep it down," I said again.

"To hell with your mother. We're gonna spruce this place up."

And then he leaned back against the wall and sort of slid down to his knees.

"What would you rather have, a pool or a recording studio?"

"Whatever you want, Dad," I said.

"C'mon, Kepler, if you had to choose, which one?"

"I still can't swim, and I don't sing."

"Jesus, you're just like your mother sometimes." And then he raised his arm and squinted at his watch. "What time is it, Kepler?"

I tiptoed out to the kitchen to check the clock, but when I got back he was passed out with a stupid smile on his face. My mother was watching more and more television, I was depressed and friendless, and my father had become a man who wanted nothing more than a good conversation about the quality of a hedge or the chance of precipitation. He seemed to think a dream was something to be manufactured, nailed together with determination and will. It was like he was asleep and awake at the same time, dreaming of Cadillacs on a street where the driveways were filled with Novas, Pintos and Volkswagens. For him, we had neighbours instead of those bastards above us. We had a lawn instead of a balcony. We were part of something that everybody wanted. And despite the hole in his sock, the sawdust in his hair and the state of his marriage, he was living the dream one beer at a time.

The next day, my parents were back to their usual sparring.

"Have you seen the Chinese take-out menu?" my mother asked, slamming the cutlery drawer.

My father was working on the puzzle, which was almost finished. "I hate Chinese," he said.

I could tell by the tone of his voice that he was looking for a fight. I got up and headed down the hall.

"You like the chicken balls and egg rolls," my mother said.

I opened the closet door and grabbed my shoes.

"I threw the menu out," my dad yelled.

I breathed in the smell of leather, dust and wool.

"What?" my mother said.

"I hate chicken balls."

I stepped into the closet and crouched down under the hems of my parents' coats, the hard cleat of one of my father's golf shoes sticking into my thigh.

"I need ten dollars," my mom said.

"I get paid tomorrow."

"We've been broke ever since we moved into this damn house."

"We've got a mall, fresh air, and a decent bowling alley up the street. What more do you want?"

My mother let out a sigh. I could picture her shaking her head. "How 'bout a million dollars, a new television, Paul Newman for a husband, Jesus, Walter, I'd settle for a stove with four working burners," she said.

I heard the freezer door open and close, and then the sound of something being dropped into a hot frying pan.

"This house is falling apart while you sit around drinking beer and dawdling with your little hobbies. Just look out the window. The lawn is covered in weeds and the eavestrough is falling off. We're the disgrace of the neighbourhood."

"Thank goodness the Queen isn't dropping by on her visit," my dad said.

My mother slammed the cutlery drawer again.

"I'll fix the damn eaves when I'm done in the basement. Now would you stop slamming every thing that you touch? No wonder the place is falling apart."

"I'll believe it when I see it," she said. "If I had a dollar for every promise—"

"At least I'm not so damn wrapped up in my own little miseries that I can't even remember my own son's birthday," my father said.

There was a moment of silence.

"Shit," my mother whispered.

"It was yesterday," my dad said.

I had read that morning that the prime minister had announced he was getting divorced. I cut out the headline and stuck it on the fridge door right next to the Aeroflot plane that crashed in Cuba, which was partially covering the headline about the two 747s that collided in the Canary Islands, but neither of them seemed to notice.

My father slammed what might have been a beer bottle down. I heard the legs of his chair scrape across the linoleum, and then before I knew it, the closet door swung open. When my father reached down to grab his shoes, our eyes met, and for a moment he seemed to look right through me. But then a smile came over his face, a sinister smile that caught hold of me, and as my father stood back up I felt like a weed stripping up little lines of earth before snapping in his fist.

"You are one weird kid," he said. "Come on, get out of there."

He had me by the elbow as he led me down the hall, and when we got to the kitchen doorway, he presented me to my mother, "The damn kid's hiding in the closet."

My mother did this odd thing where she took several tiny steps to turn her body to face us instead of looking over her shoulder. She stared at me for a moment as if I had just cancelled the season premiere of *The Mary Tyler Moore Show*, an excruciating look of disappointment that lasted until my father headed back down the hall, "Where are you going?"

"I'm going to work," he said.

"I want to see that paycheque tomorrow," my mother yelled.

My dad turned to me, raised a finger to his lips, grabbed his bowling shoes and stepped out the door.

A noticeable tension lingered for several minutes after my father left, during which time my mother opened the kitchen window and stood with her hands on the counter breathing deeply. "What do you want for dinner?" she asked. "Your choice."

I saw an open can of spaghetti sauce next to the stove, and I could smell ground beef burning in the frying pan. "Spaghetti?" I offered.

"No really," she said, "whatever you want."

"With parmesan," I said as enthusiastically as I could.

"I'm sorry," she said as she dipped a slice of bread in the spaghetti sauce. The words sounded sort of jumbled, because her mouth was full, but I was sure she said it.

"It's okay," I said. Though we were sitting at the table we had our plates on our laps.

"What's okay?"

I picked up a piece of my dad's puzzle. "I don't know, nothing I guess."

It was difficult to see her like that. More sad than angry. I wanted to hug her, and tell her that one day we'd get this house all spruced up and that ... but my father was the storyteller, I was just a kid trapped in the crumbling mess of my parents' dream.

After dinner she made me a coffee.

"I don't like coffee," I told her.

"How do you know? You've never had one."

"I don't like the smell," I said.

"Well, we don't have any dessert, so don't ask for any."

I sipped my coffee. It was sweet and bitter. It tasted just like it smelled.

"Don't drink it if you don't want it," she said.

I picked up our plates and then went and poured the coffee down the sink.

"Leave the dishes, but I want the lawn mowed in the morning," she said.

I decided not to mention that it was a school day and just try to get along.

"I'm sick of being the laughingstock of the neighbourhood," she said.

I brushed my teeth and went to bed that night without mentioning that she didn't miss anything. My birthday was still three months away.

The next morning I got up early and went out back. It was June and the lawn was covered in dandelions. To me, it looked perfect. I loved dandelions even though I knew they would eventually go to seed and lose their beauty. Everything eventually did. I knew that those dandelions were what made people keep their heads down when they strolled by, made them tug on the leads when their dogs stopped to sniff at something in front of our house. And I knew that standing out was only a good thing if it was on purpose. If you had altered something with the intention of being different, it was creative, expressive, but neglect, that was a form of failure.

The backyard was still in the shade of the house so there wasn't much light when I pulled the shed door open. As my eyes adjusted I saw the push mower jammed in sideways in a two-foot gap between a pile of beer cases and a stack of shingles. I was amazed to see just how much beer my father had consumed in the nine months since we had moved in. The other side of the shed had two sturdy wooden shelves, one holding a row of milk crates, the other stacked with paint cans and mason jars. In the corner on the left there was an old barrel with a bicycle pump, a broken lamp, a ski boot, a rake and some rusted old bolt cutters. And on the floor next to a stack of what must have been twenty years' worth of *National Geographic* I found my father unconscious.

Looking down at him like that made him look older. His hair was uncombed and hanging down over his eyes, and his cheeks were sunken. He looked a little deflated, like an old tire with some of the air let out of it. I gave him a soft nudge in the ribs with my foot. He shuddered, but he didn't open his eyes.

I nudged him again, this time a little harder. His eyes opened and closed but he didn't move. "Dad," I said. "Get up." A beer bottle rolled across the floor and stopped next to an old apple basket filled with gardening tools.

I thought about dragging him out onto the lawn, exposing him, presenting him to my mother, or maybe I'd just leave him there in the yard to rot, let the grass and weeds grow around him. I could imagine the cotton of his jeans eroding, the back of his shirt slowly disintegrating, his flesh decomposing. It would be so easy to disappear, I thought. All you had to do was let go, give up and lie there, and eventually, you'd just become part of the neglect that surrounds you.

I picked up the beer bottle and poured what was left of it onto my father's forehead. He raised his hand and sort of swiped at his face, but then he was unconscious again. I gave him one more chance. "Dad," I said. His left arm reached for the spot where I had kicked him, and when his eyes opened he was looking right at me. "Fuck you, Carl," he said. "I don't give damn if you fire me." And then he closed his eyes again.

I was raking the cut grass into a pile in the centre of the lawn when I noticed that my mother was watching me through the kitchen window.

"Kepler."

Her muffled voice came through the glass as if from under water. Once she had the window open she stood there for a moment as if she was trying to remember what she had wanted in the first place. When she spoke again, her voice was soft, and quiet. "Has your father come home yet?"

The disappointment I was moments ago feeling for my father shifted effortlessly to my mother. Even though it must be heartbreaking to wake up in a rundown old house and find that your husband didn't come home, it's a parent's job to hold it together, and in times like these, exercise a little grace.

I nonchalantly took a step to the left to block my mother's view of the shed. And even though his car was there in the driveway, I told her that he was at work—that he had got his job back at the space agency, and that he was up there now—I glanced casually upwards—gathering information, running tests on possible life-sustaining planets, collecting space dust, probing distant galaxies and whatever else it is that drunks do when they're unconscious.

I ran away from home that day. It was an ill-conceived plan. I didn't have any money, I didn't pack a lunch, and I had no idea where I was going. I spent the morning wandering through the neighbourhood—driveways, houses, hedges, finely trimmed lawns. It was all a lie. Who came up with the idea that this was a dream? More like a prison without bars.

By mid-afternoon, I found myself on the north side of Industrial Road, lifting the lids of dumpsters. I rummaged around outside a decal factory, a place that made keys, and a running shoe wholesaler. And then I came across a big clear plastic bag filled with little plastic Elvises with suction cups on the bottom. Later that day, I spotted my father's so-called special sunglasses on a rack by the cash register in a convenience store.

By ten o'clock that evening I was sitting at the table, driven back home by hunger, eating a spoonful of peanut butter. The kitchen was dark except for the light coming in through the back door window. You could hear the clock ticking and the hum of the fridge, and every now and then the whole house seemed to shudder under the force of the wind outside. When my dad came in the front door I could feel the warm air rush in from the hall. He shuffled past me in the dark towards the sink.

"Some nasty-looking cumulonimbus clouds out there," he said as he drunkenly reached for the light switch in the range hood above the stove. Even with his back to me I could tell that in some subtle way, something was different about him, or maybe something was different about the way I saw him. I watched him pour a mug full of water and then carefully pour that into the kettle before planting it on a burner. He turned to face me.

"Why are dandelions weeds?" I asked.

He took a deep breath, picked up his mug and a spoon and headed over to the window. "I got a better question," he said, "what the hell are you doing sitting here in the dark?"

"Looking up words," I said holding up the big red *Webster's* that we had inherited from my dead aunt.

"Well, what are you asking me for—look it up."

I had already looked the word dandelions up myself, but after finding him in the shed that morning it was important to have a fatherly interaction with him.

"It's too dark," I said handing him the book.

He sighed again, flipped the dictionary open and thumbed through the pages. "ABCD ... here we are," he said, tilting the dictionary towards the light above the stove. "Dandelion, any of several plants of the composite family, common lawn weeds with jagged leaves."

The kettle began to whistle.

"Shit!" my father said. "Last thing we need is to wake your mother."

"She's not home," I said.

He glanced over at the clock. "At this time of night?"

He poured the boiling water into his mug, added a spoon full of instant coffee and then stirred in two spoons of sugar, took a sip, and added one more.

"What's composite?" I asked.

He glared over at me with an eyebrow raised. One too many questions could capsize the boat.

He flipped back to page 274. I had looked composite up, too.

"Composite: put together, formed of distinct parts."

"We're a composite family," I offered.

He took a sip of coffee. "I guess so," he said.

"Does that mean we're weeds?" I wasn't trying to be funny.

He put his coffee down on the stove. "Where did you say your mother was?" he asked.

"I don't know, she was out when I got home," I said.

"Was she wearing her red coat?"

My mom had this red coat with real fur around the collar and buttons that looked like they were made out of seashells. She said she felt like a movie star when she wore it, but my parents never went anywhere fancy so mostly it just hung there in the closet getting dusty.

"Don't know," I said.

He snapped the dictionary closed, turned to the window again, and even though it was dark he seemed to be staring at something in the yard. The wind was getting stronger. I heard what I guessed was the neighbour's patio furniture slamming into the fence.

"I'm thinking of getting you a puppy," he said. "I wanted to get you a monkey, something smart that you can really play with, something you can train to use the toilet, or man a dangerous space mission, but your mother would never go for that. A dog will have to do, something masculine like a Doberman Retriever."

I knew better than to get my hopes up. And anyway, something was different now. No way I was getting sucked into another one of his promises.

"It'll be a surprise, okay?" he said.

I got up, grabbed the dictionary and headed for the hall.

"Hey, where are you going?"

"To bed. It's a school night."

My dad waved me back over to the table.

"What's this?" he said as he reached for the dandelion I had tucked behind my ear.

"It's a composite."

He twirled the wilted weed between his fingers. "I thought you were done with this queer stuff."

I turned to leave again.

"Kepler."

I stopped at the fridge.

"There's something you should probably know."

"What?"

"That's, pardon me."

"Pardon me."

"Promise you won't tell your mother."

"Tell her what?"

"Promise."

I crossed my fingers behind my back. "I promise."

He glanced down at the dandelion. "You were … adopted. I mean, I'm not sure, but I'm pretty sure."

"Adopted?" I knew what it was, no need for the dictionary on that one, but that couldn't be what he meant.

He tossed the dandelion in the sink. "It means that you're not really a Pressler."

Something that looked like an umbrella flew past the window behind him.

I could feel my eyes welling, blood rushing to my head.

"Don't be a baby about it," he said. "How old are you, seventeen?"

He picked up his mug and took it to the sink. "Your mother coddles you too much," he said. And then he headed down the hall to the washroom.

I flipped open the dictionary. Coddle: One, treat tenderly; pamper. Two, cook in hot water without boiling. As far as I could tell, my mother reserved all her tenderness for the nurturing of her nails. And then, as if on cue, I heard the front door open … a few seconds later the toilet flushed … and then a few seconds after that my mother was banging on the bathroom door.

I flipped open the dictionary again and looked up the word, cyclone. And as the tornado descended on our house, I closed the dictionary, walked over to the kitchen table and pushed the puzzle onto the floor.

I can't sit still. I get up, walk over to the bookshelf in Atwood's office and pick out the dictionary. I flip the pages. Family. All the descendants of a common ancestor; a house, a lineage. Family allowance. Family name. Family tree. Familiar. Fami— liar. Definitions are rarely enlightening. More often than not, instead of illumination, they cast a gloomy shadow around the feel of the word, draw the curtains on it. I tear the page out, crunch it up into a ball and toss it on Atwood's desk.

He looks at me and says, "Vandalism is not the answer, Kepler."

"It's not vandalism," I say. "It's symbolic."

He picks up the crumpled page and flattens it out on his desk. "Well, on the bright side," Atwood says, "it's important to get at the memories that make you feel uncomfortable."

"You want uncomfortable?" I say. "I've been sleepwalking again. I woke up in the television room last night. I was standing there in the dark like a damn idiot. I had drool on my chin. And to top it off, the television was on a channel with no reception."

Atwood rubs his chin. "Static?"

"Yeah, static..." Then I suddenly realize how certifiably crazy I sound. I can see that Atwood is ready to write down whatever it is I say next. I need to be more careful, but I can't seem to help myself. "Maybe I am crazy," I say. "Maybe I just need to be placed in a straightjacket and locked in a rubber room."

Atwood puts down his pen and starts digging around in the drawer of his desk. He pulls out some Scotch tape and waves me closer.

"Dictionary," he says.

I hand it to him.

He opens it up and reinserts the crumpled page. "Hold this," he says.

I lean forward and halfheartedly align the page as Atwood applies a long strip of tape.

"Good as new."

"Are you listening?" I say.

"Yes, but I don't think restraints will be necessary."

I'm not sure what's worse—feeling incredibly vulnerable when he writes down everything I say, or feeling ignored when he fiddles around when I'm talking.

"The uncomfortable part is, even though it was just a bunch of static, I saw an image. At first I thought it was a descrambled transmission, the ghost or bleed of the next channel, but the longer I looked at it, the more clear it became."

"Could you put this back where it belongs, please?"

I take the dictionary and place it on the shelf.

"What did you see?"

"It was an old black and white photo taken at the zoo. We were standing in front of the monkey exhibit and my father was delivering the commentary as if he knew what they were thinking. 'Look at the grumpy one there, he's not feeling well today. He knows he shouldn't have eaten that last banana. And that one over there, he's wondering when he's going to get to walk on the moon.' I could see the sadness in their eyes. It was as if they knew that this wasn't where they belonged. 'They'd be better off dead,' my mother said, and then she snapped a picture. The flash caught the three of us reflected in the glass— my father smiling, my mother sad and worried, and me, with my eyes closed as if I was dreaming a million miles away. The three monkeys in the background looked like distorted projections of our true nature captured in the cage behind our reflections. I'd forgotten all about that photo, and there it was on the television. All the other stuff, the game shows, the sitcoms, the commercials, that's the lie, the stuff designed to make us sedated."

Atwood starts scribbling away. I begin to think that I may never get out of here.

CHAPTER SIX

The notion that I was adopted made me feel grievously discon-
nected from my parents, and in the darkest hour of the night,
as the storm battered the house I had the sense that I was completely alone in the world. But this fitful anxiety was disrupt-
ed by the calm sobering realization that if I was a kid whose
whole life had been a lie, then I could create my own past, align
myself with something greater than a family of weeds.

As it turned out I wasn't the only one who had a rough
night. My father had effectively banished me from the Pressler
family tree and my mother had banished my father from the
bedroom. I could tell he had slept on the couch because his
comb and watch were on the coffee table and there was a rum-
pled blanket on the floor.

I found my father in the kitchen on his knees, tightening
the hinges on a cupboard door. He said hello without looking
at me. I ignored him and headed for the fridge.

"There's no milk," he said.

But I found a can of Carnation evaporated milk tucked
behind a bag filled with little packets of ketchup and soy sauce.
I poured some Carnation over my cereal, took my bowl to the

sink and added some water, and then headed over to the table. My dad must have been up pretty early because there was a vase of white flowers, a clear glass bowl, and a bag with two goldfish in it next to the puzzle pieces, which were now piled in the centre of the table.

As I ate my cereal I began to reorganize the Saturday paper, which my father had already dismantled searching for the comics. I tried my best to ignore my father and the two stupid fish swimming around in the little bag.

"Well," my father said, pointing a screwdriver at the centre of the table, "the flowers are for your mother; the fish are for you."

I flattened the front section of the paper in front of me. James L. Elliot, Edward Dunham, and Douglas Mink aboard NASA's Kuiper airborne observatory discover the rings of Uranus.

This was the kind of thing I would normally mention to my father, but that morning, I just turned the page.

"Don't tell me you're giving me the silent treatment, too."

I flipped the paper up so that I didn't have to look at him.

"Fine," he said.

He was still wearing his shoes so his steps were louder than normal as he walked over to the table and picked up the clear plastic bag with the fish and took it and the bowl over to the sink.

I wanted to pretend that I didn't care, but I couldn't resist peering over the newspaper. His back was to me, but I could hear him fuss with the twist tie, and then after pouring the water and the fish into the glass bowl he started talking to the fish as if they were his best friends, making fish-like kisses with his lips. But then this baby talk abruptly gave way to instructions that, even though his back was still to me, I could tell were for my benefit. "Clean the fishbowl every two weeks. Feed them a couple times a day, and you should keep the water at 74 degrees." Just as I was about to get up he placed the bowl on top of the fridge where I couldn't really see. "Their names are Venus and Mars," he said turning to face me. "They're your fish, your responsibility."

I persisted with the silent treatment.

"A thank-you would be nice," he said.

I waited until he left the room and then dragged a chair across the kitchen floor so that I could get a good look at the fish. They came to the surface with their little mouths opening and closing. I couldn't bring myself to talk to them like my father did. I mean, they'd never fetch a stick or pilot a spaceship. They were just a couple of little fish trapped in a little bowl, a thousand miles away from the ocean.

I eventually guessed my father had lost his taxi-driving job. That would certainly explain why my mother had locked herself in her room and why my dad was home and making such an effort around the house again. He had a list on the fridge of all the things that needed attention, but every time he checked something off, he added something new because the house seemed determined to fall apart as fast as he could fix it. He spent the days puttering around with a pencil behind his ear and pair of pliers in his back pocket, as if a torn shower curtain, a leaky tap, or a squeaky door were the cause of all our family's woes.

When the phone rang it seemed to hold the house in a state of suspended animation. My father would look up from what he was doing, but he wouldn't answer it—wouldn't let me answer it. "Probably for your mother," he said, "and if she wants to know who it is, she'll have to end her little antisocial campaign and come out here and answer it herself. You could feel his anger intensify with each ring, one hand white-knuckling around the handle of a hammer, the other tapping against his thigh. The space between the rings seemed to last forever, deep breaths of silence punctuated by the incessant intrusion. And then, when it would finally stop, the whole house would sink back into an uncomfortable silence, and my father would put down whatever he was holding and turn his attention to the bedroom where my mother had barricaded herself, and his brow would soften, and his right hand would unconsciously fall into his left and begin to fiddle with the gold band on his wedding finger.

When it became obvious my mother wasn't coming out of her room any time soon, my father's handyman efforts seemed to taper off and he began sleeping in. I found him each morning awkwardly reposed on the couch, his mouth open wide with his face mashed up against the hard back, his leg twitching like a dreaming dog. While I was useless when it came to wielding a hammer or a screwdriver, I did my best to keep the house clean. I did the dishes, swept the floor, and left some crackers and Campbell's Soup in the hall outside my mother's door. This was not the way parents on television shows like *Dick Van Dyke* behaved.

"This house isn't the only thing falling apart," my dad said, "and unlike this puzzle, these pieces may never fit back together again."

Five days had passed, and aside from the odd glimpse of my mother lumbering across the hall to the washroom and back,

I never saw her. The food I left outside her door disappeared, but she never returned the plates and cutlery, which meant it would only be a matter of days before there would be nothing left to put her meals on. Aside from eating it was a mystery as to what she was doing in there all day and night until I figured out that she was using the bathroom as a library when we were asleep. It took a while, but I eventually noticed a bookmark rapidly moving from one volume of Shakespeare to the next. Based upon the consistent progress of this activity I guessed that she would end her exile in two more days.

"It's a big night," my dad said, stumbling into the kitchen with the television guide in his hand.

"What's that, Walter?" I began to refer to him by his first name, which my father tolerated, I can only guess, because he was relieved that I was talking to him again.

"It occurred to me that while your mother broods away in the bedroom we can watch whatever we want on television, and, guess what's on tonight?"

"What's that?" I said again.

"Guess." he said again.

"*Truth or Consequences.*"

"Come on, it's your father you're talking to here."

"I give up," I said.

"It's an Elvis double feature, *G.I. Blues* and *Roustabout.*"

I couldn't help it. Despite the cloud of murky grey darkness that had parked itself over our house, I felt a twinge of excitement.

My dad made popcorn that night. I sat just close enough to him to reach the bowl, which he held in his lap. Halfway through the first movie I wasn't even angry anymore. As soon as Elvis started singing, my dad reached over and ruffled my hair with his greasy fingers, and in that beautiful blue light emanating from the television, for a moment, I forgot that we were trapped there in the suburbs, that my father was jobless, that I was adopted, and that my mother had become a ghost. During the course of those few hours it seemed like anything was possible. In my mind it was all so simple. It was just a matter of time before my dad would get his job back, and he'd apologize to my mother, and she'd start cooking again, and answer the phone, and tolerate my father's schemes, and she'd place her hands on his shoulders and kiss him on the cheek, and then the timer would go off in the kitchen to let my mom know the roast beef in the oven was ready, and ... then I caught our reflection in the living room window.

For a split second, I thought the roof was leaking. My bedroom was still sort of dark and there was a crack forming in the ceiling, but then I realized my dad was dripping beer on my head.

"Remember that story?" he asked.

I wiped at the side of my cheek and neck with the sleeve of my pajamas.

"The one I was telling you—why I was gone before."

If the afterglow of the Elvis double bill was still with him, I was still in the murky clutches of sleep and the vague echo of a disturbing dream.

"Remember," my dad said as he left the room, "I found the Elvis stuff, the cassette, the glasses—"

As I got up and followed him into the hall my thoughts kept drifting, struggling to focus on what my father was saying and the portentous feeling of distress in my stomach. "What are we going to do for money?"

The question stopped him at the kitchen entrance.

"What money?"

"I was dreaming, just then when you woke me up," I said. "We were starving—"

My father slammed the freezer door and held up a Sara-Lee chocolate cake. "Problem solved," he said. "This will keep us going for three days. Your mother doesn't know what she's missing."

After sitting down across from me at the kitchen table, he cut us each a big slice of cake.

"The fish," I said getting up.

"Jeeze, Kepler, I'm trying to communicate here. Do you want to hear this story, or not?"

"I have to feed them."

"Eat first," he said.

I sat back down and pushed some cake crumbs to the edge of my plate with my fork.

"So I was at the end of my shift," my dad continued, "back when I was gone. You remember, right, all those coincidences? Well, this is the part you were asking about—why I was gone for so long. I was heading back to the depot when this woman flagged me down. She was wearing a grey hat, the kind old men wear, with a small red feather tucked into the band. A nice hat. Real classy. She had a briefcase in one hand and an umbrella in the other. It was weird because it was snowing, not raining. Her suit jacket and skirt were light green, a green that would probably look grey in a black and white movie. She was wearing a pair of sunglasses, too. 'Where you headed?' I asked through the window in my best Bronx accent. 'Memphis,' she said. 'Come again?' She started spelling it out. 'M-E-M-P-H-I—' 'I know how to spell,' I interrupted. She made a little adjustment to something under her skirt and then nodded at the Elvis on the dashboard. 'I'm a fan too.' The feeling in my gut and the words that came out surprised me. 'Jump in,' I said.

"She closed the umbrella, climbed in, shuffled across the seat to the other side, and just as I was about to pull out into traffic, she opened the door and climbed out. I watched her walk slowly around the front of the car, open the back door and climb in again. Then she leaned forward, reached out and adjusted the rearview mirror, had a quick look at herself, and folded her arms over the front seat. 'Okay, now I'm ready.'

"I don't know what it was, but there was something exciting about her. I swear it felt like my cab had been turned into a chariot and we were heading for the goddamn ball or something. The whole thing had this surreal quality about it. Memphis, the umbrella … but then, when she took off her glasses and started thumbing the mirrored lens with a hanky, and I got a good look in her eyes, the spell was broken."

My dad put his fork down and started eating the rest of his cake with his fingers. "I'd heard of these people, but I'd never actually met one. I glanced back through the rearview, hoping I was wrong, but there was no mistaking it. I had a man dressed up as a woman in the back of my cab. I swear to Jesus Christ."

My mind flashed on the day my mom caught me wearing the makeup.

"So this guy—girl or whatever, says to me, 'I know what you're thinking.' 'I'm sorry for staring,' I said. I didn't want to piss him off or anything. 'I'm incognito,' he said. 'Truth is, I went on a bit of a bender and missed my ride home. Damn, this is a cold country. Can you turn up the heat?' 'So this is a disguise?' I said with relief. 'You ever heard of Rilke?' he asked. I shook my head. 'He was a German poet. He wrote the *Book of Hours, Letters to a Young Poet* … Anyway, he suffered from depression. I'm sure you've heard of depression.' 'Of course,' I said. 'Well, Rilke refused psychoanalysis because he was afraid of being cured. He was afraid that it would separate him from his creativity.'

"I wasn't sure exactly what he was getting at, but I liked what he said. I know I can be a son of bitch sometimes, but I don't want to change either. I tapped a cigarette out onto my lap and passed it to him. He took it with a slight smile that sort of tilted his lip up on one side of his mouth. I reached back and flicked my lighter. He leaned into the flame and said thanks. He took a deep drag. 'This little indulgence of mine,' he said, blowing a cloud of smoke into the back of my head, 'could probably be corrected, but at what cost?'

"'Are you some kind of a poet then?' I asked. 'Well, a poet of sorts,' he said, 'but I'm retired mostly…' His voice trailed off as he sank back into the seat enjoying the cigarette. 'Anyway, I don't want to put you to sleep with my boring life.'

"'So which terminal?' I asked. He sat forward again with a sigh and exhaled deeply. 'Terminal—oh, no, no. Truth is, I'm terrified of planes.'

"I remember the sun was just beginning to rise, but it sort of felt like a sunset for some reason. That magic that I felt when he first jumped in the car had returned. The light and air seemed to fuse. I felt giddy, like I was standing on the edge of something, teetering, afraid, but exhilarated too. Anyway, I don't know why, but I re-adjusted the rearview, turned on the meter, put the car in gear and pulled away from the curb as if driving this crazy stranger all the way to Tennessee was the most natural thing in the world. I told him I'll need to stop for gas and a map. And then we were off."

My dad licked his fingers. "Now you know why I was gone for three weeks," he said.

And even though I would have preferred that my dad had been away on a space mission testing gravitational propulsion equations or whatever, I remember thinking this was the best breakfast I'd had in a long time. I took another bite of cake and waited for my dad to finish scratching at the stubble on his chin, but then my mother, who looked like an old bear that had just awoken from hibernation, walked into the kitchen.

She stopped at the cutlery drawer, pulled out a spoon, and then placed the kettle on a burner. Her hand was shaking when she pulled open the oven door. "Where's the milk?" she said. It was as if she was sleepwalking.

I looked over at my father. He was mucking around with the puzzle, absently trying to fit what was obviously the wrong piece into the rings of Saturn.

"I can't find the milk."

"We're all out." My father shook his head, lit a cigarette and went back to his puzzle.

I got up and walked over to the fridge and opened the door. "There's only Carnation," I said.

My mother pushed the oven door closed and dropped the mug, which broke into several pieces on the floor.

"Jesus Christ," my father said.

I started to count in my head. One Mississippi, two Mississippi, three...

"Alice?"

By the time I got to seven, my father had gotten up and sort of placed his arms around her, and to my surprise she didn't pull away. She just stood there stiffly, her body slowly heaving in his arms.

"What the hell is wrong with you?"

She let the spoon in her other hand fall to the floor and grabbed my father's arm. And then, almost in slow motion, her knees gave out. I could see my father struggling to hold her weight. When her bum was just inches from the floor he let go with one hand and grabbed the counter, but she still had a hold of him and was pulling him down.

"Jeezus, Alice, let go," my father said.

Four Mississippis later, I pushed the fridge door closed, and tried my best to lose myself in one of the headlines I had taped to the door.

India's birth control efforts begin to collapse in the wake of Indira Gandhi's defeat when it is revealed that 500 unmarried women were forcibly sterilized during Gandhi's "emergency." And that "1,500 men die as a result of improper vasectomies."

And for the first time, all the terrible things going on in distant parts of the world couldn't distract me from the terrible thing that was happening right there in our kitchen.

During her eight-day exile in the bedroom my mother had taken up smoking—my father had left a carton on his dresser—lost twenty-five pounds, and, as if possessed by the spirit of Major Margaret Houlihan, decided that she wasn't taking any more crap from anybody. While my dad half-heartedly searched the classifieds, drawing circles around job listings like Make a thousand dollars a week from the comfort of your home!, my mom pulled herself up off the couch, had a long shower, spent about an hour in front of the mirror, and slipped on a pair of high heels and her famous red coat. She looked like a bruised red tomato as she marched out the door. She was gone all day, which clearly irritated my father, but when she came home wearing a new wig and with a new job, strutting into the kitchen with the fortitude of a woman who had just climbed Mount Everest, my father was reduced to a state of pointed resignation and bitterness.

"I'm a sales associate," she said, "at the Hobby Barn. I'm building my own goddamn dream from now on."

My dad stood in the doorway of the kitchen the next morning, picking at a strip of wallpaper that was buckling along the seam. "I don't know what the fuss about having or not having a job is all about," he said loud enough that my mother, who was in the bathroom getting ready for work, could hear. "The damn house is paid for, for chrissake."

But even I knew there were still bills. There was a pile of them right there on top of the fridge next to the goldfish.

"Look at her, Kepler," he said as she squeezed by him, "she's becoming a liberated woman." He said the word liberated as if it were a curse.

She grabbed her cigarettes off the counter, and this time, instead of squeezing past, she pushed my father out of the way. "I'll be home after six," she said.

I guess my mother was getting back at my father because she didn't come home till after ten every night that week. My dad and I ate a lot of mayonnaise sandwiches and pretzels. I knew that I wasn't really being parented anymore. I could see that I was simply being told on occasion what or what not to do. We became a house of roommates. The end of that school year passed without either of my parents commenting on my report card.

I don't know why I bothered to mow the lawn. The eaves were still hanging over the front window, there was a pile of spare tires and an old mattress on the driveway, and the yard was littered with the shingles that had blown off the roof. The whole thing seemed like an exercise in futility, a lame attempt to postpone the inevitable and total collapse of my parents' dream.

Despite having just left my father in the kitchen I couldn't help approaching the shed with some trepidation, as if I might find his unconscious body on the floor. The disheartening residue of that experience stayed with me. As a result, I felt a sense of irrational urgency and relief when I had successfully managed to maneuver the mower out of the shed and onto the patchy overgrown lawn. I had just released an exaggerated and cathartic sigh when my dad strolled by me and disappeared into the shed's dark doorway. He was in there banging around and swearing for about a year. When he eventually came out, he was carrying several cases of beer stacked on top of one another. I watched him drag his feet through the long grass, and then load the cases in the trunk of the car. He didn't ask me to help so I continued pushing the mower the length of the lawn while his breath got markedly heavier with each load. A dark line of sweat formed along the centre of his back, and by the fourth trip he was wheezing and coughing through the cigarette in his mouth. I imagined him collapsing on the driveway in a puddle of stale beer, his hands clutching his chest, me fishing the keys out of his pocket, popping the hood, hooking some jumper cables up to the car battery and resuscitating him with a jolt to the heart. These little fantasies in which I emerged from a number of troubling scenarios as a hero were growing more frequent. They all ended with one of my parents looking up at me with tears in their eyes and thanking me for saving their life. They'd inevitably make all kinds of promises about how things were going to be different from now on. But this particular fantasy was interrupted by a disturbingly dark cloud that had settled overhead. It had a strange foreboding quality to it, changing shape and density, an atmospheric anomaly preluding the arrival of the mysterious force that had created it. As I swung the mower around, my father was closing the trunk. I wanted to reach out at that moment, and as I struggled to string a coherent group of words together I felt compelled to apologize, but I wasn't sure what for.

By the time my father returned, I had just finished raking the cut grass into a pile in the centre of the lawn. He pulled a box of beer out of the back seat and carried it into the yard. As he squinted through a cloud of cigarette smoke, he nodded and sat down next to the mower. I glanced up at the sky, but there wasn't even a wisp of a cloud to threaten the sunny warmth of the day. My dad pulled a beer out of the box and cracked the lid with a lighter. The cap landed in the fresh cut grass at his feet. I walked over, picked up the cap and tossed it in the beer box.

"I want to talk to you for a second," he said, as he reclined onto his back.

I glanced upwards again, and for a moment we both watched a plane leaving a white vapour trail across a light blue sky. I wanted to tell him he should be nicer to Mom. I wanted to say that I didn't give a damn whether I was related to Elvis or not, and that adopted or not, this was the only family I had. But then I felt a chill moving slowly across the yard, which settled in my bones and put a temporary blight on my heart. "When are you going back to work?" I asked.

"When are you going back to work?" he repeated in a whiny and irritating voice.

I started pushing the mower over to the shed.

"Hey, hey," he said. "Come on, don't be a baby."

After dragging the shed door closed, I headed for the back door, but my dad grabbed me by the arm and pulled me down to the grass. "Come on, Kepler, it's a beautiful day. Spend some time with your ol' man."

"It's cold," I said.

"What the hell is going on in this house? Jesus, Kepler—dandelions, stuffed animals, you're even afraid of clouds, for chrissake. All this queer stuff has got to stop."

I imagined him clutching his chest again. No jumper cables this time.

My dad reclined back on the lawn again and lay there looking up at the sky. His beer had fallen over in the grass, but I didn't say anything.

"I think your mother's having an affair," he said.

I thought about that for a moment. It was pretty tough to imagine my mother sitting across from some suave guy sipping wine by candlelight. I mean, that's what an affair is right? Romance? "I doubt it," I said.

"Maybe you're right," he said. "I guess what I'm saying is, this whole homeowner thing didn't turn out the way I thought it would."

A long moment passed. I didn't know what to say, but as each second went by, my sense of empathy, sympathy and whatever other emotions make a person good, abandoned me.

"While we're confiding in each other," I said, "I'm 15."

"What?"

"I'm only 15. My birthday is in August."

"Jesus," he said, "it feels like your birthday was just a couple months ago."

When my dad came home with the glow-in-the-dark stars a couple of days later, I knew that they were both a gift and an apology. There were a million of them. He used a compass and a ruler to approximate the scale of a star chart, which I was enlisted to hold over my head while he meticulously stuck each glow-in-the-dark sticker on the ceiling of my bedroom. I knew it would be my job to erase the faint pencil lines off the ceiling, but as my dad whispered the names of the planets as he reached and measured, I was reminded that there might be purpose and structure in the design, as if the nighttime sky was a blueprint that contained thought and reason. It was moments like this that made my life bearable—when my father's obsessions manifested in an activity that brought order and beauty to our lives. But the pace was slow, and after three hours my arms were killing me and my dad was getting grumpy. "Hold the damn thing straight," he scolded when my arms started to shake.

And then, just as I was getting ready to jump out the stupid window, he told me to go grab him a beer, and that I should get one for myself too.

"Just think," he said, bouncing gently on the bed, "to someone out there, we are aliens." I climbed up on the bed beside him. He took the beer I handed him and clinked it to mine and said, "Well done, earthling."

And I liked that, the thought that we may or may not be family, but we were linked by a larger idea, an idea I didn't fully understand, but one that was both playful and serious at the same time.

"Now you get the light, and I'll get the curtains."

The ceiling of my bedroom was instantly transformed, as if the roof had been torn off our house on a clear summer night.

"What do you think?" my father asked.

I held my breath for a moment. Even though it wasn't quite real, it was detailed enough to create the illusion of depth and wonder that a cloudless night could inspire. It was beautiful and terrifying at the same time.

"We'll have to make do without satellites, comets and shooting stars, but we gotta better view here than any backyard in the whole city." He exhaled deeply. "The universe demands that we use our imaginations," he said as he sat down on the bed. "It connects and inspires the heart and the mind. In order to understand the universe you have to comprehend the depth of it. In a way, it's like an infinitely deep ocean."

To my tired eyes, there were strange and frightening things lurking in that map of light. I could imagine the anthropomorphic outlines of the constellations arching above my head, satellites, planets, shoals of luminescent fish, sea monsters, UFOs. But as the minutes passed, all the things that hurt and confused me were also exposed in the fathomless darkness above me, and I had the sudden realization that I might have to start sleeping with the lights on.

CHAPTER SEVEN

(I)

In the courtyard, they make us walk around in circles. Most people smoke as they walk, using up any cigarettes they've saved or had dropped off by visitors. Ophelia and I take a break under the tree and talk about what we are going to do when we get out.

"I want to open a bookstore," I say. "No newspapers, no magazines, no reporting or facts about the state of the world. I want to surround myself in a sea of fiction."

She takes a break from biting her fingernails. "Like an octopuses' garden," she sings. And together we close our eyes and drift. I imagine a wall of books rising up to the clouds. I wonder what it is that Ophelia will do.

"I want to get one of those hotdog stands," she says.

I guess I was wondering aloud again.

"You know, the ones with the hibachi and the red and white striped umbrella." When I open my eyes the first thing I see is the fence.

"—If we ever get out of here," I say pessimistically. "We're like caged fucking animals."

I know my memory is the key to the lock. It is up to me to put the pieces together and deliver the goods to Dr. Atwood. But so much of what fills my head—all the normal stuff like Sunday drives and Scrabble, meat, potatoes, vegetables and dessert, family photos on the mantle—are images I have only seen on television. And yet, it seems real somehow, as if television had become part of my experience, part of my memory, and therefore part of my reality. And then I realize that that is where my parents went wrong. They lost track of what was real. Somewhere along the line they started to believe the lies they told themselves, they became characters in the stories they made up. Day by day, year by year, they were chasing a dream that turned out to be nothing more than a cage.

Ophelia puts her arm around me and it feels nice and comforting.

"At least we're caged animals together," she says.

My father finished the renovations in the basement in mid-July. He made a big deal of it. The "Coming Soon" notice on the basement door was replaced with a "Grand Opening" sign. It took a lot of pleading and coaxing to get my mom to participate, but she eventually got up off the couch, turned the television off and joined us in the kitchen. "It's a family room," my dad said, "there's something for all of us." Despite my mom's grumbling, my father stopped us at the top of the stairs.

He insisted on keeping the lights out. "Okay, folks, watch your step," he said. "We are a licensed establishment, but we aren't insured just yet."

The flashlight was dim and cast a dull circle on the stairs, which eventually gave way to the newly tiled floor.

"Okay, wait here," my father said, clicking off the flashlight.

A moment later an overhead light came on and my father was standing behind his new bar with three freshly opened beers in front of him. The Elvis Russian Matryoshka dolls, the Elvis Anniversary bone china plates, the Memphis coffee mugs and the framed Elvis postage stamps were all unpacked and in their place.

"Welcome to Graceland," my dad said.

You could see the nailheads where he had driven them into the wood on the bar, the stools were mismatched, and the edges of the panelling didn't all align evenly, which gave the room the feel of a slightly crooked tree fort built out of scraps of abandoned lumber.

My father shifted his weight uneasily from one foot to the other, smiling apprehensively like a circus performer waiting for applause. It was a crucial moment, and I knew my father's sense of purpose and resolve hinged on our response so I enthusiastically took a seat on one of the barstools, unequivocally displaying my approval. My mother, on the other hand, seemed annoyed and bewildered, and for several eternities stood there looking like the ceiling had just caved in. Whether it was resignation and surrender, or the greatest performance of her acting career, I couldn't tell, but it felt like the three steps my mother took towards the bar temporarily pacified the destructive force that was now slowly loosening the bolts and screws that held our family together. What followed was a modest one-beer inauguration, half-hearted though it may have been, it was an act of generosity on my mother's part, and I appreciated the reprieve.

A few days later I was sitting on the back porch burning a hole in the step with a magnifying glass. I had read the news, perused the obituaries and noted that, despite the clear blue sky, the forecast included a severe storm warning. My father was in the shed again.

"That aunt of yours was a pack rat," he said, as he stood in the doorway scrutinizing an old straw cowboy hat.

He was trying real hard. I knew that. Both of my parents were. They weren't really talking, but this also meant they weren't fighting.

When my dad strolled out of the shed with a toolbox and an extension cord, I repositioned myself so he couldn't see that I had burned a hook-shaped black line in our rotting step. I watched him drop the tools on the lawn and then hop up past me and disappear into the kitchen. As I continued to a burn another line into the wood, I thought of my mother and how crazy she was acting. Instead of speaking, she was now using handwritten notes to communicate—do the dishes, or tell your father to turn the music down. She had taken to tucking a pen behind her ear and stuffing a pad of paper into the front of her bra. There were little yellow notes taped to the front door, the kitchen cupboards, the mirror in the bathroom, even on the front of the television guide. It was like she was disappearing, and yet at the same time she was everywhere.

My dad was carrying two kitchen chairs when he pushed open the door, a beer bottle sticking out of each pocket in his pants as he hobbled down the steps. I watched him drop the two chairs down in the middle of the lawn about three feet from each other and then gently place each bottle in the shade. When I sat down again I noticed that the lines I had burned had taken on a distinctive shape. "Today's show," I whispered, "is brought to you by the letter 'F'. Family ... Fatherless ... Fake."

My dad disappeared into the shed again, and by the time I finished burning the word "forgive" in the step, he had found a rusty old saw and had placed a couple of long pieces of wood across the back of the two chairs.

I tucked my magnifying glass into my pocket and picked up my newspaper.

"It's gonna be a doghouse," he said, catching me with my hand on the doorknob. "Never mind those fish, they're boring as hell."

I stopped, but I didn't respond or turn around.

"—Anyway, a monkey would be too much trouble," he said. "Dogs can stay outside. They can guard your property, and they're cheaper to feed."

I pulled the door open.

"Grab me that hammer over there," he said. "We'll start with the frame, and then we can put up the walls and give it a nice shingle roof. Sound good?"

I moped down the steps and stood a few feet away in the shade.

"The hammer, Kepler. C'mon, chop, chop."

"F is for fuck."

"Jeeze, Kepler, you'd think I was asking you to build a goddamn pyramid or something."

When I handed him the hammer he shook his head. "No actually, I'll need the saw first. Grab me the saw."

About a million hours later, I was standing there holding the end of a sheet of plywood with the hot sun beating down on my head. There was sawdust all over my arms, splinters in my fingers, and beads of sweat running down my temples. And even though it felt like the sun was moving closer and closer to the earth with each passing second, I kept getting this cold chill up and down my spine. I did my best to keep my end of the wood level like my father told me, but he was clumsy with the saw and his cut lines were crooked. Every time he paused to yell at me I kept checking the sky for anything big enough to cast a shadow over our house.

"What's wrong with you?" he asked.

I didn't know how to answer him. I couldn't shake the dreadful feeling that something was coming. Every time I looked up at the sky, part of me half expected to see the distant approach of Godzilla setting the horizon ablaze with his fiery breath. "I thought I heard thunder," I said.

He glanced up at the cloudless sky, shook his head and made some comment about my mother and me being afflicted by weirdness disease.

We worked in silence for a while. I fetched his tools and made beer runs to the kitchen, and did my best to stay focused on each new angle of construction. And then, after an eternity of watching my father drive one-and-a-half-inch spiral nails into the wood, it started to look something like an actual doghouse.

I still had that uneasy feeling about the sky, but when my dad peered over the rims of his sunglasses with that look in his eye and said, "Break time," I sighed with relief.

"F is for finally," I said taking a seat on the grass beside him. I was torn. I knew I'd never get a dog, despite the charade of this ridiculous construction. My father was a man of obsessive impulses. He needed to be busy. Without some kind of stimulation or distraction my father would go crazy, just like my mother.

"So what happened?" I asked.

"What happened to what?"

"The man dressed as a woman. The cab ride to Memphis."

"Ah, you see, you're hooked. That's what a good story will do."

The truth was I had sort of forgotten all about the story, but I knew the only remedy for the uneasy feeling I was having was to surrender to the comfort of my dad's storytelling voice.

I nodded and threw in a quick smile.

My dad took a long swig of beer and lit a cigarette.

"So off we went," he began, "cassette in the deck, sunglasses on, dashboard Elvis, and this strange guy from Memphis.

"After about an hour of driving and chit-chatting my passenger fell asleep. I pulled in for some gas and as I was filling the tank I was standing right next to where his head was resting against the window, and with the luxury of a good long look, I began to realize how absurd the whole damn thing was. His mouth was wide open and there was a smudge of red on the glass from the rouge on his cheek. I could see the shadow of a day's growth below the surface of his makeup. He had deep-set eyes, and his nose, though it wasn't what I'd call feminine, was sort of delicate. Plus, there was something serene and oddly womanish about his mouth. I'd never met a cross-dresser, man, woman, trans-whatever before, but snoring away like that, he looked like a damn clown.

"As I walked in the door of the gas station to pay, I glanced back through the window half expecting the car to be gone. I mean that would have figured. How the hell would I explain that to Carl? Anyway, even though it was all a crazy idea, as I got us some snacks, coffees, a carton of smokes and a map, all I could think about was that Memphis is where Graceland is located.

"Once we were back on the highway, I heard him stretch and yawn. I glanced at the meter—it was already at 64 dollars

—then back through the rearview. His eyes were taking in the rolling fields stretching out from the highway.

"'What about a flat rate.' I said. 'You pay for the gas and we split the coffees.' He nodded. I radioed Carl and told him I was driving a passenger to Memphis. There was a moment of dead air. '10-9?'

"10-9, before you ask, is radio code for pardon me, or repeat, or whatever. So I repeated. 'Memphis.' I said, 'M-E-M-P—' 'Tennessee?' he asked. 'Affirmative.' 'You've got a strange sense of humour,' he said. 'It's not humour,' I said, 'It's a gut feeling.' 'I want that car back in the depot by the end of your shift, Pressler.' That was the first time Carl ever called me by my name. I turned off the radio.

"'Your last name's Pressler?' my passenger asked. I nodded. 'Well, Mr. Pressler, ain't that a southern-fried coincidence?'"

There were several beer bottles scattered across the lawn when a big grey cloud rolled in front of the sun. My dad placed his sunglasses in his pocket and reached for the hammer. He smiled and looked up at the cloud that hung over our house. "Goddamn, meteorologist for a son," he said.

"It was a gut feeling," I said.

"We better hurry if we're going to get this built before it pours."

And though we didn't manage to get any shingles on the roof, by the time the first few drops of rain came down, it was pretty much what you'd expect a doghouse to look like. We stood back and stared at it a moment.

"A humble home for a Saint Bernard," my dad said.

"Or a cathedral for a chihuahua," I said.

And then his hand fell on my shoulder and rested there for a second, but before I felt the whole reassuring weight of it, he was jogging towards the back door. "Hang on a second," he said, and ran into the house.

I stood there looking at the doghouse feeling proud and excited for a second or two, and then got to work pushing my hopes back down into the pit of my guts where they belonged.

When my dad came back out, the cloud was breaking apart. He squinted up at the sun. "Don't quit your day job," he said. Then he removed a pen that he had tucked behind his ear and pulled a piece of paper out of his shirt pocket and wrote, buy a dog! and stuck it on the doghouse with a thumbtack. It was a jab at my mom and I knew that, but I stood there in the sun laughing with him, because at least my father's ways of dealing with the sadness and futility of his life sometimes included me.

On the morning of my sixteenth birthday, the sky was thick and grey with clouds. Though I didn't understand such things, the barometric pressure was tangible. I awoke with the feeling that something monstrous and menacing was looming just above the ceiling of cloud cover. The distant rumble of what sounded like a ten-ton bowling ball rolling across the sky followed me down the hall. There was nothing in the fridge but a couple of beers and some condiments so I tried the junk drawer, remembering that I had seen some of those little packets of jam they give you in restaurants when you order toast. I found some peach marmalade and grabbed a plate, but I had to use a spatula to pry the cutlery drawer open because the little knob had fallen off. I scooped some marmalade onto some crackers and tried to pretend that it was any other day.

My dad didn't say a word when he dragged himself up off the couch. He just made a coffee and sat himself down at the table to work on his puzzle. An hour later my mom headed straight to the bathroom, sat herself down on the toilet and started yelling through the door, "Somebody pull the laundry off the line. It's pouring out there."

My dad looked up from the puzzle, "You heard the queen, Kepler. Get the laundry before she loses her royal mind."

As I opened the back door, I was overwhelmed by the sweet and sour breath of the day, an odour from a belly bloated with the remnants of stupid kids' hopes. I stepped out into the rain, and after pulling the clothes off the line, I walked across the lawn and stuffed the wet laundry into the empty doghouse.

Two hours later, I was sitting in the kitchen on the floor with some paper and a pack of pencil crayons I found in the junk drawer with the jam. I was drawing a picture of Ham the space monkey, an American flag and a German flag joined together in the middle on the chest of the chimp's space suit. I was adding the Elvis sideburns when my mother called out again from the bathroom. "Kepler, call me cab."

"That's all she does anymore is work," my father muttered to himself. "She acts as if selling glue, enamel paint, and how-to manuals to model plane aficionados is something to be proud of. The Hobby Barn is nothing but a cult of spiteful amateurs who are more interested in super hero figurines, miniature train sets and board games than their own families. What the hell does your mother even know about hobbies? The only hobbies she has are watching television and fussing with her nails."

It was true—when my mother was home, she spent her time on the couch with an assortment of nail polishes, whispering to the characters on the television screen. She drove me crazy sometimes because once she started on her nails she'd call me into the living room every half hour. "Channel five. Channel nine. Channel two." No please or thank you. I don't know what she did when nobody else was home. And now apparently she couldn't make a phone call either.

I had already dialed the number when my father noticed that I was holding a Bluebird Cab Company fridge magnet. "No, no, not them," he said. There was already a voice on the other end waiting for my address. "Hang up," he yelled. "Call the competition. The phonebook's on the fridge."

"I'm sorry," I said into the phone as I hung up.

"And don't say you're sorry either. Those bastards don't deserve an apology."

After calling another cab, I hung up the phone and headed down the hall. The bathroom door was open about six inches. My mother had the hair dryer on, the tap running, and the radio tuned to CKEY. An Elvis song was on. I watched her as she fumbled through a cosmetic bag, opened the lid of something or other, ran it across her eyelids, patted some powder onto her cheeks, applied a very bright red lipstick, and then placed her new wig on her head and tugged on a few of the curls. It was like watching her mutate into a stranger. Maybe she was capable of having an affair after all.

"Cab's on its way," I said.

Her eyes met mine in the mirror.

"Oh, god, Kepler, don't scare me like that." She threw a wet face cloth at me and pushed the door closed.

A minute later my mom awkwardly strutted into the kitchen sliding her arms into the sleeves of her red coat, the heels of her shoes clicking on the linoleum. She stopped at the table, lifted her foot and peeled something off the bottom of her shoe.

My father had one of the last pieces of the puzzle held delicately in his fingers when he glanced up at her. "Yeah, yeah," he said absently, as if he was agreeing to some unspoken insult.

My mother looked at her watch and marched back across the floor to the cupboard. I watched her pull on a pair of rubber gloves and reach for the broom. My dad lifted his feet when she began to manically sweep under the table, banging the legs of the chairs.

"Mark the calendar, Kepler. Your mother actually did something useful today."

And with a few quick swipes she had a pile of grit and hair, a handful of cheerios, a white plastic faceplate that once covered the light switch by the fridge, and a piece of my dad's puzzle in the dustpan. The cab honked out front. She paused a moment, looked down at me on the floor, raised her finger to her pursed lips, then walked over to the cupboard and emptied the dustpan in the garbage. She unpeeled the rubber gloves one finger at a time and quickly checked her nails. We both looked at my father who was still muttering to himself, his shoulders raised in concentration.

The cab honked again.

My mother scribbled something on a pad, tore the page off and stuck it to the fridge with a magnet.

"Gotta go," she said.

And just as she was stepping out the door, she turned and called back to me. "Kepler. You're going to have to make dinner tonight. Your father won't be of any use. I think there's some corn in the freezer."

"I hate that frozen corn crap," my father said.

"I wasn't talking to you," she yelled and slammed the door.

After finishing my drawing I stood up and glanced out the window. It was raining hard. What a perfect birthday, I thought. In the reflection of the glass it looked like I was a ghost, a vague shape partially merged with the kitchen cupboards behind me. There was a flash outside the window followed by a crack of thunder. "It's here," I said.

"Yeah, well, before it blows the house down, put that thing away, will ya?" My dad was pointing at the phonebook I had left on the table.

When I turned back towards the fridge I saw my mother's note.

I thought my father had broken my heart the day I found him in the shed, but the words written on that note felt like an anvil falling on what was left of it. The words were scribbled out in my mother's awkward mix of print and cursive. I remember thinking it would have been easier somehow if she had at least taken a moment to write it out neatly, but there it was—little more than a hastily scribbled afterthought. I looked up at the two fish hovering lazily in the murky bowl, then I reread the note again. When I looked over at my dad, his eyes were closed and he was shaking his head from side to side. "No, no, it can't be," he said.

I turned back to the note, wondering how he could have possibly read it from where he was sitting.

"I fucking knew it," he shouted.

I thought I was going to vomit.

He shoved the table forward, bent over and started searching the floor. "There's a piece missing," he said.

On that August afternoon, on my sixteenth birthday, the hole in my gut expanded into a deep bottomless pit. And as I stood there in our filthy kitchen watching my father in his old blue suit crawl around on his knees under the table, I knew the dream was finally over.

"Elvis is dead," I said, and ran for the closet.

I heard the fridge door slam, followed by my father's footsteps in the hall, and then the sound of what I guessed was the radio in the bathroom hitting the wall. When I pushed the closet door open and peeked into the living room, I saw that he had unplugged his junky all-in-one cassette, radio and record player, and was piling the little speakers on top of the plastic cover of the turntable. He stood up with a groan and headed for the basement, the electric cord dragging on the floor behind him.

I could picture him down there with his homemade bar, and the crappy old patio lanterns he had strung up above it, his swivelling stools and beer fridge full of Heinekens. But I knew that somehow those things would not be enough. The monster or whatever it was I had felt in the sky all summer had arrived, and it was clear to me that this thing, this missing puzzle piece, this death of an icon, this empty space was now big enough to swallow everything.

As I emptied the kitchen garbage on the floor, I heard my dad's shaky hand placing the needle on a record and then "Suspicious Minds" coming on loud and distorted from the basement. I sifted through a mess of wet paper towels, smelly food scraps and Styrofoam containers covered in that weird orange sauce they give you with Chinese food. When I found the piece of the puzzle, I wiped it against my pant leg, put it in my pocket, grabbed my drawing and headed downstairs. I stood on the last step for a moment watching my dad slowly swivelling on a vinyl barstool studying the Elvis album cover. The music was so loud he wasn't aware of me until I was standing there in front of him. He dropped the record cover in his lap. "Jeezus Christ," he mouthed. He then reached for his beer and took a sip. His hand was shaking when I handed him the drawing.

"What's this?" he yelled.

"It's a space chimp," I said.

"What?" he yelled.

"It's for you."

He said something as he pointed at the flag on the monkey's space suit, but the music was too loud.

"What?" I said.

The surprise of being hit hurt more than the force of it. I reached both hands out to steady myself, but there was nothing to hold on to but the fractured sound of Elvis's voice all around me. The walls receded and compressed in my peripherals, a shrinking aperture until my father became a distant static image as if I was looking at him through a pinhole. Just as I was sure I was going to black out, he grabbed me by the front of my shirt and pulled me in close to him. The Elvis record cover on his lap dug into my ribs. I could feel his chest subtly heave as if he was running out of oxygen. Tears, not mine, this time, but his. The thought of seeing my father crying replaced the fog in my head with a rush of anxiety. Elvis was now acting as the soundtrack to this moment, and I worried that I would never be able to hear an Elvis song again without picturing my father this way. All I wanted was for him to behave for once in his life like a dad should. And for a moment I truly hated him, not because he had hit me, but because he had so easily been reduced to this—what my mother had called a state of uselessness.

My father held me awkwardly for a moment longer and then pushed me away from him with both hands on my shoulders. I thought he might hit me again, but instead he just wiped his eyes with his sleeve. I could feel my cheek swelling. He pointed towards the stereo and then leaned in toward me.

"Turn it down and get me a Heineken."

He took the beer from me, cracked it open with his lighter and pressed it up to my eye.

"Hold it there for a minute," he said.

A moment passed where we just sat there listening...caught in trap, and I can't walk *out*... as we swivelled silently on our stools. And then, when the song ended, he turned to me, "It's over," he said. But I wasn't ready for the dream to end. I'd hold the damn ceiling up myself if I had to. "Tell me about the time you met Neil Armstrong," I said. It was a B-side track, but it would do, because I knew he was right. I knew that if he wasn't telling me one of his stories, the whole thing would cave in and bury us forever.

Even though I could tell his heart wasn't in it, he smiled, picked up his beer bottle and held it out until I clinked the bottle I was holding to his. He still needed a little coaxing, but I knew he couldn't resist a willing audience. "It was in Ottawa," I said, "back in 1970, right after the moon landing."

I let my dad ramble without interruption. I opened his beers and flipped the records as he improvised his way through each chapter leading up to the big moment.

"Man," my father was saying, "I wish I had a camera at that moment—Neil Armstrong walked right up to me. I didn't have any paper on me so I got him to sign his autograph on a dollar bill."

My dad was quiet for a moment. He was always quiet for a moment when he got to that part, as if you were supposed to hang out there with him, being in love with Neil Armstrong's signature. But the moment lasted a lot longer than usual. And then, as "Now and Then There's a Fool Such as I" came on, he looked like he was going to cry again.

"What happened next," I said as if I had never heard the story before.

His voice was shaky. "I didn't want to hassle the man, but then I thought to myself, what the hell, this is a once in a lifetime opportunity, so I asked him, 'Mr. Armstrong, what's it like?' 'What's what like?' he asked. 'What's it like to walk on the moon?'" And then my dad paused again as if he had forgotten the punch line.

"What did he say?" I prompted.

"He told me that the whole thing was fake."

"What was fake?"

"That's right," my dad said. "The whole damn thing was done in a Hollywood studio."

My father downed the rest of his beer. "I know," he said, "I didn't believe it either. But then Neil looked me square in the eye and, I'll never forget this, he said, 'Quid credas nunc tibi pro re.' And then he walked away."

"What does that mean?" I asked sincerely.

"What does what mean?"

"Quid credas, whatever—"

When my dad finally finished staring at the empty bottle in his hand, he said, "What you believe becomes your reality."

I hadn't ever heard this version of the story. "I don't get it," I said.

"Jesus, Kepler, do I have to explain everything?"

"How do you know it was Neil and not some Latin professor?"

"It was Neil Armstrong all right. Anyway, you're missing the point. It doesn't matter whether he walked on the moon or not, the point is that if you tell the story well enough, then in a way it did happen."

I knew what he meant. At least I thought I did. And as I sat there nodding in agreement, the room tilted, and I sensed that my dad was sliding off towards the edge again.

"Anyway, none of that really matters now. Elvis is dead. And I'm nothing but a taxi driver."

I remembered the piece of the jigsaw puzzle in my pocket and was about to give it to him when it dawned on me that this whole story was a confession, a confession that I had no interest in hearing. I wanted to be as far away from what he was suggesting as I could get. I wanted to climb into a rocket ship and prove everyone wrong, but instead I did what my father did and guzzled back the beer in my hand. And then we had another—two pals in ramshackle bar telling stories. "There was a movie called *Taxi Driver* with Robert De Niro in it," I said. "I never saw it but … and, there was a song by Harry Chapin, and even a sitcom on TV."

I wasn't sure how this was relevant until I remembered that Elvis was, according to the story, driving a truck when he was discovered. But my dad knew he wasn't going to be discovered. I mean discovered for what? I'm with my mother on this one, being related to Elvis never amounted to anything that you could rub together, except a colourful and over-told lie.

"Look at me," he said, as he handed me another beer.

I swivelled my chair so that I was facing him.

"There was a complaint."

"When?"

"At work," he said. He wiped his nose with his sleeve. "I did something I shouldn't have. Actually, it's not what I did, it's what I said." He took another sip of beer. "Well, I don't remember actually saying it, but then, it's the customer's word against mine."

"What did you say, Walter?"

"I was tired, you know, I worry too much—your mother —I don't know if you've noticed but she forgets things—all those damn notes—anyway, I was just driving along you know, thinking to myself and driving, just another day behind the wheel, and the next thing I know my fare throws a ten-dollar bill at me and jumps out of the cab." My dad paused and lit a cigarette off the one he was smoking. "You gotta listen to other people's problems all day long. You gotta listen to them talk about work, their wives, where they're from, their politics, religions, what sports they like, all the places they've been to. But the minute you say anything, all hell breaks loose … Anyway, Carl's waiting for me in the office and he starts going on about policy and procedure or some damn thing. I had no idea what he was talking about.

"'One of your fares,' he says, 'told me what you said to her—are you with me?—Sometimes I feel like turning the wheel into the oncoming lane—Does that sound familiar?' I don't remember saying it, but the truth is, I'd thought it at least a million times. Carl told me I needed a good shrink, and then he fired me."

My father swivelled in his bar stool so that his back was to me again. He had lost his taxi job, and now he had lost his hero, and I had the sense that I was losing something too.

"Get yourself another beer," he ordered. "You're falling behind."

As soon as the words left his mouth we heard my mother's heels trotting across the kitchen floor above us. Our eyes went to the ceiling following her steps.

"Okay, okay," my dad said, wiping at his face with a Bowling for Dollars bar towel, "I'm gonna fix this."

My mom was still wearing her coat and shoes when my dad led her down the stairs. He left her standing in the middle of the room so he could turn down the lights on the dimmer switch. I guess I was drunk because I was having difficulty remembering the sequence of songs my father had chosen; my hand was shaking when I placed the needle on "Make the World Go Away".

I don't know if it was the dim lights, the smoky quality of the air, or Elvis's voice, but it seemed like someone replaced my father with Clark Gable, because when he took a bow and offered his hand, my mother stepped into his arms. For a moment I thought that Elvis had done it again, that even now he still had the power to keep the beast at bay. They moved with grace and tenderness as if they had been dancing together their whole lives, as if this were their true state of being. And as I watched my mother and father moving across the floor together I swear I felt a fourth presence in the room, and I imagined that Elvis himself had made a detour to our basement on his way to heaven. But then the record skipped and that little fault was enough to break a tentative and fragile moment. Suddenly they were at odds with each other again. My mother turned her eyes to the ceiling as if she was enduring some temporary embarrassment. And I looked away, too, because with her heels on, my mother was a little taller than my father, and this realization brought with it all the other irregularities that the music and the moment had hidden—my mother's crooked wig made her look more inebriated than my father, and the water dripping from her wet coat, which had pooled around their feet, had soaked into my father's mismatched socks.

When the song ended, I quickly placed the needle close to the beginning of "Love Me Tender" and my dad pulled her in close again, but she had had enough. "Careful of my nails," she said, raising both hands in the air. Though the spell never quite took hold, it was completely broken when my father placed his hand on my mother's rear end. Up until that moment, no matter what went wrong, no matter what bully might show up on the sandy shores of a Hawaiian beach, no matter what troubles may plague a travelling circus, no matter what grave force had descended on a suburban house, Elvis could make it all seem okay with a smile and a song. But the truth was, Elvis was nothing more than one more dead relative.

"Enough," my mother yelled. It was subtle, like someone pushing a cupboard door closed, but drunk as my father was, it was enough to make him stumble backwards into the bar. For a second I thought the whole structure was going to collapse. Glasses and bottles tumbled as he crumpled slowly to the floor, three empty beer bottles fell into my lap and a fourth went over the front of the bar, hit my father's head and then crashed on the floor beside him. How, I wondered, could a man used to zero gravity and the extremes of G-force be so easily tipped over? My mother raised a hand to her mouth as if she was going to scream, but then, when she caught a glimpse of herself in the mirror behind the bar she seemed to recover and stormed up the stairs. It's all just a dream, I thought—just the final gasps of my parents' dream coming to an end.

After picking up the bar stool, my father turned in a slow circle as if he was looking for the thing that had hit him, as if he expected to see a two-by-four or baseball bat as evidence of the assault. He rubbed the back of his head and then shrugged his shoulders. "Grab me a beer," he said. "That mother of yours is as cold as a witch's tit."

When I handed him a beer he stepped back and began drunkenly turning in a slow circle, dancing with an imaginary partner. I got up and headed for the stairs, but the room was shifting again. My father caught me by the arm and held on to me. I felt helpless, and simply followed the momentum as he put my arms around his waist and began moving in a slow and awkward orbit to the sound of the needle scratching at the end of the record.

When I woke up, my bedroom light was out and the house was still and quiet. The darkness around me seemed alive with energy. It was like something had paused in the shadows and was frozen there holding its breath, waiting for me to drift back to sleep. I tried to focus on the steady rain hitting the window. One Mississippi, two Mississippi, three Mississippi. The bile from the last time I vomited rose in my throat as a thin horizontal sliver of light momentarily appeared in the darkness. I heard the doorknob turn and then a silhouette appeared and vanished as my bedroom door opened and closed.

"You awake?"

My father's voice sounded deep and raspy like he had smoked too many cigarettes.

"Kepler?"

I felt his weight as he sat on the edge of my bed.

"Sorry for hitting you," he said, as he swung his feet up off the floor and lay back next to me.

I heard him push Ham to the floor.

I didn't want him there, but now that I was sort of awake and aware of some kind of a daunting presence in the room, I didn't want him to leave either.

"Now let's see," he said, turning his face up to the ceiling. "What's going on in the universe this evening?"

I focused on the vague shape of my father's arm as he pointed up through the darkness.

"North," he whispered,

I tilted my head back on my pillow.

"There's Cassiopeia." And then he drew a straight line south towards the bedroom door. "You were born under Leo. You're a fire sign."

And even though it was the last thing I wanted to do, my eyes automatically went directly below Leo to NGC 4631, the constellation of the Whale.

"Did you see that?" I asked.

"What?"

"Cetus."

"Cetus, what?"

"It moved."

"Impossible," my father said.

I blinked in the darkness and the room started to spin again.

"When Cetus was sent by Neptune to devour Andromeda—"

I tried desperately to fall under the spell of my father's voice.

"—Perseus used the head of Medusa to turn Cetus into stone."

The constellation flickered again.

"As you know, stones don't—"

But the curse that Perseus had used to hold the whale there was now broken. Cetus was free from its place on the ceiling— a rogue constellation careening through space—fluid, impossible, and like my father's story, it adjusted itself and changed direction until it was headed straight for my bed.

"...Capricorn," my father was saying. "Elvis was a Capricorn. But now he's a shining star in the sky, part of the mystery..."

I tried my best to hang on to what my father was saying, but the constellation of Cetus was now descending like a meteorite through the sky.

"The German flag has three stripes running across it—black, red and yellow." His voice sounded far away; the faint slur was gone. "What you drew is called a swastika. Don't draw that ever again."

A long and worrying moment passed. When he spoke again, I had the covers pulled up over my head.

"I wanted to tell you that I'll be going away for a while, which reminded me that I never did finish that story. When I was gone last time, remember?"

I felt his weight shift next to me, his breathing grew heavy, unfamiliar, and for a moment I thought he had fallen asleep.

"You radioed Carl, and the guy in the backseat just found out your last name."

"Yeah, yeah, I got it. We crossed the border and there was a whole lot of uneventful driving. Road trips have long spells of quiet contemplation. Anyway, I started to feel ... I don't quite know how to express it ... but I decided that something bigger than me was at work here. I never really believed in fate or destiny before, but I began to feel like there was something connected to the other end of whatever it was that was pulling me along. We passed a paperweight museum, a passenger pigeon memorial and the world's largest rubber stamp. America's filled with things like that—the world's largest this and that.

"By the time we were just outside of Kentucky the sun had gone down and the sky was filled with stars. I'd never seen so many in my life. It was as if the sky was lower down there. I just sort of stared out the window as if everything was ... hell, it was like gravity was reversed. It kind of felt like if I didn't hold onto something I'd be dragged off into the nighttime sky. And part of me wanted to go, too. To just surrender to the feeling and drift away into the night, but I held on, because I knew I had to get to Graceland.

"That morning we arrived in Tupelo and my fare starts pointing out where Elvis went to school, his favourite drive-in restaurant, the hardware store where Elvis bought his first guitar. He told me how Elvis's early days singing in a choir whetted his appetite for the spiritual, which eventually led him to someone called Krishnamurti or something like that. He described Elvis's fondness of horses, old cars, bowling, mobile homes and goddamn ice cream.

"'Wait a minute,' I said. 'Bowling. Elvis loves to bowl?' 'Hell, yeah,' he said. 'Elvis is a great bowler. The only thing he loves more than bowling is cherry cola and a slice of pecan pie.'

"As we drove along Beal Street, I counted seventeen Elvis impersonators. Some were young, some were old, some were fat, and some were as thin as the necks of the guitars they played. One was outside a church chasing a falling leaf down the street, one was arguing with a traffic cop, one was sitting on the hood of a Cadillac, one was playing his heart out to an old dog lying on his side outside of a barbershop.

"'Turn left here,' he said. When I saw the sign, things got very surreal. Everything from this point forward took on the quality of a dream. It had what looked like bullet holes in it and a couple of the letters were missing, but you could still read it, Welcome to Gr c land. Further up the road was the house. I don't know if it was because of the lack of sleep, but I swear the sky looked as if it had been scribbled by the hand of a child with a blue crayon. Next thing I knew he was standing there holding the door open. 'Can I write you a cheque,' he said, 'or would you prefer cash?' 'You work here?' I asked. 'No, no,' he said. I stared at the giant white columns rising up on either side of a classical portico.

"'C'mon,' he said. I followed him up the steps and through the door. There were three peacocks roaming in the front hall. 'Don't mind them,' he said, 'they don't bite.' The foyer opened up into a kitchen, which had the distinct smell of burnt toast. The fractured light of an elaborate chandelier danced across the walls and floor. 'You gotta have a home, Walter. A man ain't nothin' without a place to lay his hat.'

"'It's beautiful,' I said. And then he started unbuttoning his shirt. I didn't know what was going on. He undressed as if it was the most natural thing in the world. I mean he wasn't exactly in the best shape, and by the time he took his pants off, I was having a difficult time looking at him. But I swear to God there were little diamonds on the waistband of his underwear. Anyway, he ushered me along and tossed the clothes he had been wearing in a wheelbarrow. It was weird because I didn't even notice the wheelbarrow until he tossed his clothes in it. It was that kind of place. There were just too many distractions to focus on any one thing. '500 acres, 23 rooms,' he said proudly as he combed his hair back. He wasn't wearing a wig anymore.

"There was scaffolding all over the place, with sections of marble peeking out from under the curled up edges of the drop sheets covering the floor. 'It's a work in progress,' he said. 'I'm building a den in the basement. It's going to have three televisions.' He held up three fingers to emphasize the point. And as he walked me through the house I thought about how he had transformed from a woman into a man, and now he was changing again. Someone handed him a shirt and trousers. He slipped the shirt on as we passed a waterfall cascading down an interior wall. He slid a leg into each pant leg as we strolled through a long hallway and into a room with a goddamn Mona Lisa in it.

"'C'mon, Walter, you're slowing down,' he said. I followed him into an elevator which took us down one floor to a room with a mossy green shag-pile carpet covering the floor and ceiling. The room was full of pinball machines with a bar at the far end. He ordered two ice cream shakes from a guy wearing a tuxedo. 'Ah, here we are,' he said.

"And the next thing I knew I was standing next to goddamn Elvis Presley in his own goddamn private bowling alley. And as Elvis handed me a ball, he looked at me real serious and said, 'Of course, if you ever mention anything about the makeup and the women's clothes, I'll have to kill ya.'"

I closed my eyes and opened them. It was so dark that it was impossible to even imagine that somewhere around us there were four walls. My father's weight shifted, the springs in the mattress groaned, and then I heard the curtains being drawn open.

"Your mother wants a divorce," he said.

There was a moment of silence, and then as if on cue, a flash of lightning was followed by a crack of thunder. And in that split second of light I could see my father standing in front of the window with my sock monkey pressed up against his chest.

"C'mon, Kepler, get dressed. We're going to the zoo. I'm going to get you a monkey like I promised. I got it all figured out. Everything we need is in that shed. If my calculations are correct, once we're over the south fence, there's a path that will lead directly to the African Pavilion. We'll have to keep our eyes peeled for poison ivy and security guards. It'll be fun. I'll get you a damn monkey like I promised. Why the hell not?"

I knew then what my mother had known for a long time, that this man, in all his sorrow and awkwardness, was really just a child. His stories were just the fantasies he had created and held on to for so long that he eventually believed them. I knew if I stared at the stars too long the same thing would happen to me. I could feel them pulling me as well, but unlike my father, I didn't have a steering wheel or a reason to hold on to.

CHAPTER EIGHT

I haven't seen Ophelia in seven days. When I find her in the cafeteria she's hunched over her tray like a mangy giraffe nibbling on a scruff of grass. Her nose is almost touching the plate. When she speaks I am surprised to hear that her accent is gone. "I made it to the roof," she says. "I tried to tell you but—"

"What roof?"

She looks up at me. Her eyes are red and swollen. She looks about a hundred years old. I pull her cardigan up closer around her neck.

"The stairwell door," she continues, "—the lock didn't quite click—the stairs led to the roof. I wish you were with me, Kepler. It was just after dinner and the sun was setting. It was beautiful. I could see the silhouette of the Tower of London, the Parliament buildings to the west." There's a long pause. Her head drops and a line of drool connects her chin to the table. When she finally manages to raise her head again she's smiling. "The Thames was sparkling with light. It was just like I remembered, like being on stage again. And then, I don't know, there were sirens and people started yelling."

She closes her eyes, and I'm glad because I can't bear to look at her. There are dark rings under eyes. Visions of electroshock, restraint and sedation run through my mind. I reach over and wipe her lips with my sleeve.

"I feel terrible," she says as she reaches into the pocket of her sweater. "I can't remember anything after that."

Her hand is shaking as she pulls the cap off the lipstick.

"Let me," I say.

I intentionally extend the line onto her cheek. She tucks in her lips and rubs them together like my mother used to do.

I'm standing over by Atwood's bookshelf scanning the spines for electroshock therapy manuals, or studies on lobotomy, anything that might indicate what they did to Ophelia.

"Whenever you're ready, Mr. Pressler."

I ignore Atwood. I'm buying time. There are a lot of books. I pull one out called, *Transmission of Aggressions through Imitation of Aggressive Models*. I flip to the table of contents.  I need to tackle this strategically.

"This isn't a library, Kepler."

There's nothing here—at least, nothing that I can understand. I slam the book closed. "My father once told me the thrust required to pass through the earth's atmosphere is seven miles per second," I say. "Millions of dollars are spent each year researching ways to transport humans beyond the atmosphere of this planet, and yet, I did it simply by closing my eyes."

"Shock and stress can be a powerful gravity-defying force," Atwood says.

I place the book back on the shelf and then approach Atwood's desk. "But I'm not talking about shock and stress."

I stand there for a moment shaking. I can feel my eyelid begin to twitch. I grab his pen and snap it in half.

Atwood fires me a quick look of parental disappointment. "What are you talking about then, Kepler?"

I back away like a gun fighter—slowly, and then flop down on the couch. I know I'm having a little fit, but I can't seem to help myself.

"Violence and silence. Is that what this has come to?"

I raise my hand to my mouth and pull an imaginary zipper across my lips.

"Okay, have it your way…" He starts writing in his files with a pen that looks exactly like the one I just broke, "*Subject exhibits delusional and aggressive behaviour*—" He looks up at me. "Is this what you want, Kepler?"

I can't stop thinking about Ophelia's hollow eyes. I imagine them strapping me down to the table.

"I'm talking about the imagination," I say.

"Good." Atwood exhales heavily as if he was holding his breath. "Go on."

"I know that Cetus is nothing more than a constellation of large gaseous bodies which generate energy through nuclear fusion et cetera, but when it comes to the imagination, there's no instructions, no operating manual, no on/off switch."

"Once again you're focusing on the symptom, Kepler.

I resist the sudden urge to curl up into a ball. "It's a place of safety," I say, stretching my arms and legs out, holding my body as straight and rigid as I can.

"Like your front hall closet?" Atwood asks.

"Yeah, but the closet is real." I can feel the knots throughout my body unravelling, the anger and frustration giving way to exhaustion.

"Good," Atwood says. "What do you think happened that night?"

"What night?"

"The night you lost control of your imagination?"

"I don't know," I say. "Elvis died...my father disappeared."

Atwood taps his pen on the top of my file and glances down at his notes.

I imagine them hooking electrodes up to my toes and earlobes. "I honestly don't remember," I say.

"Are you familiar," Dr. Atwood asks, "with the works of Dr. Freud?"

"Cigar-smoking shrink from Austria who believed all mental illnesses had something to do with sex?"

"You know about Freud, yet you don't know what a swastika looks like?"

"Actually, I don't remember what I drew that day, but he did hit me."

"So you're—how did you put it—*making shit up*, just like your father?"

"Okay, I knew what a swastika was—it was my way of getting back at him, a cheap and pathetic shot at the German heritage he had denied me."

Atwood scratches his chin. "It seems to me that you're only telling me what you want me to know, Kepler." He waits a moment as if he's expecting me to crack.

I shrug. "I'm doing the best I can—"

"I think you need a little push."

"What do you mean?"

Atwood's hand is ready at the switch. He glances at his watch and pulls the lever. "I took the liberty of contacting your school."

I'm on my feet again, Atwood's new pen in my hand. "Who did you talk to at my school?"

I think I detect a faint grin on Atwood's face, but it's too subtle for me to be sure.

"I have talked briefly with your principal and your guidance councillor, and I have been in correspondence with Mr. Lemonitis, and if you break one more pen you will never see that typewriter again."

I don't know what's worse, the idea of electroshock treatment or having the typewriter taken away.

"Are you ready to continue or should I call Bruce?"

I bite my lip, drop the pen, and take a few steps back.

"The goal," he continues, "is to locate the cause, to excavate repressed thoughts and feelings—thoughts and feelings that are too painful to bear—"

"—Excavation. Is that what you call this?" I say. "It feels more like torture."

"What are you talking about, Kepler?"

"What did you do to Ophelia?"

"Who?"

"Ophelia, the actress. British lady."

"Oh, you mean Grace Honeywell."

"Okay, Grace...What did you do to her?"

"Grace got the same treatment you received when you first arrived. Suicide attempts are all treated similarly."

Suicide. The word feels like a scalpel slicing through my brain.

"Come on Kepler, focus. All this stuff about Ophelia is none of your concern, and all this stuff about Cetus is nonsense and you know it." He shakes his head. "This is a therapeutical exercise, not fiction."

According to Atwood, something so shocking and stressful happened on the night of my sixteenth birthday that my mind conjured the whale and retreated into six weeks of darkness. This repressed memory is an integral part of the narrative—crucial to my recovery. I have to give him something, but I don't know if I trust him. My father would have referred to this as "the crux of the situation. *An essential point requiring resolution.*"

I wish I could just sit down and tell Atwood everything that happened, but I am restricted by two things. First, I am, to a fault, my father's son, and I believe a good story takes time to tell. One doesn't just offer up a bulleted list of highlights. This isn't the six o'clock news. And so the narrator takes his time, selectively emphasizing the nuances, the drama and the tension, mixing biography with fiction. The second point is that I am beginning to suspect that Atwood is right. As painful as it is, there is a therapeutic quality to the retelling, and the one thing that I simply can't recall is the thing that I must face if I ever want to get out of here. And so here we are, somewhere in the middle I suppose, but at the crux, and as my father use to say, "Every good story should have one."

When I woke up from my Post Traumatic semi-conscious stupor, I was delirious and confused. I didn't know where I was—I tried to shift my weight, but I couldn't seem to locate my arms and legs. I took a deep breath and, when I exhaled, a feeling of claustrophobic darkness slowly contracted around me until I could feel it pressed up against the side of my face. That was the first moment that I had a sense of my body. Eventually, somewhere off in the purlieu I heard what must have been the pulse of my heart. Thump-thump, thump-thump. And then, a moment later, still farther off in the distance I heard a woman's voice.

"...Be very gentle. Your nails are made up of compacted keratin fibers running lengthwise from the matrix to the free edge. If you push them back and forth, they'll start to separate and your nail will weaken. Delicately caress the nail with single direction strokes."

I don't know how much time passed, but when it eventually occurred to me that my eyes were closed, I took another deep breath and counted to three. When I opened my eyes an intense aperture of light triggered a sudden reflexive response, which coincidentally resulted in a sharp pain that shot up the back of my neck. Every second of realization came with a degree of excruciating discomfort.

"...Starting at the outer edge of one nail, move the emery board gently, at a 45 degree angle along the edge of the nail towards the center. Repeat until your nail is the desired shape."

I pushed inside of myself, breathing deeply, stretching, trying to occupy the hollowness of my body.

"...Then do the same on the other side, working out from the opposite edge to the center."

On my second try, I opened my eyes very slowly, letting in a little bit of light at a time. Not only was it apparent that I was in some kind of an enclosure, but I could tell the source of the light was coming from somewhere near my feet.

"…Now it's time to push back the cuticles. We may have to rub some cuticle oil on them to soften them. We'll gently push the cuticles back to expose more of the lanula."

As my eyes slowly adjusted I could see that my bare feet were extended out a hole onto a checkered blanket next to a portable tape player. Each toe had been painted a very light and delicate shade of blue.

"…We'll renew the topcoat every two to three days. Now if you want your manicure to last, you shouldn't use your nails to pry batteries out of electronic devices, or loosen screws, or—"

When I finally realized where I was, I felt a sudden wave of shock that made my body convulse. I could feel the blood pulsing through my veins, my heart beating louder, anxiety and fear surging uncontrollably through my limbs. I began to heave, cough, and heave until a warm, thick flow of vomit came up from my stomach—I curled up into the darkness around me and started screaming.

The ride to the hospital was a bumpy swirling drift between consciousness and sleep. I remembered my mother's voice arguing with the paramedic. I remember the long corridor of the hospital as I was wheeled down the hall, the lights on the ceiling like runway markers. I remember being lifted into a bed surrounded by doctors. My legs felt like two-by-fours joined at the knees with rusty hinges. My hips ached and my fingertips were tender. I let out a scratchy and feeble whisper as they pried me open: my name—I knew; my age—I knew;

the date—I missed by six weeks; where I was—a lucky guess; and my address—providing we hadn't moved—I knew as well. These questions were followed by a series of requests involving the movement of my fingers, toes, legs and arms.

My first days at the hospital were punctuated with flashbacks that struck my mind like shards of broken glass—fragments of light slicing through shadow, revealing momentary images. I could see myself lying in a tub of cold water shivering, or sitting in the yard with my leg fastened to a lawn chair with a skipping rope. These memories were so fast and alarming that they left me feeling disoriented and exhausted, like a strobe light momentarily illuminating snapshots divided by slow turning pages of darkness.

My list of questions:
1. What happened to me?
2. Where's dad?
3. Why do I feel so weak?
4. Why was I in the doghouse?
5. Why are my toenails blue?

List of answers:
1. You had an accident.
2. Scratching of the head, looking at watches etc.
3. You are weak because you have been asleep for a very long time.
4. What doghouse?
5. We don't know, but it is a nice colour.

I remember my mother described my recovery as a stroke of luck, which was bestowed upon me, and that I should therefore count my blessings and not take things for granted. And furthermore, that I was indebted eternally to whatever was responsible for the distribution of my luck, which she seemed to vaguely take some credit for herself. She talked about my semi-comatose state in a tone that, one moment sounded sincere and traumatic, and the next moment sounded as if she was blaming me for something.

"It was a lot of work," she said. "I had to move you around all the time, otherwise your muscles would have atrophied and you would have gotten bedsores and such."

I had bedsores.

And then she stepped back inside of herself. "It wasn't easy for me, Kepler. I'm no nurse, but I did the best I could."

If my mother was distant before, she seemed affected now. I woke up on several occasions to find her sitting next to my bed rambling incoherently. When she noticed that I was awake she'd turn to the window or start tugging on the top of her bra, making all kinds of embarrassing adjustments. I found myself praying in those instances for a nurse to come gather me up for a blood test or physiotherapy. Hell, I would have been happy with a damn lobotomy.

My recovery was slow. One minute it was August and then it was October. I could feel the gap in my brain. A hole six weeks deep. I had to practically learn to walk again, thinking hurt, memory, at least when I forced myself back to the last thing I could recall, caused a vertiginous spin followed by the urge to vomit. And to top it all off, though I was constantly exhausted, I was terrified of going to sleep because I wasn't sure I would wake up again.

By mid-November I was given access to my own wheelchair, but I couldn't go very far because my arms tired so easily.

I roamed the hallways inch by inch, foot by foot, but I wasn't trying to move forward towards my recovery, I was searching, sifting through six weeks of table scraps and garbage for the missing piece of the puzzle.

I can't recall the name of the hospital shrink, but he was a Freud fan too. He was a stern and cold guy who asked me a bunch of disturbing questions about my relationship with my parents. He came up just shy of asking me if I had ever fantasized about killing my father, or having sex with my mother. We didn't get very far with my psychoanalysis sessions, but I do still remember the three Freudian defense mechanisms as he described them: Denial is when someone fends off awareness of an unpleasant truth. Repression occurs when someone can't remember a past traumatic experience. Intellectualization involves removing one's self emotionally from a stressful event. Sounded more like my mother than me.

I began to wonder about all kinds of crazy things, like maybe I had killed my father and that was why no one was willing to tell me where he was. But I just kept telling myself that he was probably off on one of his secret missions. Maybe his rocket had run out of fuel or crash-landed on a class nine star. And yet, when I was momentarily rocked by a flashback, I had the disturbing sense that I might not like whatever it was I had forgotten.

As the weeks crawled by between therapy sessions and visits with various doctors and specialists, I grew a little stronger. Eventually, they came for my wheelchair. It took several hours of negotiations, two orderlies and one nurse to get me

to surrender. I argued that there were never any seats avail-
able in the TV room when *Gilligan's Island* came on, but the
truth was I knew that with each stage of my recovery I was
that much closer to going home. And that was the last thing
I wanted to do.

As my mother held the door open, I was reminded of the day we moved in, and I was filled with the same apprehension and anxiety. I remembered being torn between the desire to run away and a sense of curiosity. And now, more than a year later, the house not only looked worse, but there were *for sale* signs on several of our neighbours' lawns.

My mother dragged the screen door closed behind her and shuffled into the living room with her snowy boots still on.

"Ahem," she said.

I used the tip of a crutch to hold the heel as I pulled my bare feet out of my runners, kicked them into the closet and turned to find my mother with her hand resting on top of what looked like a new television.

"It's colour," she said.

"Mom," I said, "you're getting snow everywhere."

"Oh, Christ."

While she eased herself down onto the couch and pulled her boots off, she said, "the old one is in my room—in our—your father's and my—in my room."

There it was, the same discomfort that the mention of my father inspired at the hospital. I watched her haul herself up off the couch, turn the television on and flick through the static until she found a nice clear channel. After sidestepping back over to the couch, she threw a pile of magazines on the floor and patted the seat next to her. Archie Bunker was watching television on the television, and I could now see that his chair was brown and that his hair was pure white. I wondered if his television was colour and if he could tune into our living room.

"The one at the hospital is bigger," I said. It was just a little lie, but it was probably my first real and direct lie that wasn't inspired by the need to protect myself. I wanted to hurt her for inheriting her dead sister's crappy house, for not being able to love my father the way he needed to be loved, for not being able to answer the question I had asked her in the hospital. But once again my mother shifted directions. She was standing again, looking vaguely like someone who had been slapped in the face. I watched her bend down with a groan and throw the magazines on the floor back onto the couch.

"Well, anyway, you must be hungry," she said, stepping over her wet boots and the small puddle of melted snow on the floor.

I hobbled after her into the kitchen.

The little light had burned out inside the fridge, which was practically empty except for a couple of Tupperware containers, several bottles of Cheez Whiz and a bottle of Clamato juice. My mother grabbed a flashlight from the top of the fridge and pointed it at a row of nail polish lining the egg shelf—a pantone graduation from Skylark Yellow to Lemon Zest, from Pearl to Blizzard, Radiant Blush to Baton Rouge.

"I've been eating out a lot lately," she said.

Buried behind a pile of condiments she found a loaf of bread. "There you are," she said.

I'm not sure if it was the way the filthy goldfish bowl shook violently when my mother closed the fridge door, or the fact that the note my mother left on the door announcing the death of Elvis was still there, but I remember being frightened at that moment. I looked back over my shoulder; my mother was standing by the table spreading peanut butter on a slice of bread, the puzzle with the missing piece under the plate. Time had passed, which was evident by the dust and neglect, but it looked like the house had been picked up by a tornado and dropped back down exactly where it had been. I tucked both crutches under one arm and dragged a chair across the floor. One of the fish was resting sideways on the bottom of the bowl while the other hovered near the top pleading for food. There was a little yellow note taped to the bowl. Feed the Fish.

"It's dead," I said.

"What?"

"Venus, the goldfish."

"Yes, well, are you sure?"

And that's when I saw the burn mark on the wall above the stove.

"What's going on?"

"Where?" my mother said. Her eyes darted over to the basement door.

I climbed slowly down from the chair. "The wall. It looks like there was a fire."

She looked over at the wall and stared at the charred drywall for a moment as if she was seeing the burn mark for the first time. "I'm not sure. It was a black mess when I got the fire out."

I turned my attention back to the basement, leaned my crutches against the door and grabbed the handrail.

"I haven't had a chance to clean that up yet."

My father's albums were scattered all over the floor. Most of the records had been snapped into pieces and the covers were torn. The bar stools were tipped over, the Elvis commemorative plates were smashed, the Elvis clock, though it was on the floor, was still plugged in and ticking. I looked back up the stairs at my mother. All I could see was the black outline of her, the idea of her. All the detail was gone. Why couldn't she have just danced with him that night? Why couldn't she have just pretended for a moment that she loved him?

Ham was still on the floor by the window where my father left him. It was hard to imagine that almost three months had passed. This was where the memories ended and the confusion began. I grabbed Ham and fell back on the bed, the stars on the ceiling faint but visible in the early evening din. As soon as I closed my eyes the floodgates opened. I cried for the useless lie that I told. I cried for my goldfish and how I wasn't really sure which one was dead. I cried for the missing piece in the puzzle. I cried because something was missing, something I couldn't name, something that I couldn't explain. I cried until I fell asleep, and I was still crying when I dreamt that my room was full of chimps, their teeth flashing as they chattered, shuffling pieces of paper, reloading typewriters, scratching at their armpits...

When I woke up, I found myself on the back porch in my pajamas. My bare feet were numb and red in the snow. Through the window in the door I could see my mother standing on her toes tapping the fishbowl on the refrigerator. There was an empty glass on the counter with a half-eaten stick of celery in it. I looked at the clock. It was three in the morning. When I knocked on the window my mother turned quickly towards the door, but I could tell that she couldn't see my face because it was dark outside. She pulled her old robe up tight around her neck and leaned back against the counter. It looked like she had been crying. "This isn't funny," she yelled. And then she grabbed the flashlight off the fridge and pointed it uselessly at the window, and that's when I noticed the letters t-e-g-r-o-f fingered into the condensation on the glass.

After opening the door she backed across the floor until her bum was resting against the cupboards. Her left hand came up to balance herself on the counter while the other reached for the glass with the celery in it. She took a sip and then noticed the glass was empty. "I swear this house is haunted," she said.

The next morning I sat down in the hall listening to the muffled sound of my mother crying on the other side of the bathroom door. She had spent most of the previous evening talking to the television and now she was talking to herself.

"Mom," I called out.

I heard a thump of a towel hitting the inside of the door. "Go away. I want to be alone." Her voice sounded broken, as if each word was spoken by a different person.

I scratched at the door. "I need to brush my teeth."

There was a moment of silence, and then the yellow end of my toothbrush appeared under the door. I tugged on it until the bristles at the other end dragged across the carpet. I waited a moment, tapping the brush on my knee, even though I knew the toothpaste wouldn't fit.

"Get me a drink," she said.

"A drink of what?" I asked.

"A Caesar," she said, "check the freezer, the instructions are on the bottle."

I poured what I guessed to be about a shot of vodka into a tall glass, threw in two sticks of celery and topped it up with Clamato juice and a dash of Tabasco. It was a complicated and messy affair carrying the drink while using the crutches. I used my foot to knock on the door.

"It's open," she said.

She was sitting on the toilet, a copy of the *Twelfth Night* on her lap. It was embarrassing to see her like that. She had gained weight and she wasn't wearing her wig. Her hair was turning grey and there were thinning patches where her scalp showed through. My mother glanced over at me and extended one hand, her long fingers splayed awkwardly to accept the glass. "Thank you," she said, "you're a lifesaver."

I took my toothbrush out of my pocket, slid the mirror door in the cabinet above the sink and grabbed the toothpaste. When I turned on the tap the pipes below the sink began to vibrate, which made a horribly loud noise. I apologized as I ran the toothbrush under the water, turned off the tap, and started to brush. The next ten seconds were a blur, a mindless lull, my hand maneuvering the brush in my mouth from top to bottom when I saw something move in the reflection behind me. It was just like one of my flashback hallucinations but in slow motion. I put the toothbrush on the counter, turned around slowly, leaned my crutches against the door and knelt down with my hands on the edge of the tub.

His skin was pale and wrinkled and there was an almost bluish tone to his lips, which were opening and closing like a starving fish. I leaned in closer.

"Me," he whispered.

"What did you say?" my mother asked.

"Me." I said. "He said, *me.*"

"Who?"

"Him," I said pointing at the tub.

"Who?" she asked again.

I pulled the shower curtain all the way open.

"Him."

She began rocking back and forth. "Whose horrid image doth unfix my hair, and make my seated heart knock at my ribs?" She ran a shaky hand back through her hair and took a small sip of her drink, the edge of the glass vibrating on her teeth.

I reached over and took the glass from her, and as I put it down on the counter, I could see that my hand was shaking, too.

"I think I'm going crazy," she said.

But we were both going crazy. And I could sense that if I let go, this whole room would fold into itself. I pulled the shower curtain closed.

She was crying now. Something had shifted for a moment, and even if I didn't fully understand exactly what it was, I knew that I was losing her, and at the same time, I was as close to her as I had ever been.

Later that day I found my mother scrubbing the tub with Ajax—yellow gloves and steel wool. "I want you to know it hasn't been easy for me," she said. "I lost my job. I had to quit to take care of you."

She tugged on the sleeves of the yellow gloves and sprinkled a new coat of Ajax into the tub. "That envelope's for you."

"What envelope?"

"There on the toilet."

"What is it?"

My mother was breathing hard now, her shoulders and hips undulating as she scrubbed.

I picked the envelope up.

"Don't open it," she said, glancing back at me. "Not yet. Wait till I'm gone."

"Gone where?"

"Promise you won't open it until I'm gone."

"I promise," I said.

She turned back to the tub, ran some water, added some more Ajax and started scrubbing again.

I went back to my room and opened the envelope.

Bruce is banging at the door of the washroom stall.

I've been picking away at the wall above the toilet with Ophelia's spoon for forty-five minutes. I removed one tile and gouged away about an inch and a half of grout before hitting a soft patch of drywall.

"I'm counting to thirty, and if you haven't done your business by then, you are in for an embarrassing little scene."

Privacy is not exactly one of the attributes of a psychiatric facility; it ranks up there with things like personal comfort, palatable food, self-expression and style.

It takes all of three seconds for Bruce to have the door open, me in a half nelson, and the spoon in the left pocket of his orderly uniform. As he shuffles me down the hall towards Atwood's office, he says, "You've watched too many Hollywood movies, Kepler."

Bruce releases his hold on my arm when Atwood opens the door of his office. Part of me is still in the hospital washroom scratching at the wall with a spoon, and part of me is back in the washroom at home with my mother falling apart. I want to tear this hospital to pieces, but all my energy has been expended struggling down the hall. When I see the couch, I can't help myself and fall back into its sedating comfort.

Atwood closes a book he has been reading, and then pulls my file out of his desk drawer. "This is an impromptu visit," he says.

Bruce quickly describes my activities with the spoon and steps back out the door.

I've blown it, I think. Atwood's going to take away the typewriter now for sure.

His face is blank. It's like he's staring at some point on the wall directly behind my head. I push myself up off the couch and head for the door.

"You'll be happy to hear that I checked up on Grace—Ophelia, and she's doing fine," Atwood says.

I wasn't expecting this kindness. I sit back down. "Thank you," I say.

Atwood nods. "Well, first my dictionary, and pen, now the washroom wall. You can call it symbolic, you can even call it metaphorical, but it's still vandalism, Kepler."

I wasn't planning on saying anything, but since I'd been trading my meds with Ophelia I had lost track of what ones did what. I close my eyes, hold them shut real tight and imagine a school of shiny blue fish swimming around the office. When I open my eyes the fish are still there. I try to focus. I hear Atwood's voice, but it sounds like we are underwater. I plug my nose and give my head a shake.

"—and some medications, or combinations of medications can induce hallucinatory episodes," he says. "Are you paying attention, Kepler?"

I nod. Yes, no, which is it? I blink a couple of times and my head seems to clear. "Go on," I say.

"But of course your whale and the boy in the tub are a different matter—most likely an echo of the PTS. Speaking of which..." Atwood reaches down beside his chair, and with a heave, places my gym bag on his desk, and all at once I'm back at the surface.

It looks like, well, a bunch of monkeys got their hands on it. "Is there anything still in it?" I ask.

"It's pretty heavy," he says, as he unzips the bag.

The first thing he pulls out is the bolt cutters.

"You'll understand if I confiscate these for the time being," he says, placing them on his desk. He then takes out a map of India, a copy of *Ulysses*, and a pair of sunglasses. He places them gently on his desk as well. A moment later, he's holding my journal.

"What's this, Kepler?"

I resist the urge to leap across the room, snatch the journal from his hands and tear it into little pieces. "That's private," I tell him.

Atwood leans forward and offers it to me.

Several pages fall onto his desk. I gather them up and then settle back onto the couch, flip through the newspaper clippings, the bad drawings and incoherent scribbling. The tears come hard and fast.

"What is it, Kepler?"

There's no hiding the three number ten manila envelopes.

"Pieces of the puzzle," I say.

I get up slowly, tug on the red elastic that holds the letters together, and hand him an envelope. "It's from my mother. The one she gave me in the washroom."

Atwood sits back in his chair, opens the envelope and pulls out the letter. Before I can take a deep breath and go under again, Atwood begins to read the letter out loud.

Dear Kepler, I've never been much of a letter writer, but somehow what I have to tell you seems easier this way— easier for me, maybe not for you. So much has happened in these past few months. Your father is gone, this house is falling apart and I'm losing my mind, which I think has been happening for quite some time now. Maybe that's why I need to say this—write this. I need to get this off my chest while I still can. I was folding laundry on the back porch and I heard a sound I hadn't heard since I was a little girl. I glanced up at the birch in the neighbour's yard where the sound seemed to be coming from. It took a few minutes, but I spotted a red bird near the top. It was red like a flower, or a red balloon, and for a second I felt like a little girl again, and I was transported to a time when I still had hope, a time when things were still possible. I inhaled and held my breath. I just wanted the moment to last, as if not breathing would somehow keep me there. Freeze time. But then, I looked down at you sitting in the middle of the lawn, a thin line of saliva running down your chin, and I exhaled. The moment was gone, the bird was gone, the hope and possibility were gone, and I realized that I blamed you. It breaks my heart to admit it, but I wished—

"The end of the sentence was scribbled out."

"If you hold it up to the light," I tell him, "you can still make out the words."

"—you had never," Atwood squints his eyes as he adjusts the paper in front of his lamp, "—been born."

"You wanted to hear more about my mother," I say.

Atwood leans forward, peering over the top of his glasses, picks up the Kleenex box on his desk and holds it out to me.

Ophelia reaches over and gives me an awkward hug that leaves a vermillion smudge on the shoulder of my shirt. "Your mother was a sad woman," she says. I'm not sure what this comment is in response to.

"We were all sad," I say, "I still am."

We are in the women's washroom together, looking in the mirror. Ophelia lights a cigarette and then takes a piece of toilet paper, sticks it under the tap and daubs it on the red stain on my shirt. I wonder silently where she got the lighter.

"I found it in the trash in the cafeteria. Anyway, a woman's sadness is bigger," she says. "It's bigger in the way that a sigh can sometimes express more than a scream."

And there in the mirror I see Grace Honeywell for the first time. I see her as a woman whose very face reveals the hardship of her life. She is old enough to be my mother, but she doesn't act like my mother, and though she says she has no children, she has enough passion and love to embrace the world. I hug her back and feel the end of her cigarette burning into my shoulder.

"Don't worry, we'll come up with a plan B," she says.

Plan B, *every good captain has a plan B.*

CHAPTER NINE

(I)

The plastic tree stood about three feet high; its branches, a matting of green tousled hair, were bent and flat on one side, which made it look like it had just been dragged out of a year-long slumber. The TV had been moved over a few feet to accommodate the tree, leaving a discoloured square in the carpet. It was only a year ago when the three of us sat together in front of the television watching *It's a Wonderful Life*. But then, I wasn't really sure if that had actually happened, or was it just something I had seen in a neighbour's living room window. After I found the second fish dead on the kitchen floor, Charlie Brown, the Grinch and even good old Frank Capra couldn't seem to inspire any festive cheer.

I took the fishbowl down off the fridge and dropped the fish back in the water. Had it grown so unbearably lonely in that little bowl that it committed suicide? I knew it was no substitute for the sea, just as this house was no substitute for a dream. After some thought, I concluded that it was better off. "No matter how you go," I said as I carried the bowl down the hall, "it all ends with the toilet."

I could hear my mother changing channels on the TV in the living room, so I was surprised to find that the bathroom door was closed. I don't know why I knocked but I did, and of course there was no answer. And even though I was getting used to the strange things that had been happening since we moved into that house I was still surprised to see him there—his pants crumpled down around his ankles, the same blank expressionless look on his face. His nails were painted something close to the colour of a plum or an eggplant.

"Not, what?" I asked, noticing the word written in what looked like lipstick on the mirror.

He looked vaguely distraught and bored at the same time. It was embarrassing.

"I need the toilet," I said.

He blinked but otherwise made no indication that he was going to move or talk.

"You got three seconds."

But he just sat there like a stubborn pain in the ass.

"One, two, three"... and then I tilted the fishbowl and poured the scummy water along with Venus or Mars, or whichever fish it was, onto his lap.

I was happy to find my mother in an unusually playful mood, which I put down to the festive effect of drinking eggnog instead of Clamato. She had just plugged in a string of Christmas lights that blinked in a knotted mess on the floor.

"Who were you talking to in the bathroom?"

"Santa Claus," I said.

She tossed some tinsel in my hair. "I'm not sure why we bother with all this stuff. You're not a kid anymore."

The thought of not bothering with Christmas made me anxious. I liked the lights and the snow, and even though I knew that without my dad this was going to be the worst Christmas ever, I was determined to make room for the joy and peace that the malls and Christmas catalogues promised.

"Truth is," my mother offered, "it was your father who made all the fuss about Christmas—the lights, the gingerbread house, the candy canes, the decking of the halls and such—I guess it was his way of compensating for being such a heathen all year."

"Dad was a heathen?" I asked.

She sighed. "Never mind, the point is I'm really trying here, and well, there's the presents thing, which we can't afford, so…"

I could see that she was already running out of steam, her attention drifting over to the television. A minute later she had abandoned the half-decorated tree and was on the couch, little strips of tinsel and red thread clinging to the trunks of her bruised legs propped up on the coffee table.

I was reminded of the year I realized there was no such thing as Santa Claus. We were living in some crappy old building on the ground floor, so instead of a balcony we had a doorway that led out to the parking lot. I remember the wheels skidding a bit as my father backed into his spot, spoiling the perfect white blanket of snow that had fallen while he was out. I watched him step out of the car into the cold air, rub his hands together and walk around to the trunk. When he slammed the trunk closed, he was holding the chrome handlebars of a brand new bicycle with a banana seat and red streamers hanging from the ends of the white grips. Just as he was turning towards our door, the shiny bike fully exposed, I hid behind the couch. I saw him stick his head in the door, take a quick look and then step inside. He stomped his feet a couple of times on the mat, strolled through the living room, and then headed down the hall. The rear tire of the bicycle banged into the wall leaving a black smudge. When I saw the "From Santa," tag on the bicycle the next morning my heart broke into a million pieces—not because Santa didn't exist, but because I realized that my parents were liars.

I picked up my mother's empty glass. Looking down at her snoring on the couch, I thought of how easy it would be to place a pillow over her face and smother her.

My mother was still on the couch when I woke up on Christmas morning. I turned off the television and opened the curtains. There was a fresh sprinkling of snow on the ground that just covered the exhaust-blackened crust along the boulevards.

"Rise and shine," I said.

I set three places at the dining room table, filled the cereal bowls and started making toast. I found a packet of cherry Kool-Aid, which I mixed in a pitcher.

My Christmas wish list was still sitting in the serviette holder in the middle of the table. Gone were the days of wanting train sets and shiny new bikes. Instead, my one wish was for a typewriter, a handwritten line that repeated itself several times down the length of the page until I ran out of space at the bottom. I had this image of myself with a fedora and cigarette, typing out my memoirs. For some reason my image of the writer melded with a vision of an old private eye, as if Ernest Hemingway and Humphrey Bogart were the same person. There were only two presents under the tree and neither of them was big enough to be a typewriter. I crumpled the paper into a ball and threw it at the couch. My mom groaned, heaved herself up, shuffled quickly into the kitchen and threw up in the sink.

"Hair of the dog," I said as I handed her a Caesar.

She took a sip and collapsed back on the couch.

"Mom."

"All right, let's get this over with," she said, pointing at a brown paper bag with the Coles bookstore logo on the front. I pulled it out from under the tree and tore the bag open.

What I got was one of those 100-page notebooks with a picture of a whale on the cover. My mother had written *Once upon a time …* on the first page. I feigned excitement, my mouth open as I flipped rapidly through the pages as if it was exactly what I had been dreaming of my whole life. I was determined to make the best of this day so that it didn't destroy every possibility of enjoying Christmas ever again.

"It's a journal," she said. "You can write your secrets in it. Every kid should have a journal. You can hide it under your mattress."

She was sitting awkwardly on her side with her legs tucked up under her. Her poor legs, I thought as I handed her my present. She took a sip from her drink and then awkwardly picked at the piece of tape that held the wrapping together. After a moment she grew frustrated. "You open the damn thing."

I tore at the wrapping paper, tossed it on the rug beside her and then handed the present back to her. The next layer was a cover from one of my dad's destroyed records. She unfolded it with a look of annoyance on her face. "I suppose you think this is funny?" she said.

"I thought you might want to finish it."

"Things without all remedy should be without regard: what's done is done."

"Macbeth," I guessed.

"Lady Macbeth, to be more precise." And then she dropped the puzzle piece I had given her in her drink.

I used the couch to pull myself up from the floor and made my way over to the dining room, where I sat down at the table and poured some milk on my cereal. My mother lit a cigarette, and before she made it halfway across the room, she started coughing like a madman.

"Oh my god, what a headache," she said. "Remind me to never drink eggnog again."

She was still coughing when she sat down across from me. I covered my cereal bowl and closed my eyes in case she coughed up a lung. We had Cheerios, potato chips, toast, and figs for breakfast. The whole thing was a compromise, a second-rate attempt to continue what was once my favourite time of the year. But without my father's enthusiasm, it all seemed half-baked and pathetic. While we were eating there was a loud crash in the kitchen. My mother and I turned and looked, but neither of us got up to see what it was.

Later that morning, as I dragged the range hood that had fallen down on the top of the stove out to the shed, it dawned on me. I ran back into the bathroom. The word written in lip-stick on the mirror was still there. I opened the journal my mother had given me, drew a black line across the words Once upon a time ... and below it I wrote, Forget-Me-Not.

Outside in the smoking yard, Ophelia and I watch a guy on the street buy three newspapers out of the box on the corner one at a time. He puts a quarter in, opens the box, takes out a paper, closes the door, puts a quarter in, et cetera.

"He looks just like that guy, Columbo," Ophelia says.

She's right. He has a trench coat and one whacky eye, and he's smoking a cigar, no lie. My mom would have liked that. To have seen Columbo in person, I mean.

Ophelia kicks the fence. "We've got to get out of this place," she says. And then as she bends and stubs the cigarette out on the ground I'm reminded of something, only I'm not sure if it is a memory or a dream.

My mother is sitting on the floor of the kitchen with her back leaning against the stove. It's dark, but there is just enough light coming from the television in the living room to see that she is wearing her red coat over her old blue robe. Her bare legs are stretched out in front of her. I'm stand-ing by the fridge in my pajamas. The floor feels cold on my bare feet.

She's drunk. It's obvious she's drunk because she knocks the bottle of Smirnoff's over. The bottle hits the ashtray and her cigarette rolls onto the linoleum. She rights the bottle first, then reaches for the cigarette and places it in her mouth. She takes a deep drag, and before she exhales, she takes a sip from her drink.

My mother bends her legs up and groans, and then stretch-es them out again. She mumbles something incoherently, but when I say pardon she doesn't answer. She just bends her legs, turns the cigarette she's smoking and holds it a moment over her skin just above one knee. A tear gathers in the corner of her eye. She looks up at me and pushes the cigarette down hard and fast onto her leg. I watch it bend to the filter, sparks fall onto the floor. When she drops the extinguished butt, a wisp of smoke rises up from the black circle in her skin.

"Oh my god," she whispers.

Her breath catches on the exhale. Her hands splay an inch or two above the burn as if she wants to grab it, smother it. I reach for the glass and douse her leg with vodka and Clamato juice. When she finally breathes again, there is a faint smile on her lips. "Happy New Year," she says.

Ophelia is smoking a second cigarette, which has now burned down to the filter. The smoke is swirling up around her nicotine-stained fingers. When she drops the cigarette on the ground, I stand up and start jumping up and down, crushing the butt into the hard cement.

"I always wanted to travel," my mother said, "go to Morocco, learn Spanish."

She was watching *The Littlest Hobo*.

I wanted to say that I didn't think they spoke Spanish in Morocco, but I was busy unknotting the laces of my dad's bowling shoes.

"Kepler, are you in the closet again?"

I slipped one of the shoes on. It was a couple sizes too big. "I'm right here," I said, stepping into the living room.

"I can't believe it's already 1978," she said, "I thought I would have travelled the world by now. Where are you going?"

I slipped the other shoe on and reached for the door. "I'm going to school."

"Yeah well, if I'm not here when you get home," she said, "I'll send you a postcard."

A half hour later I was staring at a typewriter in the principal's office. Mr. Waters shuffled through a folder of what I guessed were my report cards and medical evaluations. He then asked me a series of random questions: some basic math equations, a handful of multiple choice, and a number of logic puzzles. The palms of my hands were tender and itchy. I swear I'm allergic to school. I can't stand the sight of flags hanging limply in foyers, the sound of high heels echoing on hard polished floors.

"Kepler!" Mr. Waters was leaning across his desk tapping my hand with a pencil.

"Um, Forty-six sir. The answer is forty-six." I had no idea what he had asked me, but there were forty-six keys on that typewriter.

"...We take our reputation very seriously here," Mr. Waters said. He was looking at me as if I were a rare specimen of some kind. "We have a no tolerance mandate that is strictly administered." He looked at each part of me, my chest, my groin, my legs, my hands. His eyes pinning me to the seat.

I was smart enough to recognize the value of reading and writing, but I hated being graded—the long arm of the administration shuffling the students into groups—groups that were defined by alphabetized seating and subdivided into grades from A to F.

"We groom our students to be the best they can be. And we don't tolerate..." he stood up and walked around me as if looking for any damage that might reveal I was not satisfactorily preserved for the curation of his collection. He stared long and hard at my father's shoes. "...Any disruptive behaviour."

In order to survive at school you have to be versatile, keep a low profile, keep your grades down—lurk on the fringes of small crowds, lean against the wall and laugh when others laugh. You make eye contact but don't really say anything because mystery is far more alluring than awkward wit and precociousness. If other kids don't share your passions for things like astronomy, news headlines, or David Bowie, they turn hard and cold and push you further to the edge of the very group that the teacher had placed you in, until, instead of a number or a letter, you become a fraction.

"Your grades are impressive, Kepler. And that is the only reason we're not recommending you start the year over. However, you've got a lot of catching up to do. Are you up to it?"

I nodded complacently and tried to come up with a quick plan to somehow sneak the typewriter out of his office.

He then dismissed me to my first class, telling me to hurry, but not to run, as if it was my fault that I was now twenty minutes late. I pulled the pins out of my limbs, peeled myself up off the specimen board and slowly hobbled to the door. I was left with the impression that my absence from school had been documented as an academic offense, and that my return was viewed as an unfortunate manipulation of some loophole that defied the mission and mandate of the school. I stopped at the door, and as I tucked my crutches under my arms I turned to him and said, "I promise I won't run."

I was determined to make the best of it. I figured that the summer holidays and one semester might be long enough for most kids to have forgotten who I was, and if I just acted like I was the new kid who had just moved into the neighbourhood, I could keep myself under the radar. And, if nothing else, I was determined to repair my physical dexterity to the point that I could at least make it from the principal's office to class without losing my breath.

Mr. Lemonites had, what I imagined to be, the voice of some kid's friendly uncle—a voice that conjured the smell of red grapes and aftershave, heady and yet comforting. He pointed at the chalkboard where he had written his name in big bold letters. "It's pronounced, Lemon-eat-ees," he said. "And no, it's not an incurable disease." He told us that despite the noble Greek heritage of his last name, we could call him Mr. Lemon for short. We all laughed and he seemed to like that. He was new to the school, a temporary replacement for Miss Crawford who was on maternity leave.

"There must have been a power outage in town last spring," he said, "because I'll be teaching English, History and Math."

Mrs. Dixon and Mrs. Reeves were also apparently new mothers.

He seemed to believe that drama and exaggeration were the perfect tools to keep kids focused, pausing in the middle of a math lesson, he recited the Pythagorean oath with Shakespearean flare. "Nay by him that gave us the tetractys which contains the fount and root of ever-flowing nature..." He began each English class by reading to us for ten minutes from a book by James Joyce. I knew right away that I would need a dictionary. "*Ulysses* demands something of the reader," he said. "We must be patient with it, read it as if sampling a rare wine. With its stream of consciousness, puns, dream sequences, and unconventional punctuation ... it is truly an original." A long pause followed, and as that pause stretched out to the point where it could be considered an uncomfortable silence, I suspected that we had failed to react in some particular and desired manner. "Are you paying attention, people? This book," he said softly, as if letting us all in on a well-kept secret, "initiated the Modernist revolution against the Victorian excesses of civilization." He walked slowly up and down the rows of our desks, with his head tilted upwards, studying the ceiling for signs of rain, as if we were an audience of ripening olives. "June 16, 1904. One single day, people. Joyce has created a modern hero, a parody of a Greek classic. Those of you who have read Homer's *Odyssey* know that it touched exclusively upon epic and dignified themes, whereas Joyce focused on human activities: gluttony, defecation, urination, dementia, masturbation, alcoholism—a charming, and candid declaration of cultural polarity. This novel was banned in the United Kingdom and the United States. Can anyone here tell me why?"

I guessed that any attempt at answering the question would be somehow inappropriate. This was not a discussion. We were being spoken to. A sermon was being delivered. Everyone was looking at each other nervously while Mr. Lemon stopped at the front of the class with his hands behind his back. It was obvious that there was something important in the confusion of what he was saying. I needed to figure it out. In the week since Christmas my journal had become filled with random thoughts, bits of poetry, memories and questions. The observations and pictures between its covers held the key to my sanity. Its pages held proof that I existed. And there on my first day back to school as I began to take notes, I was already drawing attention to myself—a keener in the eyes of my classmates and an unfocused student in the eyes of the teacher. And I could see it from Mr. Lemon's point of view, because part of me was at the front of the class with him looking back at the rows of kids whose feet were planted flatly on the floor, hands placed neatly on their desks, minds focused, with the exception of me, second row from the right, third desk back, the skinny kid bent over his desk scribbling madly in a book with a whale on the cover.

"Care to share with the rest of the class what you feel is more important than James Joyce, Mr. Pressler?"

All eyes turned to me. I was thinking of the state of our house and how it stood out compared to the others on our street with its unkempt lawn and the holes in the driveway. The dreaded moment had arrived. There was no escape.

"It was banned because it dealt with subject matter that people thought was inappropriate?"

"That is an answer to the first question. What I asked you was, why are you scribbling in that book instead of paying attention?"

I felt like I was looking down the barrel of a gun.

"Um, the answer to the first question is what I was writing in my book, sir." And instead of the subtle click of the trigger and my life being over, there was silence, a pause. And in that pause there was a shift away from me, as if all the energy in the class drew inward upon itself. I started to breathe again. Mr. Lemon was smiling as he strolled over to my desk and glanced down at my notes.

"Close," he said, turning back to the front of the class. "That's a hand grenade of an answer, but more specifically..." He reached for a piece of chalk and wrote the word out in big white letters, T-R-U-T-H. "It was banned because it told the truth about society, about being human. And that is what literature is all about. It's not about dignity or fact. It's about truth, no matter how inappropriate that may be."

By the end of the day it was obvious Mr. Lemon should have been lecturing to a hall full of university undergraduates, not a class of hormonal 16-year-olds. But I left school feeling light-headed. Truth. I was inspired. I stopped searching for the pieces that fit, and went looking for the pieces that hurt when you put them together.

My mother was dancing in the living room when I got home—a slightly warped Dean Martin album spinning on the dusty stereo, which she had dragged back up from the basement.

"Good news," she said. She had a towel wrapped around her head, and as she raised both arms in a pirouette, I noticed her old robe now had a cigarette hole in the sleeve. "I got a job at McDonald's." Her shadow bent where the wall met the ceiling, her hands and fingers grotesquely stretching across the stucco above my head. "I'm a grill specialist." Her toenails, which were splayed with pink rubber dividers, were painted a deep yellow that I recognized from a bottle in the fridge called Lazy Susan, while her fingernails were covered in a clear glistening lacquer with tiny blue sparkles. Ash from the cigarette in her hand fell to the floor. I kicked off my shoes, dropped my crutches and let myself fall back into the couch.

"Your face, my Thane, is a book where men may read strange matters," she said.

I had learned that it was best to take advantage of her good moods before they shifted, and that if she was quoting Shakespeare she was drunk, but not too drunk, which was a good time to talk. She then stretched her arms and spun in a relatively graceful circle, her fingertips narrowly missing a lampshade. "I'm drying my nails," she said. "The blow dryer is on the fritz."

I waited patiently until she stopped spinning.

"Tell me what you remember about Dad," I said.

My mother placed a hand on the wall to steady herself, and then, when her eyes cleared, she took a couple uncertain steps towards her glass.

"Please, Mom."

"I need more celery," she said.

I heaved myself up off the couch and hobbled off to the kitchen.

"Your father was a scoundrel."

She had started without me. I hastily poured the Clamato and vodka, stirred it with a celery stick and headed back into the living room.

"There, is that what you want to know?"

I handed her the drink.

"Where did you meet?" I asked.

"We met at a bowling alley."

I could tell that it was difficult for her to get back to that place, to find the memory under all the clutter.

"It was the Shamrock at Coxwell and Gerrard, I think. Anyway, your father was a loner," she said, and then she patted me on the top of my head. "Kind of like you."

It felt strange to be touched so casually, almost lovingly. I closed my eyes and started to rock, testing my weight on each foot.

"He was bowling with his eyes closed," she said. She took a sip of her drink and grimaced. "Did you put any vodka in this thing?"

"Two shots."

She took another sip. "Sit down," she said, "you're making me nervous rocking back and forth like that."

I slumped back onto the couch.

Even though the Dean Martin record was still on, she reached down and turned on the television.

"Mom?"

"What?"

"The story—dad bowling with his eyes closed."

"Wait a second," she said. "I think my show is coming on."

I got up and turned the television off. She looked at me like I had slapped her in the face. "Jeezus, Kepler, I was watching that."

"Please," I said again.

She lit another cigarette. "He was a chain smoker," she said. "I guess you know that. He always had two cigarettes going at once, one in his mouth and one in the ashtray, with a third unlit one tucked behind his ear. My friend, Jill Clayton, no, no it was Tabby, oh God I've forgotten her last name. Anyway, it was Jill or Tabby—she caught me staring at your father, well, he wasn't your father yet, but, *ignore him*, she said. He's a dreamer. It's hard to imagine now, but at the time he was the handsomest dreamer I had ever seen. I went over and asked him for a cigarette." My mother took a drag and began to cough. "If I knew then what I know now," she added, as if this was the punch line of the story. And then she turned to the kitchen. "Something's burning."

I got up and limped through the living room as fast as I could. The element was off, but there was a pot on the stove with two uncooked wieners sitting in an inch of water. When I opened the oven door, black smoke billowed up into my face. I stepped back and pushed the door closed with my foot. After turning off the oven, I went to the sink and filled a glass of water and tossed it on the flame. I used a spatula to sort through what was left of the burnt paper bag. The burger was still good, but the fries were black, and the straw and lid of the coke were melted.

"What is it?" mom yelled.

I closed the oven door.

"It's okay," I said, "just some hotdogs."

After opening the window, I came back into the living room and sat back down on the couch.

"Are they burnt?"

"What happened next?" I asked.

"I was making dinner."

"Mom, what happened with Dad at the bowling alley?"

"I asked him out."

"He didn't ask you?" I said. At least on television, the guy always asked the girl.

"Are you sure you want to hear this?"

"It's for school," I lied.

She put the cigarette out and collapsed on the couch beside me. "Okay, you're right," she said. "It's important that you know this. On our first date he drove me out to a field by the airport. He was a gentleman. He took off his jacket and laid it out on the grass for me to sit on. He brought a six-pack and some cold chicken along, and even though I didn't really drink, I let him open a beer for me. He was pretty quiet at first. He seemed content to just sit back and watch all those planes take off and land, but as soon as it started getting dark, he started rambling on and on about, I don't know, comets and quasars or something. He was so damn passionate about some things and absurdly oblivious to others. He'd get lost in his stories. You know how he was. It was like he became someone else..."

And then I saw her shift again, doing exactly what she said my father did, drifting off to another time.

"It was a warm night, but I told him I was cold. It took a couple of minutes, but he eventually moved a little closer. I remember thinking, this is it, he's going to kiss me, but instead he pointed at the stars. 'Just look at it,' he said, 'It's a miracle.' I looked up. He told me to concentrate and imagine what the earth would look like if we were on the moon."

As my mom reached for her drink, stirred it with the celery stick and took a sip, I found myself looking up at the long cracks on the ceiling trying to imagine that night.

"At first I thought he was an incredible romantic," she continued, "but I eventually realized that Jill and Tabby were right; he was just a dreamer that didn't like to drink alone."

"To make a long story short," she said, "you were born about nine months later." And then her eyes glazed over. "Now Dean Martin, there's a man who knows how to treat a lady—such a voice, all suave and romantic."

"Where is he, now?" I asked.

"Las Vegas I suppose."

"Dad's in Las Vegas?"

"Your father? I'm talking about Dean Martin, Kepler. Haven't you been listening?"

Time was up. She was on her feet again singing into her glass.

Be careful what you ask, I thought, because you may not like the answer.

"Oh, that reminds me, I need you to take the day off school next week," she said. "I have a nail appointment at this place downtown. You know how easily I get lost."

When I closed the door of the bathroom my stomach heaved for a few seconds, tightened and then relaxed. What was worse, being adopted or being the product of drunken sex in a field? I wanted there to have been a passionate and romantic beginning. Surely, they must have been happy at some point. But truth, I reminded myself, is not about dignity or fact. And while my mother staggered in erratic circles in the living room to Dean's soothing voice and the heady lull of the vodka,

I found another envelope on the toilet seat with my name on it.

I didn't want to miss school, Mr. Lemon both intimidated and fascinated me, but I was worried about my mother. The fires, her forgetfulness, and though she had always been a little temperamental, she was so easily disoriented these days. Plus, the address of Nail Destiny was on King Street, not far, I noted, from the CN tower. I grabbed Ham, and my crutches, and hurried to catch up with my mom, who was waiting at the foot of the drive.

She tore the Nail Destiny ad out of the Yellow Pages, and as we rode the bus to the subway station she kept looking at it every few seconds and saying the address out loud like a crazy person. I started asking her questions to distract her. I learned that her favourite colour is Valentine's Kiss, which, no surprise, is actually a nail polish with a deep and passionate aubergine finish. Her favourite game show was *Truth or Consequences*; her favourite sitcom was *The Mary Tyler Moore Show*. She was acting like she was being interviewed for an article in *Time* magazine, as if her responses required clarity and justification. "Though M*A*S*H has won nine Emmys, and I simply adore Alan Alda, Mary is a single and independent woman with a career. She's a role model for women all over the world." The interview came to an end when I asked her why she needed to get her nails done when, as far as I could tell, she could simply do them herself.

"Jeez, Kepler, you sound like your father." That was her way of telling me that I was annoying her. "Nail Destiny got a five star rating in the newspaper last week. All the celebs go to Nail Destiny when they're in town."

Who was I to judge, I had a sock monkey stuffed into the front of my coat.

An hour later we were jammed on a busy streetcar and my mom had broken out into a sweat. She kept annoyingly tapping the pole she was holding with her long nails. Even though it was the middle of winter, the sun had come out and the snow was melting. It was beautiful day and I was determined to make the best of it.

"Look, there's the CN Tower." As I pointed out the window I felt a genuine and giddy excitement.

"Mmhmm."

I could tell all she wanted was a seat.

"We should go up to the top while we're here." I said. "Dad always said he was going to take me."

My mom frowned. "We're not tourists, Kepler."

I watched the tower disappear behind a building and appear again at the next intersection. We were getting closer.

"There it is," my mom said. She reached up and pulled the stop signal and started pushing her way towards the exit. I was slow getting off because the streetcar was full and it was tricky maneuvering through a crowd with the crutches, which I didn't really need anymore, but I still tired easily and I liked it when people held doors open for me.

By the time I squeezed through the narrow doors at the back of the streetcar, my mother was standing half a block away with the advertisement in her hand. Even though the Nail Destiny sign was huge, pink and illuminated in neon, she checked the address to be sure we had the right place.

The technicians, that's what my mother called them, were wearing white smocks with Nail Destiny embroidered into the front pocket. "This is no place for boys," she said, blocking the doorway, "I'll be about half an hour. I can't afford the paraffin treatment. Wait for me outside."

I started walking south towards the lake, the top of the tower guiding me as I hobbled along. I turned left, then right at each intersection, John Street, Wellington, and then after crossing Front Street I crutched my way past three hot dog vendors and one guy selling little Canadian flags. At the foot of the tower I planted my feet and opened the first three buttons of my coat so that Ham could get a look as well. I was awestruck. To my mind, it looked like a rocket ship, aerodynamic, monolithic and ready for take-off. It was absurd and magnificent, its height so impressive and opposing that it threw everything out of whack. My head started to spin.

"You're blocking my fucking sun."

I pushed Ham's head down quickly. When I turned around I saw a girl crouched on the cement. She was working on a picture of a blue person with four arms.

A quiet moment passed as she poked around in a tin full of coloured chalk. When she looked up at me again something in me softened.

"Do you like my drawing?" she asked.

It wasn't finished but you could tell it was on its way to being something worth more than the change in your pocket.

"It's beautiful," I said as I took in her straight, thin arms, the pink shawl covering her shoulders, the white hair clinging to her grey leggings, her heavy eyelids and her brown skin. "A little frightening, but beautiful."

"*She*."

"She, what?"

"*She*, not *it*. Her name's Kali."

"I'm sorry," I said.

"Kali is a Hindu god—the goddess of time and change."

"I thought God is a man." I really did—white beard, old and cranky.

"Not where I come from," she said.

"Where do you come from?"

She glanced up at me. "My mother's womb, stupid."

I resisted a sudden urge to run.

As she turned her attention back to the chalk drawing, the word India evaporated in the cool air. I tried to place it on a map. East of Africa, west of China. The Taj Mahal. An image of a pinkish palace settled in the back of my mind—a cobra, and a turbaned man doing yoga—the anxiety subsiding. "Why is she so scary looking?"

"Because she symbolizes death."

I watched her for a moment as she coloured in Kali's tongue, which was hanging out over her chin.

"Like Satan?"

"No. Death isn't evil. It's inevitable."

I pushed back the vague image of my dead aunt on the toilet—slammed the bathroom door closed and refocused on the drawing. Kali was holding a severed head in one hand, a bloody sword in the other. "Well anyway, I wouldn't want to meet her in an alleyway."

Another moment passed. I thought of leaving, but something about her was even more captivating than the tower behind me. I resorted to the same tactic that had worked on the bus coming here—another interview.

"Why aren't you in school?"

"I hate school," she said.

"School's good for your brain," I offered stupidly.

"I get in shit all the time, and besides it's too nice of a day to be inside."

It was sunny, but I was beginning to shiver just standing there in one spot.

"What do you get in trouble for?" I asked.

"Things."

"Like what?" It seemed important to know if she was a bad person or not.

"Like not standing for the national anthem."

Before I could ask why she wouldn't stand for the national anthem, she pointed a piece of chalk at my crutches. "Is it a break or sprain?"

I didn't feel comfortable with this sudden change in focus.

"I had an accident," I said quickly. "Do you have a cat?" I pointed at the white hair on her leggings.

"That's Socrates. He's a bookstore cat."

Another moment passed.

"What's your favourite television show?"

"Non sequiturs abound."

"Non what—"

"I hate television. It insults my intelligence."

I stuck my hands in my coat pockets and gave Ham a squeeze. This unequivocal hating of things was a revelation. It was exciting to hear a kid my age express such strong feelings so confidently. I had always just assumed that unedited expressions of your feelings were reserved for adults.

"What about Elvis?" I asked hesitantly.

"What is this, an interrogation?"

I wanted her to say I hate Elvis, to hear something I could never imagine saying out loud. She turned her attention back to her drawing, and as she began to shade a section of

Kali's long blue throat, she was humming what sounded like "Heartbreak Hotel."

I loved her drawing and I hated it—beauty and terror. Kali was clearly a mythical character that I could easily imagine was a manifestation of an asterism visible only from a Hindu's bedroom window.

A moment later a piece of chalk hit me in the chest. "Hey," she said, "I think that fat lady is calling you."

I was relieved to find that my mother was more worried than angry. She took a moment to present her freshly polished nails before she lectured me. I examined her hands and pretended to be impressed. "Movie star quality," I found myself saying.

"Well, you have to indulge yourself once in awhile," she said, and then she placed both hands on my shoulders. "Kepler, we have to set some rules."

I nodded.

"Don't ever disappear like that. I've been through that with your father. I couldn't bear it if I lost you, too."

CHAPTER TEN

(I)

Two weeks later, the *For Sale* sign was taken down on a house up the street.

"An African family bought the place," my mother said as she peered out the front window, the curtains clenched tightly in her fist.

I imagined an ox and cart, bare feet stepping down onto the driveway, burnished hands unloading wooden crates of pottery, carved artifacts and cages of geese, the mother with bone jewellery in her ears, breastfeeding a baby, the father with shield and spear.

"Mrs. Carmichael is worried about the property value."

"Property value?"

"I want you to stay away, Kepler. Be polite, but stay away."

"Stay away from what?"

"African neighbours, Kepler. They have malaria."

Aside from the fact that he brought a soccer ball to school in the winter, the new kid from Africa was more or less just like the rest of us. He was standing next to Mr. Lemon's desk, his foot rocking back and forth on the ball when I walked into the classroom. Once the class had settled down, Mr. Lemon introduced the new kid as if he were a long-lost cousin, pointed to South Africa on the pull down map, and said, "As you can see, Benjamin has travelled a very long way to be here with us. And so I would like you all to make him feel at home." A white person from Africa. I was disappointed. Benjamin stared back at us with a calm smile until Mr. Lemon told him to take a seat. Even though there were several empty seats at the front of the room, Benjamin expertly toed the soccer ball down the aisle to one of the desks at the back of the class. "Far sighted," he said. "The writing on the blackboard is fuzzy up close." I was relieved to hear that he did have a funny accent, which I hoped, along with his status as the new kid, would be enough to distract my classmates from further interrogating me about the rumour that I had spent the beginning of the school year in a coma after being abducted by aliens.

On my way home from school I felt something hit the back of my heel. A moment later Benjamin was walking beside me. He had the soccer ball resting on his hip, his long gloved fingers cupping the black and white hexagons. He nodded but didn't say anything. When we came to a red light across from the 7-Eleven, he tossed the ball and expertly kept it in the air with tiny kicks until he sort of passed it over to me. The ball hit my crutch and rolled back to him.

"Nice pass, Pele," he said.

"I don't really play soccer," I offered.

He effortlessly kicked the ball up in the air and caught it. "What about basketball?" he asked spinning the ball on his finger.

"Mmm, can't skate either, before you ask."

"How about golf?" he said, looking down at my shoes.

The light changed to green.

"Bowling," I said, as we crossed the road.

Benjamin sighed, "All right, no Pele for you."

"I'm more of a Billy Hardwick fan."

"Billy who?"

"He's the only man to have ever won three major PBA tournaments." My father's words sounded authoritative.

"All right, Super Billy Hardwick."

"Where are you from?" I asked eager to change the subject. "I mean, where in South Africa?"

"I was born in England, but we moved here from Johannesburg. My dad gets transferred a lot."

Aside from Steve Biko who I had read about in the newspaper, I couldn't think of one famous person from South Africa. "Are there any lions there?"

"Lions, elephants, giraffes."

I tried to imagine a herd of zebras grazing in the school-yard behind us, lions lounging in the shade of the 7-Eleven sign, monkeys swinging from light standard to light standard, hyenas lurking between the cars of the Dominion parking lot... "It must be hot there."

"I guess so," he said. He was expertly heading the ball as we walked. "Hey, what do you think of this James Joyce stuff?"

I wanted to say that I hated it, just to see how it felt, but the truth was I loved it. It was like listening to someone speaking a different language, and yet, I could sort of understand it. Listening to Mr. Lemon read to the class the way he did made me feel like I was visiting another country. "My mom says Joyce is mostly a bunch of gibberish and that we should be focusing on Shakespeare." I don't know why I brought my mom into it.

"But what do you think of James Joyce?" he asked again.

I liked that he caught me. He was actually listening to what I was saying.

"I like it," I said cautiously. "I mean, I don't really get it, but I like it."

"Yeah well, I don't really get it either. I'm with your mom on Joyce. What did she call it—gibberish?"

"Well, Mr. Lemon told us we wouldn't actually be tested on it anyway."

"But then what's the point of reading it?"

I wasn't sure. "Maybe he's trying to inspire us," I said.

We had arrived at my place—the only house on the block that had been hit by an earthquake.

Benjamin was standing at the foot of the drive in front of my house the next morning.

"Super Billy Hardwick," he said, balancing the soccer ball on the top of his boot.

I tested for ice under the snow on the driveway before putting my full weight on the crutches. I hadn't shovelled once since my dad was gone. When I got to the sidewalk Benjamin did a trick with the ball that was so quick and confusing that I failed to comprehend how the ball went from balancing on his boot to end up balanced on the top of his head. "Your house is falling apart, yeah." He said it in such a casual and matter of fact way that it didn't feel like a judgement.

"Yeah, my mom says that we're cursed."

He had the ball back in the air again, knee to foot as he walked. I hesitated then took a couple of quick hops to catch up.

"What's malaria?" I asked, using the same indifferent tone he used.

"It's a disease. You get it from mosquitos."

"My mom says African people have malaria."

"I'm not African."

"Well, my mom doesn't know much about anything except Shakespeare and nail polish."

"...And Joyce," he added. "Gibberish, right?"

As we approached the school, I was torn between our walk coming to an end and the excitement of the other kids seeing us together.

At our lockers he pulled a binder open. "Here we go," he said, and began to read from his notes. "—Ineluctable modality of the visible: at least that if no more, thought through my eyes... What is that supposed to mean?"

"Ineluctable," I said, "means, unable to be avoided. But I think he's saying something about what can't be seen by the eye."

Benjamin shoved me playfully into the locker. "Sounds sort of like Dr. Seuss on drugs." That first real taste of friendship seemed as complicated to me as James Joyce, but I liked it. I didn't really understand it, but I liked it.

That day we were given a *what I did over the summer holidays* kind of assignment. It was a semester-long thing designed as Mr. Lemon put it, "to instruct us in the systemics of composition. An amalgamation of style, plot, character and dialogue." Mr. Lemon wanted us to focus on some significant event in our lives, to incorporate an object of some kind and use it as a symbol in our story. "It's called a Leitmotif," he said. "That's French for a recurring idea or feature. Joyce uses motifs throughout his work. Can anyone give me an example?"

Benjamin's hand shot up like a spike.

"Benjamin."

"In the Siren's chapter of *Ulysses*, there is a recurring theme of music."

I could see the black and yellow stripes of his Coles Notes hanging over the edge of his desk.

"Excellent." Mr. Lemon didn't miss a beat—"Anybody else?"

Everyone stared blankly at the ceiling.

"He also used the repetition of sentence structures, such as cutting short a statement, or conversely, a stream of words running into each other ... so, I would like you to think like Joyce when you work on this assignment. I want a conscious motif that will recur throughout the essay. And I want you all to remember one thing; biographical studies are not about fact. They are about ... what?"

I raised my hand.

"Mr. Pressler?"

"Truth?"

"Correct."

Mr. Lemon put down the chalk, walked back to his desk and sat down. "People, I want you to get in touch with the drama of life. And do not try to tell me that nothing has happened to you that is worth writing about." He raised the copy of *Ulysses* over his head and held it with both hands. "Joyce wrote a whole novel around an event that takes place in a single day. You've got your whole lives to draw from. Find a theme. Add a context. Don't worry about the facts. Give me some truth."

Benjamin had the Coles Notes for every book I ever read in school, he laughed at my jokes, and his height ensured that nobody bothered me about my father's bowling shoes when I was with him. And most importantly, the next morning he was standing at the foot of my driveway again.

"How are you today, Super Bill?"

"You want the truth or the facts?" I asked.

And then we were laughing again. It all seemed so easy.

When we got to the schoolyard we sort of kicked the ball around a bit. I kept tripping, getting my dad's shoes tangled up between the ball and the crutches and that seemed to make Benjamin laugh even more.

"Man, you are clumsy," he said. I don't know exactly how, but he said it in a way that didn't make me feel bad.

"It's the crutches," I said.

"Let me try."

Even with the crutches under his arms, he was still remarkably agile. I stopped the ball with my shin and kicked it lamely back to him. As the ball approached, Benjamin pivoted forward, putting his weight on the crutches, and kicked the ball with both feet at the same time. It came straight at me. I managed to just turn enough so that when the ball hit my face, I took most of the impact on the cheek. I fell to the ground and surprised myself when I found that I wasn't crying.

"Are you okay?" Benjamin offered his hand and pulled me up.

"Now you know why I stick to bowling," I said.

"Well, it was a nice save."

"Actually, I think it was ineluctable," I said. "Which proves that Mr. Joyce has some educational value after all."

The next weekend we went to the library together. Benjamin headed straight for the sports section and I went directly to the file cards. We met about fifteen minutes later at a long table by the window. It was boiling, but I had to keep my coat buttoned because I was carrying Ham with me.

"What's all that for?"

He started reading the spines of the pile of books I had in front of me. "*Acceleration, Velocity and Instantaneous Motion, Astronomy for Beginners, Whales of the World, Gods of the Hindu Pantheon*. What are you, some kind of mad scientist?" He flipped open the astronomy book. "Johannes Kepler (1571–1630)...

"You guys have the same name."

"That too, is ineluctable..."

Benjamin tapped his fingers on the table and went back to the *Guinness Book of World Records* he was reading. "Hey," he said a moment later, "this guy was hit by lightning seven different times."

"That's what I call bad luck."

"They call him the Human Lightning Rod." Benjamin turned the page. "Here's a guy that drank a gallon of beer in 1.3 seconds. That's like, gulp, and it's gone."

"*The* Human Syphon?" I said.

While I flipped through the pages of the books in front of me I made notes in the journal my mother had given me for Christmas. Notes about the constellation of Cetus, the Greek myth, Cousteau and Herman Melville, the Japanese Whaling Association, Greenpeace. I couldn't bring myself to tell Benjamin that while my classmates were visiting the Epcot Center, Niagara Falls, or doing flips off a dock in Muskoka, I spent half of August in a semi-catatonic state. Instead, I just avoided the subject, using non sequiturs to deflect his questions.

When I got home, my mother was on the couch, a nail file, emery board, cuticle oil, cotton pads, sealant and a brand new bottle of nail polish balanced on a TV tray on her lap. I was surprised to see that she didn't have a drink in front of her.

She lit a cigarette as soon as the closing credits of *Charlie's Angels* scrolled across the screen.

"Mom," I said quietly.

She turned and looked at me. "Oh, I didn't know you were home. Be a doll and change it to channel nine, will you?"

"Have you seen dad's telescope?" I asked.

"Did you look in the closet?"

"Yes," I said flipping the channels—commercial, commercial, *The Newlywed Game*, commercial, static, *Happy Days*.

"Check the basement," she said.

The door to the basement was blocked by a bunch of horrible-smelling garbage bags. I could see from the top of the stairs that all the junk on the floor had been swept up against the wall, making a clear path to the laundry room. I found the telescope in a red milk crate along with my dad's comb, a bottle of cologne, his toothbrush, a clip-on tie and a stack of Graceland beer coasters. I spent a moment entertaining the idea that he had been vaporized and that those things were all that was left of him. What would be left of me if I were incinerated? A sock monkey. A pair of crutches. An unfinished homework assignment.

That evening I climbed the antennae to the roof of our house and stared up at the sky. I watched a few cumulus clouds that, to my tired eyes, looked like a herd of drifting elephants. When the clouds finally cleared I set up the telescope, and guided by the voices of the past—Ptolemy, Copernicus, Galileo, Joyce, I searched the sky for traces of my father's orbit, charting a course through the solar system, I checked every crater, every canyon, every gaseous ring, and then I pointed the telescope at the shed.

Dr. Atwood is sipping what he calls an Espresso Americano. I can actually see the caffeine working on him as he flips the pages I have given him.

"So the whale was the recurring theme in your school assignment?"

He doesn't miss a thing.

"I'd like to read it," he says, poking his chin gently with his pen. "I'd also like to read the second letter."

"I destroyed everything, the journal, the letters."

"Actually," Atwood says pulling open a drawer, "I have the letters right here. You left them on the couch last time you were here."

Atwood holds the envelope up.

"Busted," I say.

"May I?"

I shrug.

He starts to read.

Dear Kepler, You've been gone for 15 days now and I have been praying to whoever may be listening every night, but no one answers. In fact, I'm beginning to wonder if this nightmare will ever end. What did we do to deserve this? Why us and not the Phillips next door? Do the cosmetics of their home protect them from misfortune? I wonder if calamity, illness, and death rove overhead and selectively pick on the vulnerable, those who don't keep up appearances.

I know I sound like a crazy person; I can't sleep and I've been forgetting things. I don't know what happens, but I get distracted, leave things half finished—clothes in the washer, the ironing. The other day I found myself in the basement just standing there without any idea of what I had gone down there for, and I practically had a heart attack last week when I went into the bathroom and found you lying there in the tub. Your skin was white and wrinkled and you were shaking. I thought that maybe you were hyperthermic, but I couldn't take you to the hospital, I mean, what could I tell them? So I bundled you in towels and used a blow dryer to warm your feet and hands. I had done this to you—left you in the tub—forgotten you.

Atwood doesn't say anything for a moment.

"Do you believe me now?"

"Believe what?"

"Calamity, illness, and death roving overhead. She's talking about the whale."

"She was under a lot of stress, Kepler, so was your father. No doubt they were going through a hard time, some of which was exacerbated by a degree of bad luck, but, they were also self-medicating so that they didn't have to face their regrets. Clinically speaking, your parents were in denial. They blamed each other, but more importantly, they also blamed you. As we have been discovering, we have to face the painful memories in order to heal and move on."

I know he's probably right, but his assessment is too convenient. It is an oversimplification, a standardized diagnosis devoid of nuance, character, and most importantly, truth. He insists that everything remotely ambiguous needs to be stripped of its colour and emotion, so that whales become metaphors, and curses become figments of a diseased mind. "Okay," I say, "I'm ready to move on." That was easy.

"Prove it."

"How?"

"By answering the question."

"What question?"

"How did your father die?"

A low cloud parks itself in my brain. Over easy.

Atwood leans back in his chair. "How did he die, Kepler?"

I try my best to co-operate, but the question isn't simply a question, it is a scalpel that opens me up. I can see the whale, its hinged jaw agape as it flounders in the turbulence, but this time I don't give in. NGC 4631. The scientific naming of the constellation reduces the whale to ionized hydrogen and interstellar dust. I'm left feeling raw and vulnerable, but also a little deflated. Something so scary so easily stripped of its power. I reach for a tissue. "I'd rather do this on paper," I say.

Atwood checks his watch, sips his coffee and nods. "Three thousand words at a time."

"Kepler."

I recognized my mother's voice, but it came to me from the far corners of sleep. A moment later, I heard my name again, but this time there was a rising urgency in her tone that caught me by the front of my pajamas and yanked me to the surface. When I opened my eyes, I was blinded by a bright light.

"Kepler, wake up."

I pulled the blankets up over my eyes. I heard the soft click of a flashlight and the room went black. What the hell? I lowered the blankets and saw the faint outline of my mother in the doorway. "Get dressed," she whispered.

"What's going on?" I asked.

"Hurry," she said. And then I heard the floor creak as she shuffled out into the hall.

I threw my legs over the side of the bed and sat there for a moment in a sleepy daze. I could feel the weight of sleep pulling me back towards my pillow. And then, just as my eyes were closing, my mother was in the hall again, the beam of light flashing across the walls outside my door. A moment later, the damn light was pointing in my face again.

"Put these on," she said, and I heard what I figured was the weight of my shoes clunk on the floor. I hadn't worn my own shoes in months. I tied the laces in the dark and headed out to the kitchen. She still hadn't turned any lights on, but I could make out the dark shape of her at the sink.

"What happened?" I asked.

She turned and pointed the flashlight at me.

"Are you ready?" she said.

"Ready for what?"

The beam of light fell to my feet.

"Take this," she said, handing me a paper bag.

The light flashed across the wall momentarily illuminating a half dozen yellow notes stuck to the cupboard doors, before pausing on the face of the clock. It was 3:42.

"C'mon, Kepler, we don't have all night."

I followed her down the hall to the front door. She turned on the flashlight again, handed me my coat, and then pointed the light at a folded up lawn chair leaning against the cracked pane of glass in the long narrow window next to the front door. "Grab that," she said, and then she turned the flashlight off again and headed back to the kitchen.

I put on my coat and picked up the lawn chair.

When we were back in the kitchen she pointed the damn flashlight at me again. "Enough with the light," I said. "What is going on?"

"Enough with the questions. Just hurry up." And then she pulled the back door open and stepped out into the cold night air.

I stood at the door holding the stupid lawn chair and a brown paper bag. The cold rushed up the pant legs of my pajamas. I heard a siren off somewhere in the distance and I wondered if they were on their way to our house.

"Kepler."

I followed my mother's prints in the snow.

"Give me a hand."

I stuck my head in the shed. I didn't want to go in there. "Turn the light on," I said.

I heard her bang into something. "Shit!"

When the flashlight hit the floor it came on for a split second and momentarily flashed on my mother's face, leaving me with the sickening feeling that I was alone in this creepy shed in the middle of the night with a stranger. I heard her groan heavily as she got down on her hands and knees searching for the flashlight in the dark.

"Mom?"

I could hear her sort of snort and wheeze, but she didn't answer. I took a few steps backwards, terrified by what I might see when the flashlight came on again.

"Kepler?"

"Mom?"

"There it is."

When she came out of the shed she had a spade in one hand and a rectangular cardboard box in the other. I took several steps back into the middle of the yard. In that strange half-awake state I thought for a brief moment this is it—she's going to kill me.

She dropped the shovel at my feet. "Dig," she said. There were tiny sparkles of moonlight in her eyes. "Dig," she said again, and pointed the beam of the flashlight at the ground.

I put the paper bag down in the snow next to the lawn chair and picked up the shovel. It was cold in my hands. I placed the spade's tip in the centre of the small circle of light and kicked down on the hard edge. The ground was frozen so the spade only went down an inch or two. A sharp pain ran up the length of my calf.

"C'mon, Kepler," my mother said as she unfolded the lawn chair, "we gotta get this done before the sun comes up." The chair cracked as she eased her weight down.

After a few minutes I could feel blisters forming on my hands—red welts from prying and heaving the earth.

"Keep going. A little further. Keep going."

She told me to stop when the hole was about two feet deep. Even though she wasn't quite calm, the urgency was gone from her voice. "We don't want any dogs coming along and digging him up," she said.

Then she opened the paper bag and silently removed the contents like a magician extracting strange and magical objects from a hat. The first thing she handed me was a sandwich wrapped in wax paper. "He loved Cheez Whiz sandwiches," she said.

Actually, I loved Cheez Whiz. My father liked mayonnaise. My fingers were so numb by this point that I almost dropped the sandwich in the hole.

Next, she pulled out the pieces of a broken record, a bottle of vodka and my dad's sunglasses. She kept turning and looking around as if she was expecting someone to show up. "This is between you and me," she said.

I nodded even though I had no idea what was going on.

"Okay, Kepler."

"What?"

"In the hole," she said.

I tossed the sandwich in the hole and tucked my freezing hands up into my armpits.

"Good," she said, and placed the record pieces on top of the sandwich.

"What is it?" I asked.

"It's an Elvis record," she said.

"No, I mean, which one?"

"I don't know. It's more than one I think." And then she handed me the sunglasses.

"Why do you want to bury dad's sunglasses?" I asked.

"No more lies," she said.

I shook my head and dropped the sunglasses on top of the record pieces.

"Okay, this is it," she said as she picked up the cardboard box.

"This is what?" I asked.

"This is the answer to all your questions."

"A cardboard box?"

She leaned forward and gently placed the box in the hole. We both stared down at it for moment, and then my mom reached for the bottle. "I know he liked beer," she said, "but this is all I had." She unscrewed the lid of the vodka and poured a splash into the hole, took a big swig, and passed the bottle to me as if we were old chums standing next to a burning drum of garbage. I stood up, wiped the mud off my knees and took the bottle. I wasn't prepared for the bitter bite as the vodka splashed into my mouth. It tasted more like poison than anything someone would willingly drink. I started to cough.

"Take it like a man," she said.

I remember feeling strange, and slightly dizzy, but then the vodka warmly expanded in my chest. I held the bottle out at arm's length and wiped my mouth. My mother took the bottle, had a quick swig and handed it back to me. "Drink," she said.

I tilted the bottle to my lips and allowed a small amount into my mouth and swallowed.

"Again," she said.

I tried again. The warmth of the liquor began to swirl in my head. Tears rolled down my cheeks. I looked over at my mother. I could barely make her face out in the dark.

"I want to make this perfectly clear," she said. "Your father is dead. Anything you want to say, say it now."

I was ten years old the first time my mother told me my father was dead. My parents had had a big fight. I heard the whole thing, including the slamming of the door. "He was hit by lightning," she said the next morning. "It's just you and me now." Even though I was too young to really understand what that meant, I could feel the weight of it crush something inside of me. Whenever I mentioned my father, my mother would look me in the eye and say, "Your father's gone, Kepler. It's best to just forget about him." Six months later, I woke up to find him standing in my bedroom holding a kite that I had made at school out of wood dowels, a garbage bag and some coloured tissue paper.

"Come on," he said, "let's go for a walk."

We were living in the south end of Parkdale, not far from the lake. The next thing I knew we were running across the beach in the dark. My dad was letting out more and more string, but the kite just fluttered about six feet off the ground and then veered hard left before crashing into the water.

"Okay," he said catching his breath, "Never mind the kite. You're probably wondering where I've been."

"Heaven," I answered.

He looked down at me. "Mmm, not exactly," he said, and started walking back towards the kite.

"—The Apollo 18 mission was an embarrassment for the Academy. Do you remember that mission? It was in September—or was it October? Anyway, you have to promise you'll keep this to yourself—" he paused and took a sip of beer. There was big wet stain where he had been carrying it in the square pocket of his trench coat. "This is top secret stuff. You can't even tell your mother."

I nodded. I understood.

He stopped at shoreline where my kite lay half sunk like a capsized sailboat. "One day I'll teach you to make a proper kite," he said, and then he turned his head to the sky. "I was up there for four months. The damn Russians had to save me. There was a malfunction in the capsule ejection seat. You see, that's what a pilot uses as a last resort if his craft is shot down or one of the rockets misfires on re-entry." He was still looking up at the sky. "Get the kite," he said.

I tiptoed quickly into the water and picked the wet thing up, the cold water seeped in around the ankles of my sneakers, rivulets of cold water ran cool down the sleeve of my pajamas. I licked my finger and held it up. There was no wind. The willow down at the end of the beach was still.

"Anyway, where was I? I had just passed through the thermosphere when the damn thing was triggered by accident and I was ejected out of the cockpit into space. Luckily, I was wearing my helmet at the time, or your dear old dad wouldn't even be here to tell the tale."

I followed him along the beach as he talked. I kept my mouth shut, but my feet were freezing so I was glad when he turned and headed back towards the streetlights. "So there I was, 150 miles above earth, and I remember thinking that if I have to die, then goddamn, this wouldn't be such a bad way to end it." His hand fell on my shoulder. "But this is the thing." He looked sideways as if there might be someone else out there in the middle of a cold windless February night flying a kite, and then his voice went quiet and low. "I could see the earth spinning slowly below me. Try to picture that. It gave off this heavenly blue light … It's two-thirds water you know, and it gives off this blue … light and … and I felt like…" he nodded his head as if he was agreeing with himself… "I felt like a god, well not a god exactly, but like a star, like I belonged up there you know, looking down on the world. It was a very sobering experience, and believe me I had a few in me before the malfunction. Anyway, when you see something from so far away you become detached and connected at the same time. The Earth stopped being about specifics. I couldn't see you or your mom or the city, or even Canada. Christ, Elvis even just became part of the big picture of the planet itself. But it was a beautiful thing ... well, to see the whole wide world in perspective like that, it's a humbling experience ... but then after a while that sort of wore off and I found myself wondering, what is the point of all this? I mean my life. What good is any of it if you're alone? And that's when I thought of you. You and your mother."

I scraped the mud off the bottom of my shoes on the curb. "What happened?" I asked.

"What happened what?" he said.

"How did you get back to earth?"

"Jesus, I told you, Kepler. I was saved by the Russians." He counted them out on his fingers. "Lazarev, Oleg, Vasily and Makarov. The Soyuz 12 came along and picked me up and dropped me off at Skylab. I had to wait for the next Apollo mission to bring me back to earth." We crossed the road and headed up our street. "Anyway, like I said, don't say anything to your mother about this. The whole thing was a terrible embarrassment to the Space Agency."

He held open a trashcan lid at the side of our building and gestured to the kite. I had only finished building it that morning, and I was still convinced that it would fly had there been the slightest breeze. "I'll buy you a proper one tomorrow," he said.

I reluctantly dropped it in.

"It's all about aerodynamics," he said. "You need a harmonic balance of drag and lift to get things off the ground." He tossed in the two empty bottles that he had drunk on our walk and closed the lid.

"Mom told me you got hit by lightning," I said.

"Yeah well, that mother of yours has quite an imagination."

And now, here he was, dead again.

I looked up at the sky just as it started to snow. My mother pulled up the collar of her red coat, stood up and stamped her feet on the ground. "Fill it in," she said.

Part of me imagined I was burying that memory, two beer bottles and a kite. "So he was struck by lightning again?"

"If it be true," my mother said, "that a good wine needs no bush, 'tis true that a good play needs no epilogue." And then she jiggled the empty bottle by the neck for a moment and tossed it into the snow.

The next afternoon I pulled the kitchen curtain open and the supports that held the rod came out of the wall. I tossed the screws that fell to the floor into the sink and stared out at the fresh coat of snow. The shed door was closed, but there was a lawn chair in the middle of the yard, and there was a red blister on the palm of my left hand and one in the ditch of my thumb on the right. A few minutes later my mother came into the kitchen with a comforter wrapped around her shoulders. Her wig was a matted mess. It looked like it had gone to seed. I imagined a family of sparrows in her hair—butterflies, purple loosestrife and other roadside flora sprouting from the mess of her curls.

I sat down at the kitchen table, opened my journal and started to write. My mother was making a fuss over by the stove. Her back was to me, but I could see that she was using a dirty butter knife to pry open the cutlery drawer. A few minutes later she placed a packet of jam and plate of burnt toast on top of my journal. "What is that you're writing?" She took a seat across from me, tapped a cigarette on the table and lit the wrong end. "Oh shit."

I scraped off some of the burnt bits and took a bite of toast. "It's for school," I said.

"That doesn't answer my question," she said fingering the empty space in the puzzle.

I pushed the plate onto one of Saturn's moons and started to read out loud.

Physeter macrocephalus, sixty feet long, fifty-eight tons. From the equator to the edges of sea-faring literature, the sperm whale is a world ocean traveller. Revered and feared, it has endured more than a century of commercial slaughter. Sailors were overcome by a sense of loneliness and awe when catching a glimpse of its stony eye, great rolling back and the graceful propulsion of its flukes. In Greek mythology, it haunts the nighttime sky, feeding on satellites, space junk and the occasional dreamer.

When I closed my journal it looked like she was going to cry, but then her posture went rigid, her lips tightened into a thin red line, and her chair scraped loudly across the linoleum. As she got up from the table, a swirl of cigarette smoke stirred in her wake. She went over to the fridge and started arranging the mess of notes and newspaper clippings held onto the door with magnets. A moment later she was back at the table, "I've been writing, too," she said, dropping another damn envelope on my plate. Then she flicked me with a blue nail in the back of the head. "I've got to go to work," she added, and headed for the bathroom. I extinguished the burning cigarette she left in the ashtray, went back to bed and slept for twenty-two hours.

I don't know how long I was standing at the foot of Benjamin's driveway, but it was cold. I could feel my toes getting numb and the snot in my nose was beginning to crystalize so I began stamping my feet to keep from freezing to death. By the time Benjamin stepped out the door I was sure a couple of my toes had fallen off inside my dad's shoes.

"Hey, congratulations, no crutches," he said. I could barely see his face in the furry circle of his parka hood.

I nodded at the soccer ball. "Do you ever leave that thing at home?"

"If I'm going to the World Cup, I gotta practise every day," he said as we headed off.

"What's the World Cup?" I asked.

"It's like the Stanley Cup of soccer. Except it's every four years and it's countries playing countries, not cities." Benjamin was walking fast.

I jammed my frozen hands into my pockets and tried to keep up. "Will you play for Canada or South Africa?" I asked, pretending to be interested.

"Neither," he said. "I'm going to play for England." The cold wind was skirting off the drifts, making it hard to walk and see. "You missed school yesterday," he said. "You sick?"

"I was at a funeral," I answered. I wasn't sure if that counted as a lie or not, but it slipped out, and I instantly regretted it.

Benjamin looked down at the ball in his mitts and stopped walking. I knew it was coming.

"Who died?" he asked.

A particularly strong and cold gust of wind pushed me towards him, and as I stumbled I lost all points of reference. The sidewalk, the snow, the houses—even the stupid damn wind vanished. The question had been asked. What were moments ago simply a few words spoken in a blizzard were suddenly transformed into a meteorological anomaly.

"My father," I said very quietly. I didn't fully believe it, I mean, he had died before, and I couldn't feel the pain and loss that I was certain I would feel if it were true, and so if it was a lie, I reasoned, it was my mother's, not mine.

"I'm sorry," Benjamin said.

I wanted to tell him he had died heroically, that his spaceship had burned up on re-entry, that there was nothing left of him and his ship but a pile of dust small enough to fit in a cardboard box. But I knew that saying it would implicate me and turn the lie into something that I would have to claim as my own.

When Benjamin tugged on my sleeve we pushed on against the cold wind for a while, our feet crunching in the hard snow. I walked with my head down, following the heels of his boots until the frozen hedges and the snowdrifts gave way to a recently plowed parking lot. I was vaguely aware of where we were, and I didn't even bother to look up when Benjamin's tracks abruptly stopped. I heard the loud complaint of a door opening followed by a second tug on my sleeve. A moment later I heard the door close and the sound of vibrating glass as the wind whistled through the cracks in the phone booth.

We stamped our feet and smiled awkwardly at each other. "What happened?"

I was trapped. I took a deep breath and when I exhaled the words came out like they were sitting there just waiting to be spoken. "My dad was on a job," I said hesitantly. I could see it in my mind, a story taking shape. "He travels for work and he was down in..." the options were infinite "...Memphis," I said finally. "Anyway, on his way home it started raining, and he got a flat tire, and when he pulled over to fix it..." I could see him on one knee, the tire wrench in his hand, a low ceiling of grey broken by intermittent spikes of jagged light "...he was hit by lightning." And then, I don't know where it came from, but instead of the tears that I tried to muster, I started laughing. And as I tried to catch my breath, Benjamin's face hardened, and for a moment I thought he might hit me, but what he did was much worse: he turned, pushed open the door and walked away. And as I watched Benjamin through the dirty glass of the phone booth disappear into the blizzard, I stuck my finger in the coin return slot of the phone. It was empty.

I was an agitated mess when I got home. I couldn't eat. I couldn't sleep. I started to imagine things, okay, that's nothing new, but it seemed like the more I thought about my father and Benjamin, the more transparent I felt. I was disappearing again. I needed to destroy something. I wanted to yell and storm and exert my will against the confusion in my heart. I went into the bathroom, dug around under the sink until I found a pair of scissors and climbed into the tub. I could hear my mother flipping the channels on the TV down the hall—channel, static, channel—the isochronal white noise seeping under the crack in the bathroom door. How fragile everything was—truth, friendship, memory. It would all be much easier to simply no longer think. I gently pressed the edge of the scissors across my wrist. I could imagine the sharp pain, the blood, the panic, the mess—"To be or not to be," I said aloud. I was laughing as I drew the point of the scissors firmly across my inner arm. A red welt appeared. I took a deep breath and pushed a little harder.

It was like letting the air out of a balloon. A quiet rush. I sighed and settled back against the hard edge of the tub. I could feel my anger evaporating as the fuel gauge slowly crept to the left. The sore throat I had was gone and the light seemed perfect. I was a leaf let go of a tree—inhale—gently sway to the left—exhale—drift to the right. And in that rhythm there were no more television shows, just the constant and soothing static of numbness. I sounded out my last name pressing my lips tightly together, finishing with a flick of the tongue— Presssssler. Return to Sender, Elvis nudging a tight group of stars out of the way with his swivelling hips, making room for a memory. I closed my eyes and felt my fingers clasped through the links of a fence, a strange, deep, low growl coming from somewhere off in the dark.

"What the hell was that?" My dad's voice somewhere below.

Off in the distance I can see the dimly illuminated zoo entrance, the wooden gate, the limp flags, the antlered deer head icon.

"Jesus, Kepler, let go."

But I couldn't let go. I couldn't move.

"Kepler, let go." I could feel him tugging on my ankles. "It's the wrong fence, Kepler."

The wrong fence? It was too dark and I was too tired and drunk and scared, and I couldn't bring myself to look down at the thing that had my father in a panic. It was better to just close my eyes and hang on until I simply couldn't hang on any more. When I opened my eyes the water was lightly stained red, a smoky trail drifting away from the cut in my arm—Benjamin, my father, the lie, as vague and distorted as the darkness around me.

I exist in two worlds now. In the present, I'm stuck in this hospital like a caged animal pacing the floor of Atwood's office. All I can think about is how the hell I'm going to get out of here. But on paper I'm trapped too. I'm held hostage by Atwood's damn editorial direction. I have to get where I'm going one sentence at a time.

Atwood has a fresh cup of coffee in front of him. A wisp of steam rises up and fogs his glasses each time he takes a sip.

When he finally looks up from my file, he has a serious look in his eye. "Would you mind rolling up your sleeves?"

I cross my arms and sort of hug myself.

"We're here to dig, Kepler. This is supposed to hurt. You have to face your feelings. Keeping yourself numb won't get us anywhere."

He has me cornered and I know it. I also know where we are in the story, and I really don't want to go any further, but this is like a chess game to Atwood, and of course he's much better at it than I am.

"Okay, you win," I say.

"This isn't a competition, Kepler. It might help if you think of me as a coach as a opposed to an adversary."

"My heart feels like it's breaking all over again."

"Good," he says. "Now we're getting somewhere."

CHAPTER ELEVEN

(I)

I went to school the following Monday wearing my mother's red winter coat. The sun was shining, most of the snow had melted, and there were little yellow daffodils and crocuses blooming in the garden outside the school's main entrance. Benjamin nodded when I said hello in the hall, but he didn't stop to talk. I spent the morning in a daze wandering from class to class praying that I wouldn't be called upon to engage in any way. Mr. Lemon's English class was the worst. I couldn't focus and for the first time Joyce came across as an incomprehensible jumble of meaningless words. "*Universes of void space constellated with other bodies ... dividends and divisors ever diminishing without actual division till, if the progress were ever carried far enough nought nowhere was ever reached.*" If this was truth than was I now forever banished to the realm of lies and ignorance? Mr. Lemon closed the novel and stood there for a moment letting the weight of the Joyce's gibberish settle in. "When we look out at the stars at night," he said, "the universe expands far beyond what we can at this moment see and comprehend. Joyce is suggesting that the same is true within as it is without. When we consider the realm of the microscopic, molecules can also be reduced infinitely. And so here we are, situated somewhere in the cosmos, surrounded by infinity in every direction."

Overwhelmed by a sense of loneliness, I pulled the furry collar of my mother's coat up over my face until the sobbing subsided. A moment later I was running down the hall, an inconsequential streak of nothingness fleeing the ever diminishing dividends and divisors.

I hung out by myself on lunch break, kicking at the tennis court fence, and spent the last class of the day locked in a stall in the boys' washroom. When the four o'clock bell finally rang I was waiting for Benjamin at his locker. I had been talking to myself all day trying to resituate myself in the universe, but every angle reduced or expanded beyond what made sense until my Joycean-inspired feelings of alienation gave way to frustration and anger. I was attempting to summon a light- ning bolt from the sky when a group of people emerged from the gymnasium and settled into a small scrum at the end of the hall. As I approached I could see that Benjamin was at the centre of the crowd doing tricks with his soccer ball. He was a gravitational force and I had left his orbit—a satellite gone astray. Plan or no plan, I just couldn't stop thinking about how he had walked away from me like I was crazy. "Fuck. Shit." The words rolled off my tongue. "I hate school, and no I will not stand for the National Anthem." I adjusted my hesitant approach until I was moving quick and steady, the shadow of a four-armed blue goddess rising up behind me. Nobody even seemed to notice me until I grabbed one of them by the arm, the biggest one, the one that would retaliate with the greatest force. I tightened my other hand into a fist and swung—it was a clumsy, arcing swing, but it connected in a satisfying collision with an ear. He fell back a few steps but didn't go down as I had imagined.

"Fuck," he yelled.

I was surrounded. I remember being pushed from all sides and then my knees buckling.

In the end they went pretty easy on me. My nose was bleeding. There was a lot of blood, that much I remember, but in my version, on paper anyway, Benjamin stepped in and saved me.

I didn't go home after school that day. Instead, I took a bus to the subway station and jumped on a train. I wasn't going anywhere. In my mind, I was simply escaping. The subway map above the doors looked like a green incision across the black sky. You paid one fare and the train took you back and forth all day long from Mercury to Pluto. With a little nudge it rumbled across distant galaxies, careening through a tube of darkness. The rhythm of the track, the opening and closing of doors, the advertising lining the length of each car, everybody doing their best to ignore each other, while at the same time glad that we were not alone out there in the cosmos—old faces that might be making their final appearances in the world, overweight people with two chins whose bums took up part of the seat next to them—our bodies vibrating, the urgent rumble of a passing train, the whistle of the door operator, people coming and going whose lives intersected without complication or expectation—people applying makeup, reading newspapers, foraging for food, scratching at fleas, reaching for the bars, grasping and releasing as they moved down the car towards the doors, primates careening through space in a rocket.

It was as if I was following an invisible thread that was leading me both forward and backwards at the same time. A thread connected to my will at one end and my desire at the other. The train came to halt in the dark tunnel. The lights flickered. An unintelligible announcement garbled out of the speakers. A feeling of claustrophobia fueled by impatience unsettled the car. Time slowed, and there, past the shoulders and newspapers and grasping hands, beyond the unfathomable reaches of outer space I saw her, and I felt a renewed sense of purpose and hope which coincided with a collective sigh emitted from the crowd when the conductor blew his whistle and the train lurched back into motion.

A long red fold of satiny fabric draped over her shoulder, the sleeves of her dress embroidered with gold thread, green smudges on her olive skin under the bracelets she wore on her wrists. I maneuvered myself so that I could see her face in the reflection of the window. She smiled as the train accelerated, the yellow lights tracing through the darkness on either side of her head.

"Are you in a creating, preserving or destroying mood today?" I asked.

As she turned to face me, the bag she was holding banged against the seat and I heard what sounded like a bunch of change rattling in a tin can.

Her eyes quickly settled on the front of my shirt. "You've got blood all over you—"

She looked older. Her skin seemed darker and her tangled hair was cut short above the shoulders. Somehow she had become even more beautiful.

"Yeah," I said. "But I don't need crutches anymore."

I did a little two-step.

"Are you okay?"

"Sure," I said.

She was smiling now, eyeing the coat I was wearing. "You know, it's like seventy degrees out there?"

"It's my mother's," I said. "It's her lucky coat."

"You look like a fucking homeless person."

"I feel fucking homeless right now."

"Bad day?"

"Bad life."

As the train approached the expanding square light of the next station a million questions passed through my mind, but one seemed more urgent and prescient than all the others, "Do you ever wake up feeling like you could take on the whole world?" The train slowed. "...And then the next moment you feel like a dried up leaf waiting for a breeze to blow you to the ground?"

"This is my stop," she said, stepping past me.

I felt like a dried up leaf at that moment, helplessly adrift in a current of air, but as the doors opened she turned back to me. "I do" she said, caught in the momentum of the exiting crowd, "all the fucking time."

And there it was again—that sense of relief. I was grounded again, but it was suddenly eclipsed by the sense that I may never see her again. The mouth of the moment was still open. I tried to follow, pushing against the crowd now boarding the train, apologizing as I went, my eyes focusing on every trace of red—a purse, a tie, gloved fingers wrapped around the leather handle of a briefcase or the wooden curve of an umbrella. I wanted to freeze the world so that I could catch up. I wanted to stamp my footprint into the hard cement, but I lost her, a precious coin rolled into a sewer grate.

When I stepped out of the station, the buildings rising up from the streets seemed to sway in the currents above me. I searched among the vendors, the flower sellers, the shoe shiners, hot dog carts, the signs and the lights. The only thing that kept me from stepping out into the intersection was a taxi that had pulled up. The driver was asking me if I needed a ride when I spotted her on the other side of the road. While I waited for the light, strains of music rose up over the din of car horns and traffic—an old man with an accordion, his fingers moving elegantly across the keyboard—the distinct and unforgettable melody of Love. I kept my eye on her as she slowly moved further and further away. I was pacing, small steps from side to side until the light was green. But then, before I had even taken a step, she leapt from the curb, skipped in front of a streetcar, and disappeared around a corner.

A white cat was sunning itself next to a copy of *Gulliver's Travels* in the window of a store called Molly Bloom's. "Socrates." A little bell jingled when I pushed open the door. A dusty guy in a cardigan stared at me a moment, sipped from a dirty mug and went back to the newspaper he was reading. The white cat rubbed itself against my leg, arched its back and then strolled into the stacks, leaving a trail of white fur all over the grey carpet. I followed the cat to the back of the shop, past the poetry, history, cooking and gardening sections until it disappeared through a doorway, its tail disturbing a curtain of hanging wooden beads.

I pushed the beads aside and saw an old barber chair in the middle of the room on which the cat was settling into a nap. The walls were covered in pictures of unicorns, eagles, hearts, dragons and panthers. There was a little wooden stool and a tall floor lamp next to a sink and a small chest of drawers. The back of the room was dark, but I could make out a large floor to ceiling mirror next to another door that was curtained with a Canadian flag. I caught a glimpse of myself in the mirror and I saw what a mess I was. There was dried blood on the front of my shirt and the bruise under my eye was turning purple. I heard a toilet flush, and then a shape emerged from behind the Canadian flag. "You looking for something?"

And once again the sudden impulse to run got the best of me. My legs stretched out with each stride as I streaked down the aisle for the door, books blurring in my peripherals as I cut through the light and dust, pages fluttering as I went, chapters turning, stories beginning and ending. I made it to the front of the shop, hopped over a stack of books on the floor, and pushed the door open, where I was met by a fragmented cluster of sounds, sharp images, and then pain—car horns, squealing tires, the breath and wheeze of traffic, light reflecting off of glass and chrome, the hard fender of a car, a slow roll over a hood onto the hard hello of cement.

When I opened my eyes Milly was standing there with a small stack of books under her arm.

"Are you following me?"

"What happened?"

"You ran into a parked car."

"Sorry," I said, wiping the dirt off my elbows.

"Sorry for what?"

"For following you."

"I live in that building," she said gesturing down the street. "You can't come up, but you can walk me home—"

I followed her up the block and then around a corner onto a side street. Up close she smelled like the hallways of the buildings I use to live in—exotic, pungent—"Curry," my mom called it, but I wasn't sure what that was, except it was both intoxicating and unpleasant at the same time. When we got to the parking lot of her building she started walking really fast, weaving between the cars until she got to the loop in front of the entrance. When I caught up to her, she was sitting cross-legged on the curb, her hands resting on her books. There were clothes and blankets scattered all over the place—burgundy sheets and a matching pillow resting on the hood of a nearby Datsun, a blue striped mattress leaning against a hedge.

"Hey," I said. "We must have missed the tornado."

Milly looked up at me and pointed at an open window on the fifth floor with a pink curtain hanging from a bent rod.

"That's my bedroom," she said. "My dad...he's fucking nuts." She wiped a smudge of mascara across her cheek, lit a cigarette and then pushed the pile of books over—Kerouac, Candide, and something called *Thus Spoke Zarathustra*.

I had the sense that unless I did something, I was certain that I would regret it forever. I sat down beside her, poked at the tear in the elbow of my mom's coat, and then I put my arm around her and as she leaned in to me I felt that sense of relief and comfort again.

"Do you have any tattoos?" she asked.

I shook my head.

"Cause I'm getting a fucking tattoo. Right on my arm, none of this girly ankle shit," she said. "I already have one picked out." She handed me her cigarette, pushed aside a curtain of red and yellow silk and forced her hand into the pocket of the jeans she was wearing underneath. She pulled out a baggy and tossed it on the pavement and then stuck her hand in again, this time withdrawing a five-dollar bill, some change and a piece of paper. The image seemed to flower in her fingers as she delicately unfolded what appeared to be a page ripped from an encyclopedia.

"It's an Om symbol," she said. "It's the sound of the contemplating universe. I'm going to get that, or a pot leaf."

A tattoo. I'd never even dreamed of getting a tattoo, but I was drawn to her conviction, her determination, her skin. Suddenly embarrassed by the scars exposed on my skinny arms, I removed my arm from her shoulder, pulled the sleeves of the coat down and cuffed them in my closed palms.

"My father says tattoos are for prostitutes. He says Shiva will smite our house with his mighty wrath if I get one."

I glanced down at the pile of books. I felt out of my depth. I couldn't even imagine what Shiva smiting one's house might mean. I was so drawn to her and yet something about her left me feeling disoriented. I was too close. She picked up the plastic baggy, opened it and fingered what looked like ground oregano. Then she flattened out the Om symbol and poured what I slowly realized was marijuana into a crevice of the page.

"Do you want to get high?"

I nodded, having no idea what that would really mean either. But then I began to panic. "What about all that stuff?" I said pointing at the mess in the parking lot.

"Leave it," she said. "All we need are the books." And then she touched my arm, and as if on cue, the sun came out, and I cracked like a soft-boiled egg—my insides spilling out of me onto the ground. She led me through the parking lot and then down the street to a small parkette. There was pigeon shit all over the bench so we sat in a green patch of grass next to a water fountain. She taught me how to inhale and how to pronounce Nietzsche. She told me how she skipped a grade, how literature was ruining her life. "Have you read Orwell? That shit will fuck you up."

Looking into her eyes I was certain that I could sense the tide and rhythm of her emotions. I wanted to slip into that water and submerse myself in her, lose myself, go under and breathe. But I was scared too, because this stirring in my heart seemed to come from a place below all the hurt, where the possibility still existed of something bright and untouched. The confusion of being close to her made me feel incredibly self-conscious and relaxed at the same time.

"Nietzsche challenged the foundation of morality. He questioned everything." She took a long drag from the joint. "He was one of the first existentialist philosophers."

"Existentialist," I repeated, as if I knew what I was talking about. The word seemed so ridiculous, like a marble rolling around on my tongue. And then I started laughing.

Milly smiled. "What's so funny?" she asked.

"I wonder if he knew James Joyce."

And then Milly was laughing, too. We were laughing together. It was like surrendering to something inside of me that I didn't know was there. That laughter seemed like the perfect antidote to all the things that were so fucked up in the world.

"—And," I said, "I don't know what 'existentialist' means."

She tried to hold it in, and that made us crack up again. She had her knees pulled up to her chin, our bodies convulsing with spasms of laughter. I tried desperately not to drool. And then after I had forgotten what we were laughing about, she said, "It's the self-conscious pursuit of the meaning of existence." I looked back over my shoulder and I imagined the door of a cage swinging open. And then she was suddenly very serious. "You know, like that part of you that feels like everyone is afraid to say what they really mean, that part of you that knows that the world around you is really nothing more than the product of chance and chaos, a script written by a million chimpanzees banging away on a million typewriters."

I watched a ladybug crawl across my shoe—five black dots on a deep red shell. I imagined a blade of grass the size of an apartment building, a leaf falling from a bridge, a raindrop hitting a river. The chatter of monkeys. When shall we three meet again. In thunder, lightning, or in rain? When the hurly-burly's done. When the battle's lost and won. That will be ere the set of sun. And then Milly shifted her body and leaned back so that her head was in my lap. I looked down at her profile and that perfect spot where the top of her nose meets her forehead. "Yes," I said, and for the first time that day I knew exactly what she was talking about. Leaning forward, I felt the gentle lull of the breeze, the impulse to whisper her name pulling me into the simple perfection of her lips. I could feel the space between us, the inch and a half that separated my forehead from hers. I could measure that space without numbers. I could have swum, or flown, or kicked Benjamin's soccer ball across that divide—a distance vast enough to devote one's life to. Our brains were almost touching, separated by a universe of possibility, but this space was beautiful, more precious than touching because it couldn't be taken away.

"Kepler," she said. "I guess you're not gay."

"What?" I asked, suddenly feeling insecure again.

"I wasn't sure. Well, you're wearing your mother's coat and those shoes are pretty strange. I thought I should make sure."

"These are my father's bowling shoes, actually."

"Well, I dare say," she said in a British accent, "there's a little Oscar Wilde in you, I think." And then she touched the inside of my arm and gingerly ran her fingertips along a scab. "What's this all about?" she said.

I suddenly felt aware of the air that I was breathing, the cubic area that my body occupied in the world. "An accident with a pair of scissors," I said. I saw myself running with my eyes closed. I saw myself cutting, and I felt ashamed.

"What does it feel like?" she asked.

"I think your idea is much better," I said. "Ohm."

I feel the bittersweet echo of that day with Milly, the details of it still warm like the hood of an idling car. There was a period of about three months when none of the other stuff mattered. My father, my mother, Benjamin, the suburbs—Milly eclipsed everything. As I move the pages around, I don't really know what to believe. Is this hospital any more real than what I have written? At some point in time this will be the past, too. Fact, truth—sometimes it's difficult to tell which is which.

"Normally, we have rules against this sort of thing," Bruce says, nodding towards the pages taped to the wall. I wonder how long he's been there.

"I have no idea what I'm doing," I say to him.

"Looks like you're making a mess," he says. "By the way, time for dinner."

And then he pulls a red pen out of his pocket, reaches out and makes a mark at the bottom of the last paragraph. "Om doesn't have an h," he says.

The glint of light from the cafeteria window catches the gold band on Ophelia's left hand. "Who is Milly?" she asks.

"She was either the love of my life," I say, "or a figment of my imagination."

Ophelia smiles. "I was in love, too," she says.

"Yes, I know."

"—and I have a daughter."

"You and Hamlet had children?"

She looks at me for a moment as if she doesn't have any idea what I'm talking about.

"But...I don't even remember her name," she says.

Even though I want to put my arms around Ophelia, or Grace, or whoever she is, I just reach out and pat her shoulder and say, "Families are overrated."

And then a moment later, as if someone had just turned the lights back on in her head, she says, "Close your eyes."

"What for?"

"Just close them."

I am hesitant to even blink in this place. Just last week an old guy viciously beat a trashcan to a pulp with his cane, and a guy that usually spends his days sitting by the window like a Saint Bernard scratched the eyes out of a portrait of the queen with a paperclip.

"Okay, hold out your hands." Ophelia places something as delicate as a leaf in one hand and then what feels like a cascade of jewels into the other. "Okay, you can look."

She has drawn a heart on a piece of construction paper and cut it into the shape of a puzzle piece. It is outdone only by the handful of yellow pills.

"Happy Valentine's Day," she says.

When I told my mother I was in love, she gave me a worried look, which was a subtle shift from her usual expression, but it involved a slight widening of the eyes as if what I said was somewhat frightening.

I wanted this to be a pleasant conversation, something positive in the *calamity, illness and death* that had invaded our lives.

"What's her name?" she eventually asked.

"You already met her, that day when you got your nails done."

"The brown girl?"

But before I could say anything more she was holding me with my face uncomfortably mashed into her bosom so hard that I could practically feel her heartbeat pounding into my temple. Despite how difficult it was to breathe, I didn't resist.

There were no tears, which was a relief, but she wouldn't let me go to bed that night until I promised her that I would never leave.

Milly and I went on our first secret date the following weekend. "Let's put those crazy shoes to the test," she said. We met at the donut shop next to the Triple Blue Bowling Alley. The donut shop was a dump where guys in their twenties stood around in the parking lot looking at each other's cars. The old lady behind the counter was sitting in a fold-up lawn chair doing crossword puzzles. It took about five hours for her to get up and shuffle across the floor, hand me a chocolate-glazed donut and take my money. When Milly arrived, all the sad-looking people smoking and reading newspapers looked up at her. She threw her purse down on the table and punched me in the arm.

I said, "Hi."

Milly took off her jean jacket, opened her purse, took out a Sex Pistols T-shirt, pulled it over her head and then leaned across the table and kissed me. "You live in the middle of fucking nowhere," she said.

I sighed. "Thanks for reminding me."

"Yeah, well, if you believe in karma, you must have done some horrible shit to end up here." She stuck her tongue out, and then she added, "I'm thinking about dyeing my hair. We could do it together. You'd look great with a blue Mohawk."

"What was wrong with the T-shirt you had on?" I asked.

She sighed, "The T-shirt underneath is the one my father wanted me to wear and this is the T-shirt I want to wear." She took a bite of my donut. "This place is so painfully boring. Let's go."

"Are you sure you want to do this?" I asked her.

"No backing out now, Kepler. We are committed to the mission."

All the lanes were empty accept for one. "It smells like dirty socks and beer," Milly said as we headed over to the bar where a small group of older men were sitting around drinking and smoking. One of them had a baseball hat with a trout on it. He tapped his cigar in an ashtray and then strolled over to the cash register. "Five or ten?" he asked.

"Ten pin," Milly answered.

"What size shoes?"

"Six, for me," she answered, "but he has his own."

Milly loved the shoes. She said they made her feel like dancing. I laughed as she did a two-step across the floor with an imaginary cane. The red and black coincidentally matched the Sex Pistols T-shirt she was wearing.

We chose a lane at the very other end of the alley and spent about ten seconds trying to figure out the scorecard. "Rules, rules, rules. This kind of stuff gives me a headache," she said.

There was a loud crash of the pins being struck with authority from the far lane.

Milly approached the trough of balls. "Well," she continued, "the basic idea is to knock the pins down, right?"

"Ladies first," I said.

"Ain't no ladies present," Milly said.

She took a couple of steps and awkwardly released the ball.

I don't know why, but I was disappointed. The ball practically fell from her hand and barely made it to the end of the lane where it dropped into the gutter. She spun on her heels with an exaggerated look of sadness and reached for another ball. "Holy shit," she said, "these fucking things are heavy."

It was awkward to see her struggle with something that I could do with a degree of ease. For some reason I wanted her to be better than me at everything. "Try releasing a little later," I said stupidly.

"I know, I know, I've got to channel Fred Flintstone."

She smiled, but I saw her turning herself inside out, her feelings, her frustrations following the second ball into the gutter. "Fuck." She flopped down on the bench beside me. And I watched as her mood shifted, just as it did in the parking lot the week before.

"Patience," I said mockingly, "let the master show you how it is done."

I picked up a ball, placed my feet together, stood erect and closed my eyes. And for a moment I was my father, or rather I imagined him from the inside. I could hear his instructions in my head: never talk when someone assumes the stance, focus and envision the ball striking the pins before you actually start your delivery. I stepped forward and gracefully released the ball. When I opened my eyes the ball was about three quarters of the way down the lane and heading for the gutter where it concluded its journey with a dull thud.

There was another loud crash from the lane at the other end of the alley.

I could hear Milly laughing behind me. I grabbed another ball and again I closed my eyes. I could see the pins in my mind's eye.

"Use the force Luke," she said.

I imagined the ball curving gently from the right side of the lane and then striking the headpin. I approached and released with a twist of the wrist and kept my eyes closed until I heard the ball strike the pins. Milly was laughing hysterically. All the pins were down but I was standing about four feet past the fault line.

I heard another crash from the far lane, and as I looked through the yellow haze of smoke that hung a few inches below the ceiling, something caught my eye. There were several Heinekens lined up on the scoring table, and somewhere between those bottles I saw the smoke from two cigarettes rising up from an ashtray.

I took a deep breath.

His back was to me, but I knew it was him—elbows bent tight against his sides cradling the ball as if he were praying, one beer tucked into the pocket of his blazer.

I looked at Milly. I watched her lips as they formed the words, "that's a fucking foul."

I looked back down the alley again; the bowler at the other end was slightly out of focus, grainy like a photo of a Sasquatch or a flying saucer. A sudden chill ran up my spine. I could feel the blisters on my hands tingle. Elvis had been spotted in donut shops; it made perfect sense that I would finally find my father in a bowling alley. And then, just as I was about to call out to him, I felt the floor begin to vibrate.

I turned to Milly. She was bent over retying her shoelace.

As the shaking intensified, the lanes began to tilt, the pins teetered, and I could hear the rattle of liquor bottles behind the bar where the old men were sitting. I turned towards the exit and half expected to see a locomotive crashing through the doors. Pieces of the ceiling tiles started to come down in chunks around me. I instinctively raised my hands over my head and scanned the alley for cover. The lights began to flicker and then the sprinkler system activated.

I looked desperately back at Milly. She had a pencil in her hand and appeared to be doodling on the scorecard.

I looked to the exit sign again just as the windows at the top of the stairs exploded. I fell to the floor and started to crawl towards my father, who calmly and precisely rolled another strike, and then another, and then another, and then the roof caved in above me.

When I came to, Milly was digging through her purse, pulling things out one at a time and throwing them back in—lipstick, rolling papers, a deck of cards, loose change, until she found a mini pair of scissors, the kind you might get in a sewing kit. She was sitting on my lap, but it was like I had left my body and was watching through a camera placed in the top corner of the small white cubicle. I watched her place her purse on the back of the toilet behind me. There were tears rolling down my face.

"Calm down," she was saying, as she put her hands on my cheeks. "Kepler, look at me … Kepler." I heard the panic in her voice, but I couldn't respond. All I could do was sit there stupidly. I didn't want this. I wanted to be there with her. I pushed with all my will against the space between us. And as she looked at me, I could see that she was crying too. And then she pushed the sleeve of my shirt up to the elbow. "Tell me what to do," she whispered. All I could manage was to mumble like an idiot. She pressed the edge of the scissors into my arm and dragged it slowly back and forth, and as I watched a line of blood forming under the blade, I felt a wave of relief, and this tenderness, this thing other than the panic slowly brought me back into my body.

A minute later, someone was banging on the stall door. "What the hell is going on in there?"

"I've never been banned from a bowling alley before," she said. We were back in the stupid donut shop, sharing a cup of hot chocolate. "You really freaked me out, Kepler. You kept saying the name, Walter, over and over again. You were shaking, and I thought, I don't know, maybe you were epileptic or something, but then I saw your scars and I just knew what to do."

"Walter is my father's name," I said. My head was still a muddle.

She waited for me to continue, but I just didn't know how to explain what happened. "He drives a taxi," I said, peeling her Sex Pistols T-shirt off my arm. "He used to work for the Space Agency, but he got fired." The cut had stopped bleeding, but her shirt was ruined.

"Back in India my father was an ornithologist. Here, he sells hotdogs and French fries at a concession stand."

"That guy at the other end of the alley, I thought it was my father, but it can't be..." I was determined to not make the same mistake I made with Benjamin.

When Milly jumped on the bus to go home that day, I was so worried that I had ruined everything. Now she knew what a mess I was. She knew what Benjamin and all my classmates knew. But before she left me standing there, she held me, and kissed me, and then she told me that she had a great time, and that her Sex Pistol's shirt was even cooler now. And I believed her.

CHAPTER TWELVE

(I)

The moment I enter Dr. Atwood's office I notice that the curtains aren't drawn on the window. I take my usual seat on the couch, and as he takes his time poking around in the drawers of his desk, I gaze mindlessly at the clouds above the buildings across the street. Atwood is struggling to unlink a small tangled chain of paperclips when I spot a cloud that looks unbelievably like a whale. My impulse is to draw the curtains and take cover under a table, but then I remind myself that I have to face these things if I ever want to get out of here. I stand up and direct Atwood's attention to the window. "Look at that, flukes, pectoral fins. No way that's an accident of condensed moisture, air pressure and wind."

Atwood half-heartedly leans forward, and as he glances out the window, he says, "Oh yeah, I see it, a cloud that looks like a tuna. There's one that looks like Pierre Elliot Trudeau."

By themselves, I admit these coincidences seem insignificant, but accumulatively, they have a definite and poignant force. It's hard to accept that a guy like Atwood, who has several framed degrees on the wall, insists that the whale is not meaningful. While I'm rambling on about archetypes and symbols—I had been doing a little reading on Jung—Atwood brings up the third envelope. No matter what I offer him, he insists on changing the focus of our conversation.

"Okay, it's a cloud, nothing more, nothing less, but shouldn't we be talking about my father ... or Milly?" I ask. "I mean, did you read my last chapter?"

Atwood waves the envelope in the air like a winning BINGO card. "Who's the doctor here, Kepler?"

The wound on my wrist begins to ache, the word despair echoes in my head. "Go ahead," I say, "Let's get this over with."

"Dear Kepler" he begins ... but the first few sentences are smudged by a stain of spilled Clamato. The first legible sentence is halfway through the paragraph....

Under the doctor's instructions I was to shine a flashlight intermittently into your eyes, clap two blocks of wood together next to your ear, and touch your extremities with ice cubes—tactics designed to elicit a response from catatonic stasis. Nothing worked. You didn't blink or flinch. As each week went by, I started to get desperate, frustrated. My tests became less therapeutic. Things like putting your clothes on backwards or doing you up in makeup gave me a subtle feeling of control. Sometimes I'd sneak up behind you and scream, pinch a fold of your skin between my nails. I wasn't aware of how far out of hand I was getting until I found myself pushing the tines of a fork into the top of your scalp. I felt so horrible when four little red dots appeared, that I brought the fork down hard on the back of my own hand, the utensil creating a crisscross pattern of blood as it went through the skin three times.

The rest of the letter was illegible too, but not because my mother had spilled Clamato juice on it. It was smudged with tears.

"How are you feeling, Kepler?"

"Fine," I say.

"Come on Kepler."

"Okay, I feel like throwing up. In other words, I feel like I did the first time I read the damn thing. I feel like it was all my fault. Is that what you're after? Because it seems like that's all you really want. You want me to feel miserable and break down into an emotional wreck." And there it is, I'm crying again. "Frankly, I find this therapy as abusive as my mother ever was." My voice is loud, angry, Brando-esque.

Atwood picks up his phone and mumbles something into the receiver.

I'm on my feet. "I can't do this anymore," I say.

"Do what, Kepler?"

"This," I yell. I'm weeping like a baby. "I'm sick of all this pain and loneliness and the fucking tears."

"Looks more like anger than pain, Kepler."

I want to strangle him. I want to shake the cold indifference out of him. I want to ... I can't think because my heart is beating so loud that it sounds like a blacksmith's hammer on an anvil. The channel changes, and the next thing I know, there's a pile of books on the floor and the top three shelves of Atwood's wall unit are empty.

"Kepler," Atwood says my name calmly.

I look over at him. He's smiling.

"I want you to breathe," he says.

I exhale and close my eyes. And as my knees buckle, I feel someone catch my weight and gently lower me to the floor. The hammering in my chest is replaced by a ringing in my ears. "The phone," I say, "I need to answer the phone." I try to get up. "Please," I say, "Just let me answer the phone." Bruce has my shoulders pinned down. The phone rings louder. "Hello," I yell.

"Meet me at the 7-Eleven in five minutes," she says.

It's Milly. I look up at the clock. The hands are spinning. The sun outside the window rises and sets several times. I close my eyes, hold them tightly shut until the darkness is complete, a starless sky.

When I open my eyes, the hands on the clock have stopped. It's seven minutes after ten and I'm at home in the kitchen.

"Where are you?"

"I'm in a phone booth," she says.

I try to steady my breath.

"Are you okay, Kepler?"

"No," I say, "I don't think I am."

She was sitting on the curb outside the convenience store eating potato chips, her feet absently rolling a skateboard from side to side. She seemed pleased with herself, but she looked pale in that fluorescent light, a pollution that made her dark skin look jaundiced.

She acted as if being out this late and so far from home was the most natural thing in the world. This strange and dark unpredictability, along with her habit of ignoring traffic lights, frightened me. I couldn't keep up with her. On more than one occasion, I had felt embarrassed as she stood on the opposite curb waiting for me to cross a road. I wasn't fast enough or confident enough to challenge the world like she did. And I wasn't brave enough to go travelling across the city by myself at all hours of the night. I couldn't trust my body or my mind. But Milly didn't give a shit.

"What happened?" I said.

She had a cast on her right wrist and a bandage on the top part of her left arm, four pieces of white tape holding the cotton in place. "Want to sign my cast," she asked, "or would you rather see my tattoo?"

Before I could answer she peeled back the bandage. Her skin was red and swollen. The lines were thick—a bluish-green outline of a heart with a ribbon running across the bottom. "I didn't have enough money for the colour. I'll have to go back later."

"What does it say?"

"Read it."

She raised her arm from the shoulder; I leaned in closer ... K-e-p-l-e-r. What had she done? I swallowed hard, and held the moment for as long as I could stand it—a perfect stillness broken by a rising sense of panic. I realize now that my judgment was impaired by my overwhelming infatuation with her skin and her sense of rebellion—that and how good it felt to kiss her. But part of me didn't trust the permanence of what she was offering.

"What do you think?" she asked.

"It looks gross. Does it hurt?"

"I was going to show you when it was all healed, but I couldn't wait."

"I guess if we ever break up you can say you're really into 17th century mathematician astronomers."

"Break up?" She punched me in the arm. "What the fuck, Kepler, this is fucking romantic."

She punched me again, and then without thinking I kissed her.

"That's better," she said.

"What happened to your other arm?" I asked, looking at her cast.

"My dad threw me out."

We were awoken by the sound of the vacuum in the hallway. I hadn't heard the drone of that old thing in months. I looked over at the clock radio. It was a quarter past seven in the morning. Milly leaned up on one elbow rubbing the sleep from her eyes. "What the fuck is that?"

"That," I said, "is my mother."

I thought it was strange that she bothered to knock. She never had before.

"Kepler?"

There was an odd vulnerability in her voice. My first thought was to hide Milly under the bed, but a deeper sense of irritation and defiance prevailed.

"What?" I yelled. I had never used that tone with my mother before.

Milly's skateboard stopped the door from opening all the way.

"Kepler?" This time, she sounded annoyed.

I pulled the covers up over our heads, and we were gone together—made invisible by a single white sheet. I remember Milly's eyes being open wide, as if we were approaching the summit of a roller coaster. And as my mother pushed her way into the room I could see Milly's lips fold in, trying to hide any trace of a smile. A moment later my mother was standing at the foot of the bed, one hand holding the handle of the vacuum and the other balled around a fistful of the sheet that had been covering us.

I was a mess of mixed emotions.

"Get dressed," she yelled.

"We are dressed." We had agreed after fumbling in the wee hours of the night that we would wait until the time was right before we would fully consummate our passion for each other. That's how Milly put it, and I had no problem agreeing with what I didn't fully understand. We touched, we kissed, and we explored parts of each other's skin with our fingers and eyes, but we yielded to all buttons, clips and elastics. We made promises to each other in the dark, and we sealed every declaration with our willingness to hold on as tight as possible to this new reason to live.

But my mother wasn't looking at us anymore; she was looking at my father's things that I had carried up from the basement. His golf clubs, his bowling ball, his toothbrush, his electric razor were all placed neatly along the wall. She raised the sheet to her cheek and rubbed the soft edge of it under her eyes in a way that sort of broke my heart. The roller coaster plunged, and as my mother turned back to the door, I heard her say, "Wait till your father finds out about this." But the sound of the vacuum drowned out any certainty that I had heard anything at all.

Milly and I sat at the edge of the bed for a moment and stared at the sheets on the floor, the whining drone of the vacuum making my head spin until Milly stretched out her leg towards the vacuum and hit the off button with her toe.

"She's just a little bit crazy," I said.

"I don't know," Milly replied, "I thought that went pretty well. If this was my house, we'd both probably be dead right now."

While we ate breakfast that morning, I waited for Milly to comment on the puzzle covering the table, or on the plywood showing through on the floor where the square tiles had come unglued, or on the thousand notes taped to the cupboards and walls, but she just held her plate in her lap and smiled. I felt embarrassed and relieved at the same time. The sooner she saw how it was, the sooner she would leave me, and the sooner that happened, the less attached I would be, and therefore the less pain I would have to endure. But it was too late. Looking at her sit there at the kitchen table like everything was perfectly as it should be, made me love her, if that was possible, even more.

I was imagining us on the roof together, sipping warm cups of hot chocolate, taking turns peering through my father's telescope, when Milly pitched the idea that we should run away together. My head was still in the stars. "Yeah," I said jokingly, "we could hitch a ride like hobos to the north. We could eat rabbit and deer that I would kill with a bow and arrow fashioned out of branches and kite string. We could live off the land like wild forest dwellers, and then when we needed to, we could venture into random towns to steal supplies and go bowling."

Milly quickly amended my offering, striking out the living in the forest part. "We're not monkeys, Kepler." The menu was also altered. She was a vegetarian. The sobering tone of her voice made me realize she was serious. She thought we should get jobs, get our own place, buy a pickup truck, but we wouldn't have kids because the world was a fucked up place and we wouldn't want to fuck them up and— "What the hell do you want to go bowling again for? Anyway, we'll leave in the summer when school's done."

So this is how it happens. Life suddenly pulls up like a carnival, unloads its wagons, raises its tents, draws its curtains and overwhelms you with the dazzle and confusion of promises and dreams. It batters you with unendurable feats of wonder, stirs your heart, fills your head with ideas, kicks at your shins, all the while saying choose, choose, but one choice leads to another, and little by little you lose track of where you are, which way you are facing, and then one morning you wake up and there is an empty space where the big top used to be, and you are left with a broken heart and bruises all over your body, trying to figure out how the hell you got wherever it is that you are. The whole plan was crazy and frightening, but the idea of actually getting a job worried me the most. I didn't really feel useful enough to get paid for anything.

"You can stay here," I said. "We have a spare room—"

"That's sweet, Kepler, but I have to go back home to straighten things out with my parents."

I didn't want her to leave, but I knew my mother would probably draw the line anyway. I could hear her now, "What do think this is? Some sort of flophouse for street kids?" And then, as if on cue, my mother wandered back into the kitchen, placed her empty glass on the counter and dropped a spoon loudly in the sink. I tensed up. My mother was always making some kind of a loud noise before she lashed out. I closed my eyes and hunched my shoulders as if I was about to be struck from behind. But instead of a verbal assault, my mom scribbled something out on a piece of paper and slammed it against the fridge door where she secured it with a magnet. I knew that I couldn't leave my mother. I was all she had. And so I sat there like a child, rigidly hunched forward trying desperately not to cry. I heard a chair scrape across the floor, footsteps moving farther away, and when I finally looked up, Milly was already out the door.

Her father hung up on me every time I phoned. And after about the hundredth time I called, he even threatened to call the police. That was funny. Jail was just another cage, another set of bars. There seemed to be no end to the metaphor. The only escape was in my head. I looked up at the stars at night and tried to imagine Milly looking out her window at the same time. I stood in the parking lot outside of her building after school. I communicated with her telepathically, willing her to call me, but the phone didn't ring and no one came to the door. I eventually turned my frustration and pain inwards. I slept in, went to school late, forged my notes, spent hours scribbling in my journal. The sink and counter slowly disappeared under a pile of filthy dishes and garbage. The house creaked and complained, gravity, decay and neglect having their way. I spent the evenings on the couch with my mother staring out the porthole of a spaceship watching the world slowly turn. I just sat there because I didn't really know what else to do. And somewhere between the sitcoms and the commercials and the variety shows and the soap operas, and the odd thump and crash of something somewhere in the house falling apart, time went by.

And then, after what seemed like a million years, Milly showed up at my door. I took her hand and practically dragged her into my room. She threw her arms around me and held on tight. My feelings had never been met head on like that before. I had never been part of something so reciprocal. I had never felt so relieved—to be held so earnestly.

"My dad grounded me. I'm not supposed to talk to you ever again," she said into my ear. "I thought it was so romantic that you called so many times. That really pissed him off."

I was smiling and holding on and thinking this is a dream, this must be a damn dream.

"Kepler."

I could have stayed like that forever, just holding her and being held.

"Kepler."

I felt her hands on my shoulders.

"Kepler, you're hurting me."

When I let go, I felt the waves swell up and pull her a few feet away.

She had a worried look on her face.

"I'm sorry," I said.

"Guess what?" she said, as she picked Ham up off the floor.

"What?"

"Guess, Kepler."

"You ran away again?"

"I got a job at the bookstore."

I looked down at Ham. "Maybe we should forget about the job thing and just go," I said.

"Kepler, what the fuck?" She took a few steps further away until she backed into the closet door.

The truth was, I had forgotten about the plan.

"What are you crying for?" she asked.

"I'm not crying," I said, as I dragged my sleeve across my cheeks.

"Don't fall apart on me, Kepler."

"Who's going to hire me?" I asked.

She was holding me again. Gently.

"We can do this," she whispered. "Don't be a fucking baby."

I applied at the Bluebird Cab Company, but they told me I needed a license and a driver's abstract, which confirmed my argument that I was unemployable.

"You have to be realistic, Kepler," Milly said. "You won't get your first job at NASA."

But when she took me to McDonald's, I felt depressed the moment I walked in the door. I tried to imagine myself as the other kid behind the counter wearing that ridiculous outfit, the smell of grease thick in the air. What would be worse, standing at the counter taking orders or stuck back there in the kitchen flipping hamburgers with my mother? I couldn't decide. I intentionally wrote down the wrong name and phone number when I filled in the application.

"You don't have to like the job," Milly said. "Think of it as acting. You just pretend that you care about your job and then at the end of each week they hand you a paycheque. You put that in the bank and eventually you can tell them to shove it."

I ended up working at a theatre in the mall. Milly secretly filled out an application with my name on it when I was using the toilet after we went to see *Grease*. They caught me off guard. Left a message with my mom. The note was taped to my bedroom door. I went in for the interview the next day and, despite my efforts, they hired me.

As it turned out, it wasn't such a bad place to work. When I wasn't tearing tickets, I had to make sure people weren't smoking in the theatre or putting their feet up on the empty seat backs in front of them. And as an employee, I was allowed to see movies for free. I got to see parts of "R" rated movies like *Omen II*, *Annie Hall* and *The Deer Hunter*. I took to the movies like my mother took to vodka. The sense of distraction and escape that the big screen provided seemed like the answer to all my problems. I loved the intensity of the drama, the stark emotion, the romance and the righteous delivery of revenge. I began to live vicariously through the struggles and triumphs of movie stars. Something was changing inside of me, the lines between reality and fiction were blurring. I was becoming my father's son.

When I wasn't at school, or with Milly, or at the movies, I was mixing random pills I stole from the bathroom cabinet with shots of vodka. I wasn't really sure what I was doing, but by June I had a twitch in my right eye, was having difficulty sleeping, and I hadn't saved a penny.

"What is that?" Milly asked one day as we stood at the cash of a convenience store. She was always buying books, but now instead of literature, she was buying magazines like *Vegetable Gardening Made Easy*, and she was particularly fascinated by a magazine called *Harrowsmith*.

"What is what?"

"You keep blinking all the time."

"I guess I'm tired."

The cashier cleared her throat.

Milly reached into her pocket and pulled out a twenty-dollar bill.

"Damn, that's the smallest I got. Can you get this, Kepler?"

I stuck my hands in my pockets.

"I always preferred libraries," I said.

"Libraries are fine," she said, "but what's that got to do with anything?"

"Why do we have to buy these magazines? It all just feels like a waste of time," I said.

"What's a waste of time?" she said. "We need to be prepared..."

"I can't explain it."

She had what was becoming a familiar worried look on her face. "Try."

I measured my words. "All this planning just seems to get in the way of enjoying the time we have together."

"Um, excuse me." The cashier was standing there with her hand out. "Do you two lovebirds want the magazine or not?"

We left the magazine on the counter and walked out onto the street.

"Be patient, Kepler. You have to believe in the future. Do you know what that is?"

"Yeah, it's a rhetorical question."

"I'm fucking serious, Kepler. You have to make plans. You have to make sacrifices." And then she looked at me with that worried look again. "You are saving money, aren't you? I can't do this on my own."

"Don't worry about me," I said.

"I am worried about you, Kepler. I feel like you're not all there half the time."

We walked a couple of blocks north and with each step the silence between us took on a physical presence. She was intentionally walking really fast, so I intentionally slowed down until she was about twenty miles ahead of me. I was reminded of the day when Benjamin left me in the phone booth. Once again, I was being punished for getting my hopes up, for believing that I could fit in. I am disappearing, I thought. The world around me had a strange vagueness to it. I could see it, but I couldn't really feel it. When I finally caught up to Milly she was sitting in the curve of a giant sculpture in front of the art gallery.

"C'mon," she said, "we're going inside."

We went straight up to the Canadian collection where she sat me down in front of a painting.

"Okay," she said, "that's the future. That's where we're going."

There was something demeaning about the whole thing. I felt like a child being dragged around by the collar, forced to confront something that I couldn't understand. The self-pity I was feeling was atmospheric, safe and complete. I raised my eyes reluctantly and shrugged. But then something happened.

The painting was a surreal landscape of tranquility and wonder—an impossible, soft-edged dream where intensely coloured rocks and wind-blown trees were mirrored in a clear lake reflecting a smoky yellow sky. It was frightening and beautiful and perfectly contained in a frame that made it seem complete and possible, like a window to another universe. The painting seemed to be a visual expression of that line between what is real and what is fantasy, the fact and the lie. I could recognize the trees and the rocks et cetera, but they did not look exactly like any trees and rocks I had ever seen. This was a visual manifestation of the world where anything is possible, a perfect articulation of the thing I had been searching for. It was a place a called truth.

And that's when I told Milly about Ham, not the sock monkey, but the real monkey that had been sent into space to see if astronauts could carry out their jobs during launch, weightlessness and re-entry. I told her how Ham was able to perform his tasks almost perfectly, but then his rocket malfunctioned and boosted his capsule off course. I told her how he landed sixty miles from the nearest recovery ship and that the capsule was beginning to submerge when the Navy rescue helicopter pilots found it. I waited a few moments to let the gravity settle in, as if I was reliving the moment myself. And then I told her that Ham was all right and that he retired. "Well, actually, they put him in a zoo somewhere." I was out of breath.

"What does that have to do with—"

"That's how *I* feel. Like Ham. It's as if I have returned from an impossible place, and even though I can use words to describe it, the feeling and the look of the experience don't quite fit. Just like this painting." I unbuttoned my jacket and pulled the one-armed sock monkey out and handed him to her.

"He's yours. I want you to have him."

"How long have you been carrying this thing around with you?"

"My whole life," I said.

I would like to say that it was me who was leading Milly astray. But she was a born troublemaker really. Not only did I lack Milly's discipline and courage, but her intensity and passion frightened me sometimes—I couldn't keep up. My mother was acting very strange, all those notes were one thing, but she was also having trouble remembering the names of things. She referred to mustard as the yellow ketchup. Her vocabulary was shrinking, the lines of stress and worry deepening in her face. By the end of the school year I was a nervous wreck. Even though I wanted nothing more than to escape from the worry and stress of that house, I was too frightened by what Milly called the future. I was still lost in the past and I had failed to hold up my end of the bargain. My inability to save money and commit to the promise of another life, an idea that I realized wasn't really my own, had created a rift between us. Something I began to think of as a sort of unspoken lie. I had been using my assignment for Mr. Lemon's class as an excuse to avoid Milly and the thing that I couldn't admit to her. My journal was now filled with images I had cut out from magazines, photos and paintings photocopied from books in the library, but the truth was still eluding me. I felt like a fraud, and even though I knew I would be exposed for the inept fool that I was, the inevitable assault came from straight on.

"What time is your break, handsome?" Milly said.

I didn't much like it when she showed up at my work. The maroon uniform I had to wear made me feel like an impostor. I glanced at the clock. "I get a break in twenty minutes. I can meet you by the record store."

She leaned across the little podium where I deposited the torn tickets, kissed me quickly and said, "Good, I'll be there."

Milly and I had our second fight right in the middle of the mall.

"Tomorrow's the last day of school," she said. "How much money have you saved?"

I stopped walking and turned to stare into the window of a shoe store.

"What's wrong with you?" Milly asked. "Why are you crying?"

"I'm not crying," I said. "I'm looking at the shoes."

She stood next to me and met my eyes in the window's reflection. "Look at me, Kepler."

I looked at her.

"This is not a dream," she said. "This is reality. You have free will. Stop fucking hiding."

"I'm afraid," I said.

"Afraid of what?"

"Losing."

"Losing what, Kepler?"

"My mother." She quit or lost her job. I knew because she was stealing the money I was saving in a pickle jar under my bed. She always left the change and the twos, but any bill five or higher disappeared within the week. I never actually saw her take the money, but well, you didn't have to be Sherlock Holmes to figure it out.

Milly's fists were clenched and for a second I thought she was going to slug me.

"Okay, okay, I've got it," she said. "Let's figure this out. What are our options?"

My first thought was to buy a bunch of lottery tickets.

"We need the money now, Kepler. We've got to get you out of that house."

"I'll get the money," I said.

"How?"

"From the theatre?"

"What?"

"I'll hold the place up," I said matter-of-factly.

"No, Kepler, fuck. You can't go around stealing," she said. "Fuck, you've been watching too many movies."

And it was true, I was picturing myself with a fedora and a Thompson machine gun, a toothy Warren Beatty smile on my face. All right, hand over the loot and no funny stuff. I'd make a discreet getaway in a 1934 Ford sedan. Head for the hills. But the romance of it wouldn't be the same without Bonnie. And then I thought about the painting at the gallery. It must be worth a fortune. The cat burglar worked alone. I knew it wasn't rational, but I was desperate, and before I could say, "Why, worthy Thane, you do unbend your noble strength, to think so brainsickly of things," I got it in my head that I would go to the art gallery, steal the painting, find some rich millionaire to buy it, stuff the money in a sock and make it to Mr. Lemon's class in time to hand in my assignment. No movie stars involved at all.

"I'll get the money," I said. "I promise."

I didn't sleep. Couldn't sleep. My mother was vacuuming again, manically dragging the machine throughout the house. You could tell the bag was full because the machine was whining like an over-revved engine, occasionally emitting a coughing, bogged down stutter every time it hit a piece of furniture. Whether it was the insomnia, the vacuum or the pills, my mind had become fixated on the puzzle—the empty space that seemed to contain not just a section of Pluto, but part of my memory, Elvis, my father, six and half weeks of my life. I could feel myself being pulled in two directions. Milly, with her heels dug into the carpet, trying to drag me out the door, while my mother had me by the collar trying to keep me home. Part of me wanted to surrender to embrace the future Milly was promising me, while part me wanted to stay behind, fall into the black hole in the puzzle and disappear again.

When my alarm went off at 7 am I was sitting on the edge of the bed, dressed and with my shoes tied. I neatly extracted the pages from my journal that collectively made up my essay and stapled them together. I then gathered up the bolt cutters, flashlight, gardening gloves, a pair of scissors and duct tape that I had stored under my bed and neatly placed each item in the gym bag. The door dragged on the carpet when I pushed it open. The house was quiet except for the television; the white noise from a channel off the air filled the morning. I stepped over the abandoned vacuum, inhaled the two pickles slices and four cold French fries I found on a plate on the coffee table in the living room.

I got to the gallery about half an hour after it opened.

The Plan:

One. Buy a print of the J.E.H. MacDonald painting in the gift shop.

Two. Casually stroll up to the Group of Seven exhibit, and then, when the coast is clear, use the scissors to cut the canvas out of the frame.

Three. Replace the painting with the print.

But somewhere between three and four my mind began to drift...

After removing the painting from the frame, I opened my gym bag to discover that the replacement print wasn't the right size. Step three had to be abandoned. I left the frame and the print on the floor, grabbed the bag and started walking quickly across the gallery to the fire exit. But then, just as I pushed the door open, I heard my name. I turned back and saw my father, who was standing there in a security uniform. "You forgot these," he said. He was holding a bunch of bananas. "Truth is, you're gonna need them if you're going to set them free."

When I opened my eyes I was standing in the middle of the gift shop with a large hardcover book in my hand called *Canadian Perspectives*. There were people all around perusing key chains, ashtrays, and postcards. As I began to flip the pages, I discovered that the whole book was filled with prints of surreal landscapes that more or less all looked the same. Was truth that common, or had I imagined it, a trick of colour, light and paint. My hands began to tremble. I suddenly regret- ted giving away Ham.

"You'll have to leave that at the coat check."

When I turned around I was face to face with a security guard who was nudging my gym bag with the toe of his boot.

I felt the foundation tremble, a display of ballpoint pens, corkscrews, and bookmarks began to vibrate.

I had no choice but to abort the mission.

When I opened the classroom door, Mr. Lemon, in his tweed London Fog blazer, was collecting the students' essays. The tremors were getting stronger, closer together.

"Kepler?"

I stood in the doorway. That's one of the safest places in an earthquake.

"Are you okay, Kepler?"

Hairline cracks began to form under my feet. The ceiling tiles began to fall. I heaved my bag over my shoulder and headed down the hall. I could hear the floor cracking behind me, the ductwork groaning, florescent tubes smashing, but I stayed calm. I would improvise, every good storyteller does. I turned left, then right, and despite the chaos, I made my way to the principal's office. I was fast, determined, in and out.

And as the school slowly collapsed into a heap of rubble, I was running across the school parking lot stuffing the typewriter into my gym bag.

CHAPTER THIRTEEN

(I)

My mother was sitting at the kitchen table with a mug of coffee in front of her. The kitchen was a mess, but she looked nice. She had on an olive blazer over a white blouse with ruffles down the front. Her hair looked brushed and she had lipstick and eye makeup on that made her look ten years younger. She was holding an envelope in her hand. "I went to the doctor's this morning."

"I didn't know you were sick," I said.

She began to tap the edge of the envelope on the table. "He says I have to go back for some tests—blood work and a CT scan."

I stepped over a busted up piece of plaster on the floor and lifted a pot of burning beans off the element. There was another can of baked beans and a carton of eggs resting precariously on the pile of dirty plates that covered the counter.

"They think I might have something called"—I could hear her unfold a piece of paper—"Mild Cognitive Impairment, but it could be a vitamin deficiency."

I found the can opener in a coffee mug in the sink, secured it on the rim of the unopened beans, and as I started to turn the handle, I knocked the carton of eggs on the floor. My mother twisted in her chair and watched the three eggs that hadn't broken roll across the floor. There was a definite slope towards the back door, leading me to speculate that a supporting wall in the basement may have collapsed. My mother lit a cigarette, turned to the window and scanned the sky as if she was looking for something. "Doctor says I can't drink anymore. I have to change my diet. I have to exercise."

Even though I could hear the hurt and fear in her voice, the naming of what she had been denying for so long came as a relief. I asked the question. "What's Mild Cognitive—"

"—It's a memory problem."

It was clearly more than a memory problem. There were a billion notes all over the house, a thousand bottles of Cheez Whiz in the cupboard. There was a pair of slippers in the fridge, four bags of sugar in the freezer. There was a notice from the telephone company threatening to cut our service.

"I can't always remember things," I said.

She started to laugh. She was still looking out the window. "I once said to your dad that if I ever got cancer, I would kill myself." It was as if she was talking to herself. "I hadn't ever given it much thought beyond that. I just imagined myself going to sleep, as if suicide was a decision, like a heartbroken animal that simply closes its eyes and passes. But the idea of tying a rope to a tree, or dragging a kitchen knife across my throat all seems so dreadful."

"You don't have cancer."

"No," she said, "it's something much worse." She lit a cigarette off the one she was smoking and stubbed the first butt out in the ashtray.

I dropped a tea towel on the mess of eggs on the floor.

"I need to talk to you, Kepler. About what the doctor said."

It was the first time I had ever heard my mother sound so sincere. I walked over and sat down across from her at the table.

She turned back to the window and frowned at the eaves-trough hanging from the roof. "I have these memories, like the exact moment when I realized I wanted to be an actress. Did I ever tell you this?"

I shook my head.

"I was five or six and my mother had given me a haircut. It was outside in the backyard. I was miserable—I used to have beautiful curly hair, but there was an outbreak of head lice or something at school so we all had to have our hair cut short. Anyway, when my mother held the mirror up, I didn't recognize myself. Without the curls I wasn't Alice anymore. I was a stranger looking back at myself—separated from what I was seeing—as if I was the audience. Does that make sense?"

She reached across the table and touched my hand for a second. "I can remember so many details from my childhood, and yet I don't remember what I had for breakfast." She took a long drag from her cigarette, a plume of smoke obscuring her face. "I don't really understand it," she continued, "but I have the feeling that something awful is happening."

And then, as if we were breaking for a commercial, she leaned over, picked up the three eggs, threw them at the wall and stormed out of the kitchen. I could see that the envelope she left on the table had my name on it, but this time it wasn't my mother's handwriting.

Dear Kepler, my father has gone completely crazy and has decided to send me to live with my uncle in Bombay. My father says this place lacks the depth of history that I need. He says children here have no discipline, no sense of culture.

It is a snake eating its own tail. He blames Canada for my bad behaviour. Am I bad? I feel like I am two people. In my house I behave myself, respect my parents. I don't complain. I am happy helping my mother in the kitchen. We speak quietly and laugh about my father's rules when he can't hear. But then when I step outside I feel like a different person, as if I've been asleep. I feel angry and I get mad at people. My father says I am reckless and that my behaviour is shameful. Maybe he's right, but there is still something inside of me that sees the beauty in things. I see the beauty in you.

I will contact you when I escape,

Milly xo

Milly's father was frowning when he answered the door. A pungent and aromatic odour wafting out into the hall made me feel light-headed as I introduced myself and searched for a sign of Milly in the apartment behind him. He shook his head from side to side and then started waving his finger back and forth as if he was trying to hypnotize me. "This is none of your business," he said.

The slamming door felt like a punch in the face.

I closed my eyes and pushed against all the frustration and disappointment I felt in my heart. What had I done wrong? The only thing I could measure was the edge of all the anger I was feeling.

I knocked again. This time he didn't open the door. "She's gone. Go away," he yelled.

I wanted to kick the door down and empty the cupboards, push their stove off the balcony, tear down the coloured fabrics and brass decorations that I had briefly seen on the walls of their living room. I wanted to curse their gods, rage against their sense of family. I wanted to remove every detail of their culture until they were stripped bare, vulnerable, with no past, no future, no identity, no one to love them back. I wanted them to know what it is to have your whole past be a lie. I wanted them to be stuck in the present, without roots. I wanted them to know what it was like to be Canadian. I pounded on the door one more time.

"I'm ringing the police."

I stumbled down the hall and reached for the elevator button. There it was again, as if I was looking through the wrong end of a pair of binoculars, everything was stretched out of proportion. I turned and looked back down the hall to find Milly, my mother, my father, and Benjamin, each one waving from a different apartment door. A bell rang in my skull as I fell sideways into the elevator. I was trapped, cornered by images of all the people that I had lost. I searched desperately through my pockets, rolled up my sleeve and pressed the serrated edge of a key against my flesh and started sawing. There was no pain, just the diffusion of anger into a lukewarm state of shame. The elevator doors closed and swallowed me.

Ophelia and I are talking in hushed tones. We have developed a sign language that makes our secret conversations more private. The latest plan is based on some foggy three-part notion about creating some kind of diversion so that I can scale the fence in the courtyard, steal a car, and bust her out. We both know that our plan is ill-conceived and desperate, but lately it has taken all the control I can muster to keep from completely falling apart. I tell her I have to go. I have an appointment with Dr. Atwood. We shake hands and then hug. I feel our bodies twitching, our eyes trying to focus as we step back and quickly go over our coded hand signals one last time.

I've been chewing my fingernails. They are bitten back, jagged and tender. The tips are sore as I scratch at my armpit. Am I getting better? I can't tell. I'm sitting on the couch. Atwood is sitting in his chair. I'm listening to him talk. He says we are making progress. He says my therapy sessions are unearthing the layers of buried truth, the stuff at the core of my illness. But it feels like I am digging around in the bloody mess of my heart. I lost my father and my mother, and in the end, I lost Milly as well, but more importantly, as Dr. Atwood reminds me, I lost myself.

The word lost echoes as it ricochets off the walls of a deep, deep well. And what begins as a slight cramping in my side turns into a phantom anaphylactic reflex. I can't get enough air into my lungs. I begin to hyperventilate. And before Dr. Atwood can pry himself out of his chair, I'm out the door.

I am halfway up the fence when Bruce grabs me by the back of my pants. I hear Ophelia screaming, telling Bruce to let me go. He has me pinned up against the fence, holding me there so that I don't fall or climb any higher, while, with his other hand, he tries to block the bunches of dry leaves that Ophelia is throwing at him. And when I hear the words, "Let go, Kepler," I feel the stitching come undone, the glue cracking along the spine, and all the pages start falling like straw from under my shirt and the cuffs of my pants. I feel like I am getting thinner, my identity, my memories, the very idea of me is blowing away until all that is left of me is a single memory.

On the night that Elvis died my father pulled me out of bed, and along with his telescope, a dozen beers, a lawn chair and a pair of bolt cutters, he loaded me into the car. My mother was at the front door in her robe threatening to call the police as we pulled out of the driveway. My father was manic. "A promise is a promise," he kept saying over and over. I was half asleep and still pretty drunk from the beer I drank. I remember pulling into a parking lot, the cool chill of the night air as my father opened the car door. I remember staggering through the dark following my dad's urgent and agitated directions into a forest. I remember him cursing as he worked the bolt cutters on a locked gate.

"Hold the damn flashlight still, Kepler."

And then I was hanging on to a fence, my father pushing me up from below.

"Come on, Kepler, keep climbing. You're almost there."

But it was high, too high, and too dark to see.

And then I remember the sound of something hitting the fence below me. I heard my father swearing, "Jesus fucking Christ. Jesus fucking Christ," and then he was pulling hard on my pant leg. "Let go, Kepler. Let go..."

But I couldn't let go. I had been holding on so tight for so long. The idea of letting go paralyzed me. I kicked at him, tried to free my legs. I was yelling back at my father, telling him to let go. And then I heard the thing hit the fence again, and when I looked down, I saw the shape of it crouched in the dirt on the other side of the fence, its tail swaying, its yellow eyes visible in the murky gloom.

I let go.

I'm not sure how much time had passed, but when I opened my eyes again I was lying on the hood of our car, my head resting back on the windshield. I heard my father mumbling, half singing, half talking, and then the familiar sound of the cap being knocked off a beer with a lighter. I felt the car sigh and rise as my father lifted his weight from the fender.

"That was definitely not the fucking monkey cage," he said.

He emptied the beer with a quick tilt of his head and staggered into the beam of the car's headlights where his telescope was set up next to a lawn chair. He unzipped his pants, and after relieving himself, he kicked the lawn chair over and headed out beyond the beam of the headlights.

I closed my eyes and imagined a warm blanket pulled up to my chin, and as I sank down into the comfort of my exhaustion I heard my dad flipping the locks on the tripod's legs, the plastic limbs sliding up into each other. He was saying something about Elvis being somewhere up there now, somewhere behind those damn clouds. I rolled my head to the left again as he dismounted the telescope and wrapped it in an old blue towel.

I could hear beyond the dull ache in my ankle and the sharp edges of the cuts on the palms of my hands, the sound of a distant siren. I heard the crack of another beer being opened—more swearing, and then the door whined and the car sank again. My body slid further down onto the hood until I could feel a windshield wiper against the back of my head.

When the engine turned over beneath me, it sounded like it was under water. Even the Elvis song that followed sounded like it was being transmitted from a submarine. I managed to twist my head until I could see my father through the windshield, his shadowed face eerily lit by the blue glare of the dashboard lights. His eyes were closed tight, his head resting on the steering wheel. He looked like he was going to cry. I wanted to tell him that the clouds were clearing, that I could see a star, but as I lifted my head through the exhaust that had curled around the front fender, I felt the vehicle shift into gear, the weight under me jolt, the rear tires spitting up gravel. And as the car accelerated in reverse, the empty beer bottles my father had drunk were illuminated by the flashing lights of a cop car. I slid with a squeak across the hood, the clouds parted, and then one by one, the stars that made up the constellation of Cetus flickered brightly in the darkness, and as the whale opened its mouth, I closed my eyes, and my father was gone.

My hands loosen on the fence, and when I feel my feet on the ground again, arms pull me in. "It's okay," a voice whispers. Is that an English or a Danish accent, I wonder. And I fall into those arms and I feel the comfort that I have always longed for. I'm a child again, a little boy being rocked gently in a loving embrace, and I keep my eyes closed because this time I don't want to wake up.

"First things first, Kepler," Dr. Atwood says. "You can leave any time you want. You are a voluntary patient. There's really no need to climb the fence."

A smile slowly creeps over his face. The corners of his mouth push the skin up until his cheeks become fleshy and round. Deep lines form on his forehead. His eyes sparkle. I realize it's the first time I've ever seen him laugh.

"It's all right here in your file. You signed the conditions of your stay here yourself."

"I can leave any time I want?"

"Yes, but I recommend finishing what we started here. This is important stuff and I think we're finally getting to the heart of the matter."

I look over at the door. All I have to do is tell Atwood to fuck off and I can walk right out of here. "Fuck," I say.

"Excellent," Atwood says. "Let it out."

I want to tear up the carpet, throw a chair through the window, stuff Atwood's coffee cup down his throat. I can feel my temples pulse, my hands tighten into fists. Breathe, I say to myself.

"This is your moment, Kepler. You can run away from what you feel. You can find something to cut yourself with, you can pull yourself inwards and shut everyone and everything out, or you can find the courage to face the pain—what are you going to do?"

I look at the door, and even though all I want to do is run, I weigh the consequences of each option that Atwood has just mentioned. "I'll go with number four, Bob." I am a contestant on my mother's favourite game show. "I'm going to tell the truth," I say.

Three hundred and sixty-four days after Elvis died, I found myself in the bathroom dragging one of my mom's pink plastic razors across my skull, hair falling in clumps into the sink, blood dripping from my eyebrows. There was no resistance, no excitement, no fear—just the methodical reduction of myself until there was nothing left but what had been forgotten.

"*Only in the world I fill up a place, which may be better supplied when I have made it empty.*"

The water in the tub was stained yellow with urine; the ridges of his fingertips were pale, swollen and porous.

I turned around and threw him a towel. "Get out," I said.

I had been in the tub for approximately seven hours when my mom opened the door. I can still see the glass of vodka and Clamato juice hitting the linoleum, my mother reaching into the tub and pulling the plug, her arms taking hold of me, picking me up, stronger than I could have imagined.

In a matter of seconds she had me in the hall, my wet socks leaving dark stains on the carpet. She shoved the front door open and pushed me out onto the porch. My soaking pants were heavy as I stumbled down the steps.

As she dragged me down the driveway, I heard the neighbour's lawn mower switch off, Mr. Phillip's voice strained and uncertain behind us. "Everything all right, Alice?" But my mother forged on across the street and into the park. When I tried to stop, she just looked fiercely into my eyes and tugged on my arm. I decided that it was best to stop struggling and just try to keep up with her. We passed the schoolyard, the swing sets, we marched through the baseball diamond, a softball bouncing to the left, a young girl sprinting to first base, some-one in the bleachers yelling, my mother's perfect nails digging into my skin. Even though there were plenty of people staring at us, no one moved in our direction. Eventually her grip loos-ened, but her pace did not let up until we came to an intersec-tion where she finally stopped and pointed at the road.

"Look!" she demanded, transferring her grip to the back of my neck.

I was surprised again by her strength.

She forced my head downwards. I crumpled. The cement was hard on my knees. I had an intimate view of the ground—little bits of glass, brown like a smashed beer bottle, clear like a shattered headlight.

"Your father is dead," she whispered. "He drove his car into this pole."

Even though my mother wasn't holding me anymore I couldn't seem to get up. It was as if the sky had crashed down upon me, or maybe the earth had smashed me into the sky. Vomit spilled from my mouth onto the pavement in front of me; I could taste beer, not vodka, in the acidic residue in my throat. Something had come unstuck.

"He took you to the zoo that night, and when the police came he took off, and he left you."

I looked up slowly, half expecting to see the remains of the collision there in the intersection, my father's crumpled body against the windshield of his car.

My mother was hyperventilating, one hand flat against her chest. "He was trying to break into the tiger enclosure," she said.

"Monkeys," I corrected.

She shook her head angrily. "Tigers, Kepler."

I realized I was seeing my mother as she was and as she would never be again. The fear in her eyes was as real as my father's depression. Some monsters lurk in closets or on the ceilings of children's bedrooms, but the worst ones chew at you in the broad daylight of your life—bit-by-bit, day-by-day. My father was dead. She had said the words. I got up slowly, wiped the dirt off my knees. It was too late for us, but it wasn't too late for the monkeys.

I didn't say goodbye. I didn't try to hug her or say I was sorry. I just walked back home, picked up my gym bag and headed for the zoo.

EPILOGUE

After a year in a mental hospital I have come full circle. In the good doctor's opinion, I am no longer suicidal. I have overcome my righteous animal liberation tendencies, and I have exposed enough of what was hidden of the iceberg. I have finally touched down. Like Ham, I have returned to earth. Although things went terribly wrong on my mission, I managed to face the strange and frightening things out there in the cosmos and steer the ship back to reality. But it is not my fate to retire in a zoo and spend my days behind bars. I am free. I shake Atwood's hand, nod at Bruce, knock on Ophelia's door, kiss her wrinkled cheek and then, I click my heels.

The sun is setting, but even in that orangey glow the house looks terrible. The eaves are rusted and hanging over the living room window. The hedge has gone wild, the patio stones are buckling and nature has reclaimed every crack of the lot. I wait a few moments, and then open the front door. As I pass quietly through the living room I see that the television is on but the volume is turned down. A series of severe cracks have splintered the walls, and the floor groans and creaks with each step. I stick my head in the kitchen. The puzzle is still there, though it is barely visible under a mess of newspapers and dishes. The refrigerator seems to be sinking into the floor on one side. When I open the door a horrible odour hits me in the face. I kick the door closed and a pile of mail falls on the floor. Mostly unopened bills. A beam of yellow sunlight illuminates the fractures in the cupboards.

The door to my mother's bedroom opens with a slight drag on the brown carpet. The curtain and the rod are on the floor amongst a scattering of clothes, paper bags and Styrofoam containers. My mother's red coat is hanging in the closet, her suitcase at the foot of the unmade bed. What a mess. As I step back out into the hall I see that the bathroom door is closed. I continue on to the spare room. The wall is still partly painted and the brush my father was using as a microphone over two years ago is lying there next to the paint can and tray. My bedroom looks pretty much like it did the day I left except the door is awkwardly hanging by one hinge and the light switch no longer works. The walls are still covered in newspaper clippings, but several of them have fallen onto the floor. In the dim light I spot an envelope on my desk. I pick it up and move towards the window to take a closer look. When I pull the curtains open, the streetlights flicker and something hard strikes me violently on the shoulder. A second blow strikes the back of my head. The roof is collapsing, I think as I instinctively stagger through the hall towards the kitchen. I turn, just as my mother swings again. The spade leaves a deep gouge in the cupboard door. "Get out," she says, "shoo."

I can feel the back of my head swelling as I run out onto the back porch and leap down onto the lawn.

"No more ghosts," she yells, and slams the door.

For a second I feel compelled to laugh. The sight of my mother in that same old robe, her perfectly pedicured toes, the madness and determination in her eyes... And then I feel a trickle of blood running down the back of my neck. For a moment I think I might pass out, but then I remember the envelope and my head clears.

I am hesitant at first. Letters in my experience have always meant bad news, but I also know that I have to face it. No more running away. Inside the envelope I find the essay I wrote for Mr. Lemon's English class. I shuffle through the pages and begin to read.

I know that the evening didn't end there in my bed that night. I know there was a collision of some kind—an act of remembering and forgetting which sort of cancelled each other out, leaving an empty space in the middle. I know that it was a journey inwards, a tucking into oneself, a folding over so that the seams were inaccessible to the prying fingers of those outside. I blocked out the events of that night in an effort to protect myself. This was no knee scrape, or fractured bone, but rather an atomic boom somewhere in the chamber of the heart... The following six weeks were lost to me. Memory and time didn't seem to exist in the digestive juices of Cetus's gut. Instead of plunging into the sea, the whale set a course straight into the void. It took me beyond the ceiling of my bedroom, out past the field of telescopes to a constellation called amnesia.

And after several paragraphs of Joycean inspired nonsense the essay concludes:

For every child who has ever felt misunderstood, let down or humiliated, there is a parent who can match that hurt with their own childhood. Every lie, every bruise, every mistake needs to be forgiven. Otherwise they form scars that break open every time we look back and remember them … but when I look back all I see is a puzzle with missing pieces, because even though memory is integral, it is unreliable. There is no veracity in the past—there is nothing there but the story we tell. Truth, I conclude, does not exist in the words that are written or spoken, but rather in the intention that creates them.

I look up and see my mother standing in the window of the kitchen with a mug in her hand. There's a strange look in her eye. "Kepler." It takes a second before I realize that there is no screen or glass in the window. The torn curtain flutters next to her face. Her voice is soft, almost childlike. "Is your father home yet?" she asks.

The first thing I do is glance up at the roof. I half expect to see him up there with a beer in his hand. The sun has set. The sky is clear, but there is nothing there, nothing but a bunch of stars.

"Yes," I say, "He is home. We all are."

ACKNOWLEDGEMENTS

First and foremost I am indebted to my partner Rain Bone, whose support, tolerance, and quiet understanding are so deeply appreciated.

A warm thank you to Calvin Wharton, and Shane Neilson for their efforts on my behalf, and especially to Annabel Lyon whose generosity and support fortified my belief in this manuscript and at times in myself as a writer.

Thanks to the Humber School for Writers, and the University of Guelph's Creative Writing MFA program.

Thanks to Devon Code and Ivano Stocco for writerly conversations, and to Nancy Lee for her last minute efforts.

I am also grateful to Carla Elm Clement, Sarah Parkinson, and Christine Fischer Guy who provided insightful feedback in early stages of this manuscript.

And last but certainly not least, a big hug to John Vigna for his friendship, integrity and encouragement along the way.